ANTARES TRAP

OTHER BOOKS BY ANJULA EVANS

Illustrated Children's Titles:

I Kicked the Ball in Gym Class: Self-esteem & Identity

School Day Worries: The Link Between Thoughts & Anxiety

The Anti-Bullying Project

Twins: One Black & One White

Where is My Gigi? Dealing with the Loss of a Loved One

I Go Away...I Go Home: Emma's Journey Through Foster Care

The Super-Hero Survival Guide

The Super-Hero Survival Guide: Red Alert!

The Super-Hero Survival Guide: Close Encounters of the Green Kind

Illustrated Young Adult Titles:

Living with an Acquired Brain Injury

Living with an Acquired Brain Injury: Adapting to Change

ANTARES TRAP

Scorpius Chronicles

ANJULA EVANS

Second paperback edition 2019
First hardcover edition 2019

Cover Art by Gareth Brown
garethnbrown.co.uk

Paperback ISBN 978-1-7770249-0-1
Hardcover ISBN 978-1-7770249-1-8

For all the young family members whose names are hidden in this book.

Zac, you were my inspiration for Reagan's character.

Susan, thank you for showing me how to put my ideas together.

TABLE OF CONTENTS

MAP

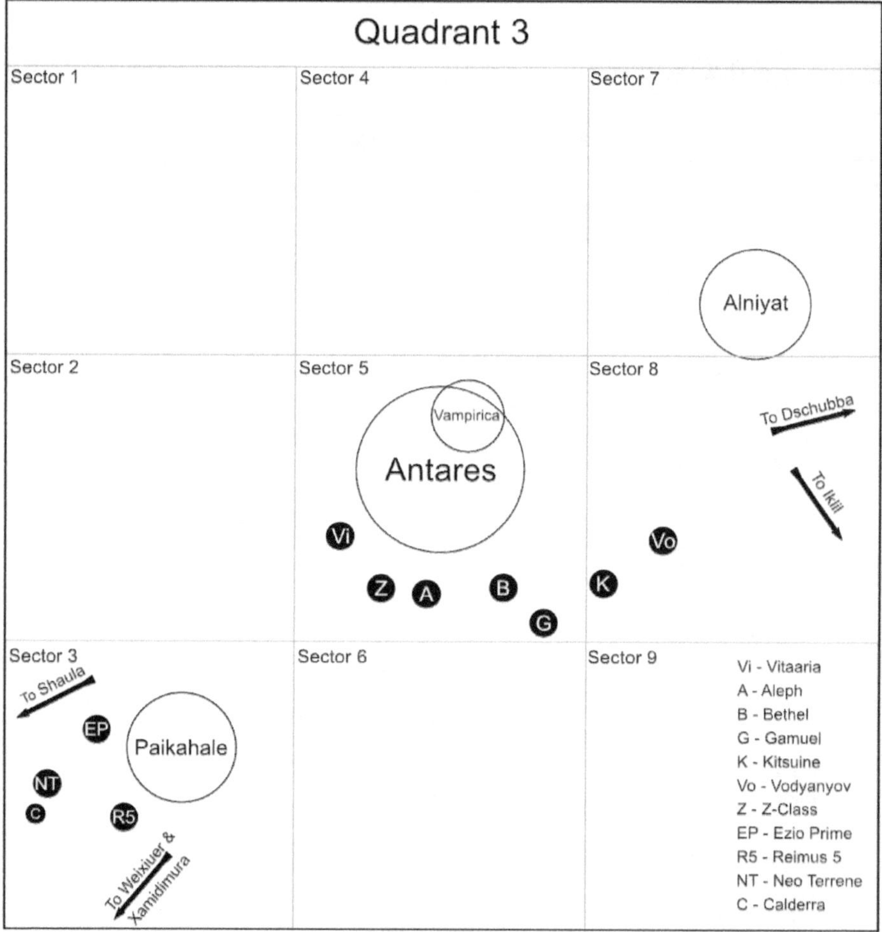

Map is <u>not</u> to scale. Planet sizes are much smaller. Planet positions are variable.

OUTPOST

CHAPTER ONE

*Wisdom is gained by learning from those around us. A fool
believes there is nothing left to learn.*

Lord Mykel Vasilios, Protector of the Isidorian Throne

Reagan woke suddenly in his cryogenic chamber, and realized that decompression and climatization had started. Finally, the ship was close enough to its destination to trigger the thaw.

He felt groggy as he awoke. A month in a stasis pod would do that to you. As he stretched, he felt wobbly, as if trying out his legs for the first time. Another effect of deep space travel. As sensation returned to his limbs, he contracted and released his muscles to familiarize his body with movement.

Reagan was anxious to prepare for his first major assignment offworld, at the Galactic Investigations Bureau outpost, known as the GIB. Quadrant 3 was comprised of corporations and colonists who were constantly in conflict, and he was to help manage the disputes. Reagan had been assigned to this position to gain experience in one of the most difficult regions of the empire.

Reagan used the console to tilt his pod from sixty degrees to an upright position, then extended his leg, putting his full weight down on it. Now able to weight-bear, he stepped forward, grabbed a towel and set of dry clothes from a locker, and changed. He then walked to the bridge.

"Greetings, Governor Vasilios." The android on the bridge was monitoring systems, as he did several times daily. It was strange to Reagan to hear his father's title directed at him.

"Good morning, Lincoln. Anything I should know?" Reagan ran his hand through his short, damp, chestnut hair.

"Just a routine flight, some turbulence on the way due to an asteroid storm and solar flares, but otherwise smooth sailing."

"Any repairs necessary?" asked Reagan.

"All done during your cryo-sleep," answered the android. "Those new bots on the hull were a wise improvement. They repaired a breach within seconds."

"Something breached the hull?" Reagan was surprised.

"Yes, one of the larger asteroid pieces during the storm. The sensor array had already been damaged, and didn't pick it up in time to outmaneuver it. In all fairness, it was as big as the ship, traveling at incredible speed."

"What part of the hull was breached?" asked Reagan.

"Just the cargo bay, nothing lost. It was good to finally see the new bots in action," the android commented.

Reagan assumed position in the captain's chair, and tapped his fingers on the console to see their current position. A large holographic map popped up between the room's other consoles, above the emitter in the center of the floor. The ship was built to accommodate an entire crew, or it could be run by one android, synched with the ship.

"A few hours until we get there," Reagan declared with renewed energy. "I'm looking forward to getting started."

"Nice to see you again, Governor Vasilios." Deputy Governor Tarek Shaw was shaking Reagan's hand. "Your father was a fine leader and mentor. It was a loss for us all when he left for Isidore, so it's good that you are here in his stead. Although your father will no longer be working directly with our unit, we'll still be taking orders from him."

"It's good to see you as well, Deputy Governor Shaw. My father has always spoken highly of you. He thought of all of you as brothers-in-arms, not just as your governor. I've heard many stories of your work together over the years."

Shaw laughed. "No doubt your father exaggerated our role in some of the stories he told you." The other men smiled. "He always downplayed his own role and gave more credit to others than was due."

Reagan smiled. As he and Shaw walked towards the briefing room while the other men followed, he was glad to be with this unit that was so loyal to his father. His goal now was to ease into his role, learning what he could from these men.

During the debriefing, Deputy Governor Shaw was proud of Reagan for immersing himself immediately, asking questions about each situation. Reagan had grown from the young boy he had known on Isidore, into this fine young man. He was receptive and keen to learn from those more experienced. Reagan would be a great governor. Shaw would ensure that.

"So there are current investigations into this rumor of slavery on Reimus 5?" asked Reagan.

"Yes, we've uncovered what may just be a few isolated incidents of enslavement, but we are continuing to investigate in case there is more going on underground," answered Officer Marshall Jennings.

"Good, let's continue to investigate. Keep informant ears open at space stations and on planets close to Reimus 5. We need to nip it in the bud, to avoid repeating history," Reagan said.

The Secretary of Bureau Investigations recorded "Action Required" on the console that fed to the large screen. He then made a note of what actions were required and by who.

"Next, there's a minor issue that may need some routine follow up," said Deputy Governor Shaw, who was chairing the briefing. He looked over at Officer Slate Beckett. Reagan nodded for Beckett to proceed.

"One month ago, a group of colonists complained that working conditions in the mining operations had deteriorated. They stated that the corporations aren't following through with terms of their contracts. We started investigating the complaints, but were then told that conditions had improved.

"The three companies we received the most complaints about were the Aurora, Leo, and Asher Corporations. We contacted the corporations as well as the colonists who filed the complaints. The corporations and some colonists said the conditions had improved, but many of the colonists were unreachable. It's possible the conditions have improved," Beckett sounded doubtful, "or the corporations may have paid people off."

"And no additional complaints have come in since then?" asked Reagan.

"No. No more complaints have come in," said Beckett.

"But you question if the conditions have truly improved. Why so?" wondered Reagan.

Deputy Governor Shaw noticed that Reagan was perceptive, and was quick to address issues. Shaw smiled.

"The Miners' Guild originally allowed us to set up imaging as part of the investigation. Visuals haven't shown any new equipment or machinery delivered, which was part of the complaint." Beckett shuffled papers and read, "Lack of safety equipment and updated machinery."

"I'll look into it personally, since I need to acquaint myself with the corporate leaders and colonists," said Reagan. Secretary Cohen put "Action Required" on the screen. He made a note that Reagan would be following up with the complaints.

"Any other issues to add before we close?" asked Shaw. No response.

"Meeting adjourned."

Back in his office, with Deputy Governor Shaw standing by, Reagan attempted to reach the Aurora Corporation.

"Ah, it's the new governor, finally arrived," said the director of the Aurora Corporation. "Welcome to Quadrant 3."

"Greetings, Director Finley, and thank you," said Reagan.

"What prompts you to give us a call?" Director Rowan Finley asked.

Reagan answered diplomatically, "I'm doing routine follow up of some complaints that were made against your corporation one month ago. It's our responsibility to investigate each complaint that comes in."

"Ah, yes, we were able to come to terms with the Miners' Guild, and conditions have improved for them." The director smiled, but it looked like he was gritting his teeth. It was apparent that he was an impatient man, used to getting his way.

"That's great to hear," said Reagan with a genuine smile. "I'd like to close this case, so will be investigating. I wanted you to be aware of the reason."

"Well, thank you for the notice. When you interview the miners, you'll see conditions have improved since our talks," said Director Finley.

"That would be the best result in this situation. You wouldn't want tensions to disrupt the daily flow of your business profits," said Reagan.

"Well hopefully you'll be able to close the case quickly." Director Finley changed the subject. "How has your trip been so far? You must miss family and friends from back home. Too bad the distance is so far."

"Well, it's my first out-journey, so not too bad, and I would like to explore the quadrant. I'd like to discover how life here compares with life back home, and what our people could learn from those in Quadrant 3," Reagan said in a friendly manner.

"Well, that's great to hear. I have many contacts. I'll let them know of your wishes to see more of the quadrant. Perhaps you will receive invitations from some," said Director Finley.

"They would be well received," said Reagan.

"We'll be in touch," said the director. "Transmission end."

VITAARIA

Chapter Two

Those who obsess over wealth and power climb over others, forcing them down in the process. They attract others with the same obsession who will do the same to them when opportunity arises. It is a road of emptiness and betrayal that many young Vitaari have embraced.

Lord Bartholomew Sullivan, Owner of the Nicos Trading Company

K'vaal Ianov, of the reptilian race known as the Vitaari, thought so highly of himself that he had built a fantasy world inside his mind where the lovely Lady Isla was with him because she actually chose to be. As a result, he acted more as a suitor than her captor. He gave her special freedoms and indulgences, believing she would eventually fall in love with him.

He looked at his scaly face in the mirror and attempted a smile, but all it did was bare his teeth into a type of snarl. He would have to keep practicing.

He straightened his purple plaid bowtie so it sat properly over his white shirt with the lacy sleeves. He donned his long, fancy, purple dinner jacket to complete his outfit. His tailor had ensured his black pants and purple jacket sat properly over his thick tail without bunching up. His previous tailor had been "dismissed" due to ineptitude.

He thought of the Lady Isla, her beautiful elven form. She was of the Elanisse race, a beautiful and powerful group of beings.

K'vaal didn't like the idea of using Lady Isla for her abilities, so he put that out of his mind. He was taking her to the party as his companion. If she chose to use her power to benefit him, that was a sign of her devotion.

Gone were the days when she had been kept on a pretty golden leash attached to the necklace with jewels. He had enjoyed parading her for private audiences as his newly acquired pet. It wouldn't do to take her out like that, since he might be accused of slavery. But to own one of the Elanisse, and one of the royal family at that -- that was true power.

Months ago, he had surprised her and purchased her younger sister to live as a Lady on his estate, in his care. Lady Isla was speechless, and showed her appreciation by gently planting a kiss on the right side of his snout.

This evening, K'vaal was hoping the new governor would be introduced to Vitaari society. The young Governor Vasilios would be an important ally, if they could forge a bond. However, if he was anything like his father, he wouldn't be susceptible to bribes. But there had to be a way he could be distracted to look past some of their practices, K'vaal thought.

Suddenly, K'vaal had an idea. He would have Lady Isla's beautiful younger sister, Lady Cia, join the party as the governor's companion. Lady Isla would be absolutely delighted by the arrangement. This would be a major step, he thought, not just in gaining the governor's favor, but in winning his Lady Isla's love.

The first of the invitations came a few hours after Reagan's conversation with Director Finley. Reagan was sitting back in his chair at his cherry wood desk, hands behind his head. He was studying a smaller holographic projection of the planets of the Antares system, watching them revolve and rotate in fast time. He and Shaw had been discussing the current tensions between the Vodyanyov and the Kitsuine dynasties.

A minute later, a communication was hailing him.

"Transmit on screen," said Reagan.

Reagan saw a lizard-creature, ridiculously overdressed, in a gaudy purple coat with embroidery and white lace at the end of the sleeves.

"Good afternoon," said the creature. "I am K'vaal Ianov of the Vitaari Community. We wish to invite you to join us this*ss* evening on Vitaaria to meet *sss*ome local dignitaries."

"Why, thank you," replied Reagan. "I will be sure to attend. Please transmit details. Thank you," he ended.

"Transmission end," said the Vitaari.

"Interesting," said Reagan to Shaw, "I wonder where this will go."

"Dealing with the Vitaari is like dealing with a nest full of vipers," said Shaw. "They are vain and self-serving."

"Then this will be a good introduction for me," said Reagan. "I'll join them tonight, and when I'm out that way will try to get hold of the Miners' Guild in that sector. I want to be able to make arrangements to discuss issues with them over the next few days."

Reagan slowed down the holographic projection and zoomed in on the planet Vitaaria.

"Good idea, Governor." Shaw stood and shook Reagan's hand. "I'll let you prepare then."

The Antares system was a binary system with two suns, a large, older red giant and a small, young greenish-blue sun. The small blue sun, Vampirica, was amassing energy from Antares and was the source of heat for the solar system. The system contained seven planets, Vitaaria, Kitsuine, Vodyanyov, Colonist Planets Aleph, Bethel, and Gamuel, and a Z-Class planet insufficient to sustain life.

As Reagan approached Planet Vitaaria's surface in his shuttle that night, it was nearly as bright as day, due to the artificial lighting. The Vitaari seemed to have a very busy night life.

There was movement everywhere, traffic, shuttles coming and going. There were lighted entertainment novelties on top of buildings and in the open squares. Everywhere you looked, there was light in different shapes and colors.

He made his final approach, docking at the coordinates he had been given. He exited the shuttle, bracing himself, expecting he was about to walk into the lion's den.

He was led down several corridors to a fancy ballroom, the like of which he'd never seen. He took in the beautiful chandeliers, the elaborate crimson window dressings, dark antiques, classic paintings and tapestries. They all complimented a gold and crimson theme with deep purple highlights. His host, or his decorator at least, seemed to have good taste.

Although the colors were warm, Reagan shivered as he entered the room, as if he could sense malevolence in the air. These creatures were cold, very cold and calculating. He could see it in the glittering eyes that gave him piercing glances, apparent even under the low lighting. Some glanced up momentarily from their drinks or away from their companions to take in the newcomer. Calculating, those eyes were, always calculating.

At the same time, the creatures were almost comical to Reagan. All fancied up, stuffed into elaborate costumes. But Reagan kept a straight face and focused on the undercurrents, subtle torrents he knew could pull him under if he wasn't cautious.

The Vitaari had a sinuous way of almost slithering over to him, undulating in rhythm with the low tones in the background music. Reagan's presence was announced in an amplified voice to all those in the room:

"Governor Reagan of Houssse Vasssiliossss." Some gave a cursory glance at the man in dress uniform, others didn't break eye contact with those they were conversing with, still others stared.

Reagan stepped forward, ready to mingle with this hungry crowd, and stopped short. His eyes locked with the most beautiful creature he had ever seen.

Apart from her delicately pointed ears, Reagan would have thought she was from his own home world. Her eyes were large pools of purple, the shape of almonds, and she had the most beautifully shaped mouth. Her nose was straight, and her looks indicated an ancestral link to Isidore. She looked to be his own age. Next to her stood a lady with similar features but with darker hair, that Reagan surmised was her older sister.

Her sister's arm was held by a Vitaari with snake-like eyes, with an upturned sneer. Or perhaps he was attempting to smile. Reagan recognized him as the host of the gathering, the one who had sent him the invitation. He had been deep in conversation with another Vitaari, no doubt calculating and plotting. The majority at this gathering clearly had a lust for power, and were lobbying to gain more.

K'vaal Ianov was trying to pull himself free, as he kept glancing up at Reagan. "Pardon me," Reagan heard K'vaal say, hurriedly. "I mussst attend to our newessst guessst. We can continue thisss converssation later."

The Vitaari and the two ladies walked up to Reagan. He received a bow and curtsies, as K'vaal introduced "his" Lady Islanda, and the younger Lady Cianna. Reagan extended his arm to K'vaal to shake his hand, *(Or is it a paw? Reagan thought to himself)*, thanking him for the invitation.

"You are very welcome," K'vaal replied. "Lady *Ccc*ianna will be happy to be your companion for the evening."

Although regal Lady Isla exuded a dignity possessed by no other in that room, it was the younger Lady Cia who captured Reagan's eye. "Such a beautiful...party," he almost gulped with embarrassment, as he'd lost himself for a moment.

Reagan was slightly flushed as he held out his arm for Lady Cia. She gave him a shy smile, delicately placing her arm in his.

One of the Vitaari asked Lady Isla a question, and she moved into discussion with her companion and his acquaintances. Her musical laugh rang out as one of her company made a joke. Her companion also snickered at the comment. It looked as though those around Lady Isla sought her approval. Reagan noticed her glancing over at Lady Cia and himself from time to time, *Most likely as the older, protective sister,* he thought.

The host and his lady were objects of attention for those at the party. However, Reagan and his companion received a fair share of attention themselves. Vitaari were sidling over to them one after the other, attempting to draw Reagan into conversation, in order to meet the new governor.

Reagan observed faces of stone and unreadable expressions. He knew there were questionable motives behind many of them.

Regardless of the current political tensions between them, there were several in attendance from the Vodyanyov and the Kitsuine dynasties. They were in discussion with each other, as well as with the Vitaari.

The Vodyanyov were greyish, round-bodied, amphibian creatures with fat, moist, frog-like faces. They let off a muddy scent and tended to be loud and crass. Once in a while you would hear one of them belch in the middle of their laughter. It was a natural habit they were not ashamed of, so many people tried to avoid evoking a lot of laughter. Unfortunately, the Vodyanyov found many things to be amusing.

The Kitsuine were the exact opposite to the Vodyanyov. Tall, regal, and slender, with red-golden shiny fur, they were generally serious and perceptive with their fox-like eyes. They kept clean, and prided themselves in shining their fur with pleasantly scented oils. They were polite and formal in their dealings with others.

Reagan accepted two glasses of some type of liquid from one of the servers. "My Lady," he held one out to Lady Cia.

"Thank you, Governor Vasilios," she said, accepting the crystal glass.

"Call me Reagan," he said. He devoted his full attention to her, looking into her purple eyes. "So tell me about yourself." Reagan was very curious to find out how two Daughters of the Elanisse had ended up here, in Quadrant 3.

"Not a lot to tell, really," she said cautiously. "As you can guess, my sister and I are from planet Elanissia, close to Isidore."

"Do you miss your homeworld?" asked Reagan.

"Very much so," sighed Lady Cia. "However, currently neither my sister or I are in a position to travel back."

"Ah, business out here?" he asked. She nodded. "Do you know how long you will be staying here?"

"Well, currently our stay is indefinite in this quadrant. K'vahl has taken it upon himself to provide rooms for both my sister and I on his estate."

"That is kind of him to do so." Reagan sensed something troubling in the affirmative nod of her head. Perhaps she was missing her homeworld.

The servers were circulating, offering food to the guests and drinks to those with empty glasses. Reagan didn't intend to drink or it would dull his perception. He observed that other sharp-eyed attendees hadn't touched their drinks, or just took an occasional sip. Others, especially the Vodyanyov, were constantly trading empty glasses for full ones as servers floated across the room. K'vaal had very attentive servants, Reagan noticed.

A man at least twice Reagan's age walked up to them. He looked familiar. "Good evening, Governor Vasilios," he addressed Reagan, shaking his hand. He introduced himself. "My name is Bartholomew.

"Ah, and the lovely Lady Cianna." He held Cia's hand and kissed it. "I hadn't known until recently that Lady Islanda had a sister in this quadrant." Lady Cia flushed as she made a little curtsey. Reagan was surprised that he felt a pang of jealousy.

"It's nice that you are finally here. I know your father well," he addressed Reagan, "he is a good man and was fair when dealing with local disputes."

Reagan smiled at the mention of his father. "What trade are you engaged in?" asked Reagan.

"I'm just that. A trader, with my own fleet of trading ships." Bartholomew spoke freely. "I suppose some here would love to steal my cargo." He smiled, while gesturing not-so-subtly around the room.

He raised his hand pretending to whisper to Reagan, but spoke with a loud voice. "I have to admit that wine from Graffias is worth stealing." Reagan saw one of the Vodyanyov lick his thick lips, with the mention of Graffias wine.

Bartholomew laughed. "But jesting aside, I prefer to stay out of interworld conflicts and deal with trade between quadrants instead. Less hassle that way."

Reagan suddenly recognized who this man was. The trading company had been dealing with his own quadrant for two centuries. It was an ancient, established company, respected in many outerworlds.

"You're Lord Sullivan, owner of the Nicos Trading Company," Reagan said with wide eyes. "What are you doing with this group?" Reagan gestured to the party.

"You mean with these questionable characters? I could ask the same of you," Bartholomew chuckled. "So many interesting personalities though! Besides, K'vaal always throws a good party." He laughed.

"Actually, I'm here to broker the best deals I can get, which isn't to say much, since so much greed rules here. This is my least favorite quadrant to travel to, but it must be done. There are necessary resources here that other worlds need. Cava beans for one," the trader remarked. "And what brings you to Sector 5?" asked Bartholomew.

"Right now, Lord Sullivan, I'm doing follow up on a dispute that looks to be resolved, between the corporations and miners. It's a good opportunity to meet the parties involved," Reagan said.

"Just call me Bartholomew," he said. "That's a wise move, to familiarize yourself with future players. Perhaps you'll uncover what's *really* behind this corporation-colonist dispute," said Bartholomew, cryptically. "As I mentioned before, greed is a huge motivator in this quadrant. Follow the paperwork and you'll find out some interesting things." Reagan listened carefully then nodded.

"Call on me if you ever need anything," he said with a serious tone in his voice. "My lady." He smiled and waved to a group that had signaled him over, walking towards them with a hearty laugh.

Next they were approached by a random Vitaari who wished to make Reagan's acquaintance. He seemed quite amused at what was going on between the Vodyanyov and Kitsuine.

"Amazing how *ssso* many of u*sss* -- even current enemies -- can gather pea*ccc*efully at one pla*ccc*e, isn't it?" His grin was too large to be natural and actually looked like a wide grimace. "Although, if the opportunity arose, *sss*ome wouldn't hesitate to kill another if they could get away with it." He grinned with too many teeth, then moved on.

K'vaal and Lady Isla moved over to talk with Reagan and Lady Cia. "At Lady Isla's request, *sss*omeone mu*sss*t give you a tour of the area tomorrow," said K'vaal. "Would you like to *sss*stay in my gue*sss*t quarters tonight?" he asked Reagan.

"Oh, I wouldn't want to impose," replied Reagan.

"It would be no imposition at all," insisted K'vaal. "*Sss*stay with us, and Lady *Ccc*ia can give you a tour in the afternoon."

Reagan was eager to spend more time with Lady Cia to get to know her better, and to explore Vitaaria. He agreed to K'vaal's proposal.

"It'*sss* *sss*settled then," said K'vaal. "You'll join u*sss* for the midday meal and then you and Lady *Ccc*ia can *sss*set out for the day." K'vaal had no worries that secrets would be divulged. He had emphasized certain things to Lady Cia during the afternoon. She wouldn't want to put anything at risk. He was sure of it.

Reagan rose during the late morning, after a short night of sleep. The party had gone on until the wee hours of the morning. He couldn't understand how the attendees stayed up so late, night after night. However, they did like their double shots of cava. Drinking that would keep anyone awake.

He yawned as he turned down the bed, then gazed through the picture window at the sights below. This was the least active time during the day. Most activity would start in five or six hours from now, when it was dark again. The Vitaari were on a twenty hour clock, but twelve of those hours comprised the night.

As Reagan dressed in uniform, he stared out the window at the zoomcars below. The lanes were very similar to the busy cities on his own planet, zoomcars flying in both horizontally and vertically spaced lanes. Except he could tell that they weren't regulated here by electromagnetic grid.

Reagan couldn't understand why some planets preferred manual control of vehicles to orderly, streamlined transportation. On Reagan's planet, accidents only occurred due to mechanical malfunction, and vehicles were required to be inspected regularly. On planets like this one there were speed demons everywhere, people pushing passed others or forcing other vehicles out of lanes. Accidents just waiting to happen.

Of course, Reagan preferred to steer clear of the big cities in general. He enjoyed living in the country, and missed his home with green fields, gardens, archways, and trellises adorned with flowers. Much calmer there, and a place where one's mind became more productive.

Reagan was tying his brown leather vest at the waist, when there was a knock at the door.

"Come," said Reagan.

A young servant girl wheeled in a cart with a carafe of cava. The warm scent filled the room.

"Courtesy of the Lord and his Lady," she commented as though rehearsed, curtseyed, then backed out of the room. Her eyes were downcast at all times.

"Thank you," said Reagan, as the door closed. Reagan walked over and poured himself some cava. He took a sip from the intricately decorated mug. The cava was very good, definitely Cavienna brand.

He held the mug while gazing out the window again. He was thinking about the Lady Cia. There were so many interruptions last night that they barely had a chance to talk. *What was her story?* he asked himself. He was curious to know. Possibly he would get to know her better over midday meal. He was looking forward to it. He gazed out the window again.

The buildings here were tall and sleek, but decorated in a gaudy manner, each one trying to stand out more than the next. Just like those at the party last night. As if showiness would give them self-worth.

Reagan knew that as quickly as someone could rise to power, they could fall out of favor. He'd already seen one empire fall during his own lifetime, and had read of many others.

Thinking of books, Reagan walked over to a wall of leather bound editions. Reagan pulled out a volume titled *Dragons: Real or Myth?* He sat in the elaborately embroidered chair, placing his mug on an equally decorative round table, crossed his legs, and began to read.

Just after starting the third chapter, there was another knock on the door.

"Come," called Reagan.

The same young maiden, her eyes averted downwards, opened the door and delivered the message, "My Lord and his

Lady are ready to receive you, Governor." She closed the door again.

Reagan walked down the plushly carpeted stairs into the foyer. He was shown into the dining room by a formally dressed Vitaari, standing at the ready.

"Ah, hello, Governor Vasssiliosss." K'Vaal, Lady Isla, and Lady Cia stood in greeting. Reagan was placed opposite Lady Cia and next to Lady Isla, and they settled into their seats at the lengthy dining table.

"How are your rooms?" asked K'vaal.

"Very nice, thank you," Reagan replied.

"Ah, that*'sss* good," remarked the Vitaari, as he began to eat his meal.

Lady Cia looked up from her plate, venturing a glance at Reagan, then gave him a demure smile.

"You'll enjoy this dish. Decopidia," remarked Reagan's host, gesturing to his plate.

Reagan filled his fork with the deco and took a small amount into his mouth. It was indeed delicious. His host attempted to fill the conversation with small talk, but Reagan's attention had been captured by the beautiful Lady Cia. He answered and made the right comments and gestures to his host, but really his mind was elsewhere. On her.

"Do you prefer the countryside over the city?" asked Lady Cia perceptively. Reagan's host hadn't picked up on the few comments he'd made that suggested he preferred the countryside.

"Yes, I do," remarked Reagan.

"As do I," Lady Cia said. "It reminds me of my homeworld."

"Doesn't it get a bit tediousss though? The lack of crowds, excitement, parties, and all that?" asked K'vaal in a disdainful voice.

"No, not at all," laughed Reagan. He and Lady Cia then proceeded to talk about the fields, lakes, views of the mountains, and the places they'd seen. K'vaal was clearly bored by the conversation, but allowed it to continue without interruption. He saw that Lady Isla was enjoying listening.

By the end of the meal, Reagan and Cia were laughing together, and Reagan felt a type of camaraderie with her. Lady Isla just looked very thoughtful, but Reagan could see K'vaal calculating behind the scenes.

"Well, Lady Cia must give you a tour of the outskirts, not just the busy city then," smiled Lady Isla, as they were finishing the meal. "I know of some beautiful areas that I can recommend."

"I'd really like that," smiled Reagan.

"How boring," mumbled K'vaal, but then quickly followed up with, "But if you're *ssset* on it," he suddenly seemed very indulgent of Lady Isla, "then we shall have them go, my Lady." Reagan noticed a strange dynamic between the three of them, K'vaal, Lady Isla, and Lady Cia. He knew that K'vaal was clearly trying to impress Lady Isla, but as for the other, he couldn't put his finger on it.

Taking a zoomcar from the city was a wild ride. As they whipped from lane to lane, Reagan couldn't believe they hadn't been in an accident yet. The driving was insane.

Although they were switching to and from track, level, and lane constantly, their driver outmaneuvered and avoided the collision Reagan thought was imminent.

Reagan's stomach felt like it was in his throat, but at the same time, he felt a sense of exhilaration.

"Don't worry," Lady Cia who was sitting next to him whispered. "K'vaal hires only the best in the solar system." This relaxed Reagan...a bit. He still preferred the predictable system back on Isidore, with their electromagnetic grid.

Reagan and Lady Cia were dropped at the outskirts of the city to begin exploring.

"I haven't been here before, but this is one place Isla discovered that does remind her of home," said Cia.

Reagan looked at the pastures in front of him. It was very peaceful. "Then we can explore this new area together," he smiled, taking her hand.

The two of them started up the pathway to the right, and up to the top of the ridge on a hill.

"Ohhhh." Cia was scoping the area, taking in the sparkling crystal lake, the gardens, and the statues.

"This reminds me of Isidore," remarked Reagan.

"It is beautiful isn't it?" Cia spoke dreamily, as she breathed in the sweet air.

"Very much so," agreed Reagan. But he wasn't looking at the landscape. He was looking at this beautiful creature, walking beside him. Eventually Cia turned her head, and shyly looked up at him.

"I'd really like to see the lake," said Cia.

"Then let's head down there," said Reagan, smiling down at her.

Reagan led Cia down to the lake, making sure she didn't lose her footing on the pathway that wound down. He wanted to hear her laugh, to see her genuinely enjoy herself.

Reagan could tell she felt free and happy, as she walked beside him in her pale green, ruffled skirt, eyes shining. It was amazing what a change of scenery had done to her, Reagan was thinking.

They sat by the lake on a curved, white stone bench with a hedge behind it. "Isla says that people rarely come here. The

Vitaari mostly love the cities and the nightlife," she said, as she watched the lake shimmering in the sunlight.

"Well, it's nice to feel a piece of home. This is a place I will definitely plan to visit often." Reagan put his hands on the back of the bench, and leaned slightly backwards, just relaxing in the cool breeze. "This planet is really very beautiful in the daytime," he said, looking around him, "but you haven't done much exploring here yet? Did you arrive recently?"

Cia hesitated. "I've been here for a while," she said. "I just haven't been out much."

"Oh okay," said Reagan. "Well, I'm glad you're out now. It looks like getting out today has been good for you." He looked at her rosy cheeks and bright eyes. It was like life had been breathed into her, coming to this place.

"Thank you for sharing all of this with me," she said, shyly.

"Oh, it's my pleasure, really," said Reagan, smiling down at her.

The two of them spent the afternoon, just enjoying each other's company and the beauty of nature around them. When it was time to go, Reagan offered his arm, and they walked back up the path from the lake to meet K'vaal and Lady Isla.

Cia waved to them on the way up.

Lady Isla was smiling. She could see the change in her sister. She was indebted to K'vaal for purchasing and bringing Cia into the household as a free Lady. Although the Vitaari tended to be cold-hearted and greedy, she had seen a change in K'vaal during the time she had known him. Little did she know that it was because of her that he had changed.

Cia and Reagan took the zoomcar with them back into the city. Reagan tried not to outwardly cringe during the whole ride. Cia just looked amused every time she glanced at Reagan.

Apart from the rides in and out of the city, Reagan had enjoyed the day immensely.

As he prepared to depart via his shuttle, Reagan asked Cia if she would mind if he dropped by to see her again sometime. Her face blossomed into a beautiful smile. "Of course, I would love that."

He thanked his host for his hospitality, and hoped to drop by again soon.

TREACHERY

CHAPTER THREE

To be involved in treachery is to sign a contract with fate.

Lady Isla of Elinissia

Reagan was finally able to reach the Miners' Guild, and started conducting video interviews. However, he was hearing the same story in rote. The miners looked fearful and nervous, and offered no complaints. Reagan wasn't convinced they were being genuine. After the third interview, Reagan decided to travel to the first colonist planet, Aleph, to see conditions for himself.

Reagan set his shuttle down on Aleph an hour later. He took a look at the working conditions in and around the mine. He saw that they were less than ideal, even archaic. The safety equipment and machinery hadn't been upgraded in twenty years and it looked in need of serious repair. Evidence of manual equipment lying around was an indication that the miners were no longer using some of the machinery. The rusted machinery verified that suspicion.

Living conditions were poor, and the colonists were not doing well. There was sickness among the children especially resulting from inadequate heating and medical supplies, and limited rations.

Reagan documented everything with voice recordings and visuals, which would later be referred to in his report. Each

interview was also recorded, to assist Reagan with further investigations on individual statements or circumstances, should he see fit. Lord Bartholomew's words were stuck in his head. As a result, he was intent on investigating the situation thoroughly.

He knew he wasn't going to get to the truth of the matter through the interviews, but he wanted to develop rapport. He wanted to encourage people to anonymously contact him if they should wish to discuss things at a later time. Reagan didn't put any pressure on the miners in his discussions. He called them "friendly chats". Sometimes the first interview could be a bit intimidating for people, but he hoped that they might open up in a later discussion. Reagan doubted anyone would come forward this time, but there was always that possibility.

It wasn't until Reagan got hold of the actual contracts and questioned the bookkeepers that he became aware of what was really going on. He was going to have a lot to discuss with Director Finley and the other corporation leaders.

The second colony that Reagan visited had contracts with the Elizana and Jorati Corporations. There he found a very different picture. He was given a tour of the Elizana mining facility and the Jorati processing plant. The two corporations had given the colony the ability to process their own metal at cost. Overall the operation was excellent.

The Elizana and Jorati corporations clearly provided machinery. Everything was in good working condition, and he could see that miners were well-fed and clothed. The living area itself had grown into a modern city, well planned out with good infrastructure, community buildings, and adequate housing.

Reagan was very pleased to see this type of support from the corporations. From the interviews, he gathered that the two corporations were fair, thoughtful, and ethical. Payments were made in full, on time, and concerns were addressed in a timely manner.

The miners seemed genuine when asked about contracts and treatment, and there was no fear of speaking their minds. Naturally, there were a few "complainers" in the bunch, which usually occurred when people didn't grasp how good their situation was.

Overall Reagan was satisfied. The contracts had been renewed repeatedly over the last century, showing stability, and Reagan could tell the companies had treated the colonists well.

Reagan visited two more colonies that day, then contacted K'vaal Ianov, as he wished to visit Lady Cia.

"Well, visits to the colonies on Aleph have shown that the miners have inadequate modern machinery and safety equipment to accomplish the type of work you are requesting of them," said Reagan to Director Finley.

Director Finley look flustered. Reagan could see on the screen that his face was turning a light shade of pink. He hadn't expected Reagan to actually go out of his way to visit the colonies. He thought Reagan would rely solely on video transmission interviews. "Look, Governor. It's the miners' responsibility to provide their own equipment for the mining operations. If the equipment is outdated, it's due to the Miners' Guild's own mismanagement of the funds we graciously allot them, to support their colony and their business."

"However, based on last year's records," Reagan pulled up the numbers on his console from the Aurora file, "it shows that your payments didn't even meet a minimal standard of living for the colonists. They didn't have enough to support themselves, let alone purchase equipment necessary to complete job quotas."

"*Governor*." Director Finley was more than visibly irritated now, and used the title 'Governor' as if addressing one of his inferiors. "If the colonists declare they no longer want to work the mines, then you know the procedure. We bring in our own workforce and stake claim to both the mines and their land. The agreement is clear about that."

"Please let me finish, Director Finley. The amount you are currently paying them is dated back twenty years. You have not increased the amount of payment, even though the 'cost of living' has risen multiple times since the original agreement." Reagan would not back down.

"I know what's in the agreement," barked Director Finley. *But I didn't think you would find the 'cost of living' clause! That could ruin us!* he thought. "The bookkeepers are currently in discussions about the amount to increase the payments since the original agreement."

Reagan could tell Director Finley was lying, and the Aurora Corporation had hoped that clause would continue to be overlooked. He thought it was ridiculous that the corporation still hadn't paid the amount for increased cost of living. Director Finley knew it was ridiculous as well. The Aurora Corporation was trying to "legally" take over the mines and the colonists' land by giving them no other choice.

If the colonists went back to focusing on becoming autonomous in other ways, without working the mines, the corporations could swoop in. Reagan knew there would be nothing to stop corporation dominance on a planetary scale. He had seen it before. However, if the colonists continued to work under current conditions, they would continue to live in poverty.

If the Aurora Corporation paid up the amount owed for the last twenty years, the colonists would be able to purchase the equipment and machinery. They would be able to raise their quality of living significantly, as well as hold on to their land and way of life.

"See that your bookkeepers sort out the percentages sooner rather than later," said Reagan, "or else I will have no choice but to give the case directly to Magistrate Kian Anderson to deal with."

Director Finley was too incensed to answer. "Communication end," he said forcefully.

Reagan had been visiting Lady Cia whenever he could during the week he was investigating the colonies. When he was too far to make the trip, or needed to honor an invitation, they spent time in video calls together. On his way back to the Galactic Investigations Bureau outpost, he dropped by to see her. They were sitting in their favorite spot, by the lake on Vitaaria. Reagan had asked Cia to show him her Elanisse abilities first-hand. Lady Cia placed her hands gently on Reagan's cheeks. She asked him to close his eyes, and she closed hers to concentrate.

"Think of something that causes you anxiety," she said to Reagan. Reagan thought about riding in a zoomcar on Vitaari.

"Okay, now I'm going to cause a mind-shift. Tell me what you feel," Cia said. Reagan suddenly felt relaxed, even though he was still thinking about his ride out.

"I feel like my anxiety just faded away." Reagan was in awe. "What an incredible gift you have, Cia."

"This time I'll demonstrate how thoughts can be planted," said Lady Cia.

She placed her hands gently on Reagan's cheeks again, and Reagan closed his eyes. She then concentrated.

Reagan said, "Peace. The thought is of peace."

"That's right," smiled Lady Cia.

"Can you do it in reverse and read what someone else is thinking?" asked Reagan.

"I can usually sense their emotions, but not specific words," Cia said. "I'm not as skilled as Isla yet."

"See if you can sense what I'm feeling," suggested Reagan. He asked her to close her eyes, then he placed his hands gently on her cheeks.

A moment later, she started to blush.

Reagan gently moved his face closer to Cia's, and his lips softly brushed against hers. Cia's lips responded to his, and she put her arms around him. They touched noses, drawn together in a tender kiss. They kissed again. Reagan held Cia in his arms, close to his chest.

Of the twenty-two mining colonies that Reagan investigated while he was in Sector 5, only four had favorable conditions. The other eighteen colonies he visited were living and working in impoverished conditions.

Only five corporations were meeting their workers needs. Of the other fourteen corporations Aurora was the most diverse, with contracts with eight different mining colonies in the Antares system.

As he travelled from Vitaaria, Reagan finished writing his thorough report. He had detailed facts based on financial reports and his own observations, and had reinforced his points with visuals. The Aurora Corporation wasn't the only corporation that owed "cost of living" backpay.

Reagan had outlined his requirements under each contract in order for those corporations to avoid sanctions. They included machinery replacement and backpay for missing wages, which for some was an exorbitant amount of money. Reagan set up a reasonable payment schedule with deadlines.

Once he was done, he saved it on the ship's computer. Then he sent his report as a communicae to the nineteen leaders of the corporations. An hour later, he was hailed by Director Finley, who wanted to meet with Reagan in person.

Reagan entered the ship's boardroom, ready to answer questions the directors had about his report. The Aurora Corporation had extended its courtesies to Reagan and the other directors to join them for a "Question and Answer period". For some reason, Reagan felt uneasy.

"Take a seat, Governor," the leader of the Aurora Corporation directed, while gesturing towards an empty chair.

"We wanted to talk about some changes that we'd like to see in your report," said Director Rowan Finley, hands folded under his chin, staring Reagan directly in the eye.

"Changes?" Reagan couldn't hide the surprise in his voice. "What kind of changes?" he asked cautiously.

"Well," spoke the director, "we, the corporations, are going to assume that this is your 'preliminary draft', and not the final report that will be submitted to the Galactic Investigations Bureau."

"Okay, let's just say it's a preliminary draft." Reagan wanted to find out what their game was. Suddenly, the tension lessened in the room. "What changes are we speaking of?"

"First of all, there is the payment schedule," said Director Finley. "We'd like that recommendation removed. We can negotiate payment with the Miners' Guild ourselves."

Reagan's face hardened as he listened to this weasel dictate terms to him. He could see that the director had a long list in front of him, which he proceeded to go through. The list eliminated every significant recommendation Reagan had made.

"Pardon me for interrupting, but are you speaking on behalf of all the corporations mentioned in my report?" asked Reagan. Around the table, the corporate heads nodded, most avoiding eye contact with Reagan. Only the Aurora, Leo, and Asher Corporation directors actually made eye contact, and their eyes were hardened.

"Yes, the corporations represented *in this room* are now operating officially as the new, unified Corporate Alliance," smiled Director Finley, with a shifty gleam in his eyes.

Suddenly, Reagan noticed that the five corporations he had spoken highly of in his report didn't have representatives in attendance. Had he just walked into an ambush?

"The normal procedure, which I believe you'll find reasonable," said Reagan in a quiet voice, "is to present your arguments and reasoning as an addendum to my report. Your comments will appear directly beside my recommendations, so the council and magistrate will be aware of where you stand on matters. If your logic is good, then they may override the recommendations I've made, and go with your suggestions instead. Other than those added notes, the report stays as is. I'll not cover up the truth."

Director Finley's face had been hardening as Reagan was talking, and now he looked outraged.

"Are you sure you want to go down this route, *Governor?*" He spat out Reagan's title in a mocking tone of voice.

The same corporate directors were gazing at him with hardened faces. The others averted their eyes, some looking embarrassed, others as though they wished to be elsewhere.

"If you do, then you won't like the result," warned Director Finley with a menacing tone.

"Are you threatening me?" asked Reagan in the same quiet tone. "I said, the report stays as is, except I will add your own comments *as your own*. I'm ready to add in your own recommendations whenever..." Reagan never had a chance to finish his thought.

In the middle of his sentence, Reagan felt a blinding pain in the back of his head. He heard gasps and saw shocked faces on some, and sly smiles with knowing eyes on others. Some in that boardroom had been aware of Director Finley's plan, whereas others apparently hadn't been aware. It was a skilled move on the part of Director Finley's, to make the others complicit. Now they would be forced to side with him in future dealings. If the director was willing to dispose of the governor, then he would have no qualms against "removing" the head (possibly literally) of a corporation with little or moderate power.

Reagan vaguely felt himself being carried from the boardroom to the shuttle bay. He was in and out of consciousness, and time didn't seem to exist. He felt like he was floating on air, then felt the hard grips of the two men transporting him.

What seemed like a lifetime later, he felt himself sitting with a harness on in the pilot's seat of his shuttle. *How did I get here?* he wondered. Then he was seeing black again.

"Hacked in...locked in on autopilot...unable to change course...I've disabled both manual and safety protocols..." Reagan heard a voice say miles away. He passed out again.

When the shuttle left the docking bay, Reagan wasn't aware of it.

Z-CLASS

CHAPTER FOUR

When Reagan came to his shuttle was hurtling downwards. He jammed on the controls and pulled up on the handle. But it was no use, the controls had been disabled and a crash was now imminent.

He scrambled to find a space suit and parachute. Being bounced around by turbulence in his condition complicated things. His sense of balance was thrown off, making coordinated movement difficult as he clambered to the back of the shuttle. He hoped he would find what he needed in the cargo hold.

Thankfully, the corporate lackeys hadn't checked underneath the floor panels in the small cargo hold. His extra suit, survival pack, and parachute were there. He removed the panels while hanging onto a cargo net to prevent himself from slipping down to the front of the shuttle.

At 12,000 feet Reagan put on his space helmet, and pounded the "eject button". He was forcefully ejected upward and away from the shuttle. He deployed his parachute and was floating in the cloud cover when he heard the shuttle crash. He saw the orange flash of the explosion reflected in the clouds.

As he pulled on the levers and descended more rapidly through the cloud cover, he didn't know what to expect below. "Calculate Barycentric Celestial Reference System directions. What planet is this?" Reagan asked.

He checked the console on his inner left arm and his heart sank. This planet had been deemed centuries ago to be a Z-Class planet. It was uninhabitable by humans, and incapable of sustaining life.

When he cleared the invisibility belt, he was able to get his first glance of the planet's surface. Though his scope was limited, he could see that he was descending towards a desert. There was a rocky plate next to it, and further away what looked like vegetation. It looked like there was a lake in the middle of the vegetation. This was surprising, as records said this planet was incapable of supporting life. His heart was lifted, but only slightly.

"Calculate Cardinal Directions based on Polaris System," Reagan ordered. As he descended further, he saw the desert became rocky the further north he got. Using the handles, he steered towards a small pool of beige that looked relatively smooth. Preparing for a hard landing due to the merging rocky plate, he was pleasantly relieved that the impact was light. He must have touched down on some very soft ground.

After detaching the cables, he began rolling up the parachute. The readings on his space suit indicated that the air was safe to breathe, a combination of 74% nitrogen and 25% oxygen. His fingers clicked on the metal catches on the neck of his helmet, and the air release valve in his suit closed as his helmet opened. Between his survival pack, parachute, and helmet, he had quite a bundle to carry. He strapped everything to the survival pack, then lifted it onto his back. It was surprisingly light.

Reagan's first priorities were to find water to preserve what he had, and to find protective shelter. He had water in his survival pack, a water-purifying canteen, and an emergency shelter tent. He decided to travel on the rocky plateau and take shelter overnight, part way across. His goal was to get close to the vegetation and lake.

"Map the terrain according to Polaris Cardinal Directions," Reagan ordered.

He lifted his right foot to step north, and his walking stride put him into more of a bounce. The gravity was much less than he was used to. Travelling was going to be much faster than what he had originally anticipated.

He set off north to cross the rocky plateau, hoping to find protective shelter before nightfall. Although Reagan had no idea when nightfall would be, the sun was more than three quarters of the way across the horizon. He didn't want to stay close to the desert side of the plateau because it looked like windstorms had caused the erosion there.

Reagan noticed the sand particles were large and coarse compared to what he had seen back home on the expansive beaches. He took some geological samples. He felt himself moving from lower-impact sand, to stones with rock underneath, and then finally to rock. He couldn't identify the rock, but its texture was similar to slate and it was the color of tar. He took more samples, in case he ever got off this forsaken planet.

He was getting used to the gravitational change, and became more accurate in his stride. Clearly the planet had less mass than Isidore, as each step was taken with ease, and the burden on his back felt light.

This isn't too bad, Reagan thought to himself. He was going at a good clip, about twice his normal pace. He knew that a long-term stay on the planet would weaken his bones, but a short-term stay, being able to move this quickly, might not be too bad.

As he sped across the rocky ground and moved further north, Reagan saw different rock formations developing. He had always been fascinated by geological change due to acute natural catastrophe or long-term development. Erosion, tectonic plate movement, changes due to extreme weather formations, it all interested him.

As time flew by, he tried to imagine what had caused this planet's terrain to develop as it had done. Well, at least this small area of the planet's surface. The rest of the planet might be very different than what he was experiencing.

Reagan's suit was equipped with a map-tracker, and it began automatically charting out the area. The device measured distances between landmarks, mapping out direction and distance so those places could be easily found again. He had started at ground zero [0,0] and was now at [5.7,0] north, according to his map-tracker.

He estimated that he would need to travel to [6,0] to reach the vegetation, but finding protective shelter looked hopeful here. He was looking for an indentation that would keep his survival tent out of any severe weather storms, and give him some good cover. Then he could continue later to the vegetation.

A large rock formation had caught his eye, and Reagan slowed down.

Looking good, Reagan thought. At the base of the small mountain, there was a cavernous opening that went deep into the rock. Reagan set his map-tracker to mark it as a landmark and to map the cave inside. He then ventured inside the tunnel, turning on his torch once inside.

The cave diameter was about the same as Reagan's height. He could stand up, spread his arms out wide, and still have a bit of room to spare. He didn't venture in too far. If vegetation was thriving on this planet, who knows what else could be living here?

Reagan noticed that the light and temperature had both dropped. *Perfect timing,* he thought. He wouldn't want to be outside if there was a severe temperature drop, especially if wind or snow accompanied it. His suit was regulated, but it was only effective to a certain degree. Although there looked to be vegetation on this planet, Reagan couldn't be sure what its temperature thresholds were. It might just go dormant if the temperature hit below freezing.

The temperature was falling quickly. Reagan decided to go deeper into the tunnel in case there were violent night storms on this planet. He turned a corner, and his map-tracker continued to map out his path. He found a suitable cavern for his tent, with three additional tunnel openings around it.

The temperature seemed to level out at above freezing inside the cavern. Reagan began setting up his survival tent. He went back and placed a sensor at the cave opening, and three more at the tunnel openings in the cavern. Although he hadn't seen or detected anything living on this planet yet, apart from the vegetation to the north, he didn't want to take any chances.

Reagan opted to sleep without his helmet on. His suit would wake him if there was a severe temperature drop that penetrated his survival tent.

He had covered a huge distance today. It had been so exhilarating, traveling with less gravitational pull, that Reagan hadn't noticed his own muscle tiredness. He realized now that he was sore and tired, and his body needed to rest. He thought of Cia and the several visits he'd had with her. Then he drifted off to sleep.

Reagan was awakened three hours later by a strange sound, a howl in the distance. He sat upright and alert, holding his breath so he could listen carefully. It seemed there was other life on this planet, possibly some type of animal?

Again came the howl, this time closer. Reagan scrambled to stuff his things into his pack, deflate his tent, and strap it to his pack. He put on his helmet, clicking in place the metal clasps as he did so. He set his suit on "filtration mode" in case he encountered poisonous vapors in the tunnels. As he put his pack on his back, he heard the noise again. He backtracked, and listened to another howl at the cave entrance, but couldn't tell which direction the noise was coming from. Sounds were bouncing off the rock formations outside the cave.

Reagan ran deeper into the cave and down the left tunnel he thought of as tunnel A, helmet torch turned on. His map-tracker automatically recorded each turn he made. "Label tunnel A," he commanded the map-tracker. He would easily be able to retrace his steps without getting lost, if the need arose. Reagan set his helmet to project a holographic layout of the cave system. The map-tracker recorded it and constructed possible openings based on the current layout.

Strangely, the signal wasn't able to penetrate past the walls of the tunnel he was in, so he'd have to rely on probability. He followed twist after turn. Unfortunately, being able to leap further than usual didn't really benefit him inside these tunnels. Once in a while he purposely dropped a sensor when the tunnels branched.

For a while, he didn't hear anything else. He pressed himself against the cave wall, resting for a minute, and tried to slow his heart-rate. Perhaps it was just a dog. Maybe it was hunting something else. Or maybe it wasn't hunting anything at all. For all he knew, that noise could be part of a mating ritual, assuming the creature mated.

Suddenly, the howl repeated itself, but this time it reverberated through the caves. It was answered by a bunch of faint barking sounds. *Okay, it sounds like there is a pack of dogs behind me,* Reagan thought. At that moment, one of the possible openings turned out to be a dead end, which corrected itself on the holographic map. The hole was too small due to a cave-in. Reagan ran back the way he came to take the next turn. He could still hear a faint barking, and the holographic map marked the opening sensor. That meant the pack had passed the first marker at the entrance.

Reagan delved deeper into the labyrinth of tunnels. He seemed to be going uphill. He saw that the pack had crossed all three of the tunnel markers at the branches. Maybe they knew these tunnels and were planning to cut him off. Every once in a while he heard a faint low grunt from the animals that seemed to be tracking him, from somewhere in the tunnels.

Reagan was far ahead of them, and moving at a good clip. However, he thought he should get a better idea of what was following him, if it meant not needing to backtrack. He found his opportunity high up in one of the expansive caverns. There was a small hole there, just big enough to put his head through. He heard movement in the tunnel next to his, from a tunnel he had passed through some time ago in this labyrinth.

Cautiously, Reagan scaled the wall, using indentations and outcrops for hand and footholds. When he got to the top, he looked through the hole, shining his helmet torch on the mob below him. He was surprised to see they weren't dogs or wolves.

A large reptilian creature glared up at him and sounded a loud bark. The rest of the creatures stopped and looked up, but were blinded by the light and couldn't get a good view of Reagan. Reagan noted although these reptiles were a bit shorter than him, if he was cornered there was no chance of survival. He could see strong muscular reptilian forms with thick skin, sharp teeth and claws.

One of the smaller reptiles reared up on its hind legs, turning its head as though listening for something. Suddenly, it flew at the wall, scrambling up its side, using its huge front claws to pull itself up and back claws for balance. The snapping jaws missed Reagan's helmet as he jerked back, and half slid, half jumped down his side of the wall.

Thankfully, the reptile's head was too large to maneuver through the hole. There was no way its body would fit through either, so Reagan was safe, for now. Reagan started running, picking up the pace. There was no way he was going to let himself be caught.

The pack still had a distance to go before they caught up with Reagan. There were multiple twists and turns in the maze which would keep slowing down their pace. However, Reagan heard the pack speed up with a renewed energy.

Reagan hoped for no more dead ends. He thought to himself, *A dead end here would literally be a dead end for me.*

Reagan looked at the holographic projection made by his map tracker. It had mapped out the tunnel, and he could see a pattern. He was moving inward, towards a center point. Reagan hoped that didn't mean a dead end or intersection with one of the other tunnels.

"Map out possible routes for tunnels B and C," ordered Reagan. The holographic projection showed possible routes in red, whereas actual routes were in blue. "Remap out possible routes for tunnels B and C," ordered Reagan. Both times it showed tunnels B and C heading towards the center of the maze, just like his own tunnel.

There was a red blink on the hologram. Another sensor had been triggered. The pack was closing in more quickly than he'd hoped. He saw their current position, and realized he was in a "do or die" situation. He ran uphill as fast as his legs could carry him. Instead of watching where he was going, he was relying solely on the holographic projection. He trusted the map tracker to sense the walls with sonar before he ran into them.

The map-tracker was constructing possible routes for tunnels B and C while he was running through tunnel A. All three tunnels would eventually merge or surface close to each other, since the space was being compressed as they moved towards the mountain top.

Reagan could hear evidence of the reptiles in the other tunnels, a slip here, stones being dislodged there. No holes in the walls were large enough to worry about an ambush. He must have taken the longest tunnel, as it seemed the reptiles in tunnels B and C were keeping pace with him.

Then Reagan heard it. A deep, low rumbling was coming from the center of the cave system. Simultaneously, a low screeching sound echoed through the caverns. Reagan stopped in his tracks.

As though in response, Reagan heard howling and barking from the reptiles. He tried to cover his ears, forgetting he was wearing a helmet. Stones showered on him from the wall behind him. Reagan could hear part of the pack quickly retreating. Whatever was in the center of the caves was clearly a threat to the reptiles.

Reagan shivered. If he went back to the outskirts of the caves, he would either encounter reptiles on the way or at the end. The pack would be waiting for him. But going further in would mean facing the creature that made that low, screeching sound. If the pack had retreated because of it, it was something they feared. He heard barking behind him getting closer. It looked like he didn't have a choice. He started towards the labyrinth center.

Suddenly, he felt a breeze coming from the center, and heard a swooshing and flapping sound. The smells floating with the breeze from the inner cavern were not pleasant. It smelled of death, decay, and rotting flesh. Reagan tried not to gag.

Then the breeze and flapping subsided and there was enraged screeching.

Although there was a soft glow at the end of his tunnel, (*A way out!* he thought), Reagan saw no shadows on the wall of his angled tunnel. That meant nothing dangerous was directly beside the opening. Knowing that some reptiles were gaining ground in tunnel A, he realized he had no choice but to scoot inside. He would find a hiding place or go directly for the exit. He felt his fate was precarious, as though he stood on a precipice and was about to fall over the edge.

Reagan ran out of the tunnel at full speed and skidded across the floor to the right. He then tumbled into a corner of the dimly lit cavern. The stench now hit Reagan full force, and he vomited in his helmet, as he realized he was sitting in a pile of what was once another reptile. The substance he had skidded on, was that reptile's entrails, stretched out over the floor.

Reagan tried to clear the outside of his helmet off so he could see what he was up against. The roaring and barking was deafening.

Then he saw them. He watched in awe as two gigantic, winged reptiles on the other side of the room pulled a reptile apart. The book he'd read at K'vaal's popped into his head -- these winged reptiles looked like dragons! Apparently, the other two tunnels emptied into this room. He saw reptiles charging into the room, trying to jump on the dragons. They were using their razor sharp claws, without much effect. The dragons, however, were snapping up the lizards and tearing them apart. Reagan wondered if he'd been inadvertently caught in some territorial battle. That was until he saw a dragon headed his way.

Reagan ducked down and rolled in the lizard goop, sliding part way under the dead reptile. He then saw that he hadn't been noticed yet. The reptiles from his tunnel had caught up and were running into the room. They were targeting an area close to Reagan which he had overlooked in all the chaos. A group of six baby dragons huddled together about twenty feet from Reagan. They looked overexcited and were squawking and chirping, tiny wings flapping.

The dragon snapped up the reptile just in time, before it landed on the baby dragons. The babies were half as big as the reptiles, and didn't have thickened skin, sharp teeth, killer claws, or killing experience. They were defenseless.

More reptiles spilled into the room from the tunnel. The dragon grabbed another and tossed it hard against the cave wall, stunning it. Both dragons moved into a defensive position around the nest, but the reptiles kept coming.

Reptiles were being thrown, scrambling to get up, then resuming their attack. But they had no apparent effect on the large dragons. One of the babies was so excited that it tumbled out of the nest. The dragon on the other side looked back and growled at the baby, who scrambled to get back inside. The dragon pushed it in the rest of the way with its snout.

Two of the reptiles took that opportunity to jump onto the dragon's neck, and take a flying leap towards the nest. The dragon used its wing to block their way. The reptiles were able to slice through the thick skin of the wing using their hind, sickle-shaped claws in a slashing motion. Apparently, the scales on the wings weren't as thick as the dragon's other scales.

The dragon was thrown into an enraged frenzy, snapping at the two reptiles with its jaws. The reptile claws ripped more of its wing.

Reagan was watching this amazing battle through his vomit-soaked helmet. Or he *was* watching until a reptile was thrown backwards into his corner. The reptile lay upside-down and looked dead, but Reagan kept an eye on it even in all the chaos. After a few minutes, he saw it open its eye and blink. Then it rolled over onto its front, shook its head, and shakily got back onto its hind legs. It was in the perfect position to make a leap onto the nest.

Reagan knew he was dead meat. At least he was to all the reptiles in the cavern, including the one three feet away from him. He smelled like dead meat, was wrapped in dead lizard meat. In effect he had erased his presence.

He racked his brain to figure out what to do. He didn't want to see the infants harmed. And although this wasn't his fight, he'd prefer to sneak out of a dragon's nest than face these vicious creatures. He had no viable weapon, as his knife wouldn't slice through the lizard's tough skin.

The lizard shook its head again, and tried to focus on what was going on around it. Then it spied the nest. At that moment, Reagan played a recording of the barking he had heard earlier.

The reptile looked over confusedly at the dead lizard lying by its feet and on top of Reagan. Most importantly, the closest dragon looked backwards sharply, saw the reptile, and snapped it up before it could attack the nest.

Reagan could see the dragons were tiring, especially the one that had the torn left wing. They had already taken out over thirty reptiles, killing or disabling them, and the injured dragon was stumbling slightly. The dragon on the left looked at his companion and made a low rumbling noise. Then it suddenly stretched upright, arched over, and dove straight forward towards one of the reptiles. Using its plated head and horns, it railed into it and those behind, smashing all five against the opposite wall. Three of the reptiles were dead, and the dragon then detached its horns from the dead ones, and snapped the necks of the other two stunned ones, using its teeth and claws.

The dragon then drew itself up into that majestic position again, for another charge. The remaining reptiles fled down the tunnels, barking as they ran. The dragon went to each tunnel opening, roaring, perhaps as a warning. The tunnels were too small for the adult dragons to fit through, or the healthy one might have pursued the lizards. The dragon then soared across the cavern to where the injured dragon was lying down in front of the nest. The healthy dragon covered the other with its wings, huddling their heads close together, and settled down to rest. A low growl and pointed look settled down the excited chicks and they stopped chirping. The family settled down to sleep.

Reagan lay there in the corner, behind the dragons, and wondered what he should do. He was glad he had been in his protective suit before entering this "cavern of death".

He knew he would have to work quickly and quietly, or it was all over for him. He carefully wormed his way out from underneath the lizard carcass, then crawled forward. This would eventually place him next to the adult dragon that had fought in front of him. However, it was the best way to the center of the cavern, beneath the giant hole in the ceiling.

The dim light coming through the hole was that of a morning sunrise. It seemed that night was only five hours long here. Reagan wondered how long the days were. If Reagan was correct in assuming these dragons were nocturnal, he had the best chance of making it out alive sooner than later.

In his survival pack, Reagan found a coil of rope, which he quietly pulled out. He unfolded and attached a grappling hook to the end and hoped his aim would be true.

Reagan swung the grappling hook on the rope, trying to avoid slipping in the sea of reptile goo, then hurled it upwards. Unfortunately, it rebounded with a "clunk" on the cavern floor and landed with a "sploosh" in reptile remains. One of the adult dragons stirred slightly, but Reagan had nothing to worry about. At least that's what he kept telling himself.

Reagan picked up the grappling hook, gathering the slime-covered rope. He threw the hook again as high as he could. It went through the large hole and caught on something. *Yes!* thought Reagan. Now he needed to get out quickly.

Reagan tested the rope before his ascent. He wrapped the rope around one leg to anchor himself, then draped it across the top of the other boot. He hoped it would provide enough of a brake as he climbed. The rope fed easily, but he had to clamp hard on the slimy rope to make sure he didn't slide. It wasn't the fastest way to get up a rope, but it was the safest way.

At the top, Reagan's body was halfway onto the ground when his movement brought down a shower of stones. One of the baby reptiles startled awake. Within a few seconds, the little one's chirps had awoken all the babies. They became excited when they saw movement at the top of the cave. *Oh boy,* thought Reagan, as he pulled the rest of his body onto the ground. He headed down the side of the mountain in leaps and bounds. He left his rope and hook there, having another set in his pack.

Drops of rain started falling. Within a minute, it was a steady torrent.

Reagan looked backwards and saw one of the adults' heads poking out of the hole. Shaking its head groggily, blinking in the sun, it clawed its way out frantically. The dragon perched on the edge of the ceiling opening, and let out a mighty roar. Reagan saw a crevice, and half-slid, half-slipped right into it, not slowing his pace. He could see the silhouette of the giant reptilian head against the sun, with its extended snout and glittering teeth.

The dragon sniffed the air, then the ground, unfurled its wings, then began searching the mountain-top. Reagan silently waited, hoping the dead reptile remains and rain would keep his scent hidden. He still smelled the terrible stench of death and decay that was caked on his suit, and the dried vomit in his helmet. Reagan tried not to gag again, but his body moved involuntarily, and his helmet bumped against the rock.

The dragon suddenly looked over in Reagan's direction, its eyes narrowed. With a growl, the dragon gathered itself together and slid down the side of the mountain. It used its wings to keep an even pace, and its claws to navigate over the rocky surface. It was headed straight for Reagan's hiding place.

Reagan held his breath, then moved as far backwards as he could. The space was just high enough for his body to wiggle back a few more inches. The dragon reached the outcropping and tried to get at Reagan, using its large snout. However, it couldn't open its jaws since the rock above and below prevented it. The dragon pulled its head back to breathe without inhaling the accumulating rain water, then attempted to get at Reagan with its razor-sharp claws. Its arms were not quite long enough to penetrate that deeply.

Realizing that it couldn't get at Reagan, the dragon let out a roar. Then it turned around, and Reagan thought maybe it would return to its nest.

But then came a scraping noise. The dragon was trying to claw through the rock! Reagan knew he'd be okay as long as he stayed deep within the crevice. The water had covered the outside of his helmet, blurring his sight. He switched over to "oxygenation mode" before the water from his suit leaked into his helmet. There were risks, switching from filtration mode in a suit partly filled with water, but he felt it was a bigger risk to surface for air, when there was an angry dragon hunting him.

Reagan expelled his breath, then inhaled, laying there for a few minutes, when suddenly a loud bang sounded above him, and the rock started to shake. Reagan groaned. The dragon was pouncing on the rock, trying to crush him. Thankfully, the rock was too solid to crack.

As the sun rose higher and the rain stopped, suddenly the banging and shaking stopped. Reagan saw the blurry image of a dragon drawing back from the outcropping, and moved his head forward to see better. The dragon's eyes were blinking rapidly in the sun, its wing shielding its face, steam rising off its hard, leathery skin. It then fixed its yellow eyes angrily on Reagan in the crevice and let out a mighty roar. After that, it flew upwards to the cave where its mate and the young ones were resting.

As soon as the dragon had disappeared down the hole, Reagan surfaced. He decided to make a dash down the mountainside. Easier said than done. He took a tumble in his waterlogged, imbalanced suit. He hid behind an outcropping where he drained the water.

The dragon would have to be highly motivated to pursue him, but his heart was still pounding. Reagan hoped the dragon was too tired after a night of protecting its young from invading reptiles.

Further down, Reagan found a place where the water had pooled from the rain, and cleaned the vomit out of his helmet. He'd need to disinfect the filtration system. Well actually, the entire suit.

After a minute's rest he clipped the helmet to his pack, inhaling the fresh, clean air. He then started down the mountain, skidding and slipping due to wet rock. Reagan was aware he was about to hit the vegetation. Then he saw them.

A pack of reptiles was at the north side of the mountain, slightly to his left. *There must be a tunnel exit around here,* he thought. He was about to slow down to find somewhere to hide, but it was too late. One of the reptiles started barking, and the others turned their heads to look in Reagan's direction.

Still running full tilt, he took a giant leap of faith. His foot touched the ground between the thick, steamy vines that covered marshy ground. It seemed to be some type of humid jungle floor, but he'd never seen plants like these. His only option was to outrun the reptiles, get to the lake, and hope they weren't swimmers.

Before he leaped again, he felt something loosely slither around his leg. The sensation was gone once he was in the air again. He looked back at the pack, and saw the most extraordinary thing he had ever seen.

Half the reptiles had charged after him in a frenzy, but the other half were hesitant and stepped back. As those in front launched into a run, leaping into the vegetation, suddenly they were snapped up in giant red jaws -- no not jaws -- what were those *things?* A pink foamy ooze was coming out of the jaws filled with reptiles.

The slithering over his legs continued, and he felt something loosely grasp him. *The vines?* he asked himself. The vines were trying to grab him, and he could see they were anticipating his moves. He must get to that lake, and quickly!

Reagan avoided stepping on the vines and strangely shaped flowers, and gravity allowed him to do so for the most part. However, he couldn't avoid them completely, stepped on a flower, and a substance was released into the air. Reagan saw the lake up ahead, but the vines rapidly snaked towards him.

The vines in front of him shot upwards, and in one fluid movement, Reagan grabbed his second rope and hook, and threw it at the bunch of vines. The grappling hook spun around the tentacle-like vines, securing them together. In the effort to remove the rope, the vines just became more entangled. Then Reagan landed right beside them and took off again in another flying leap.

This time, he skidded on marshy ground, and into the deep blue lake. Reagan yanked hard on the rope to pull himself out of the water quickly. As he scrambled onto the bank, the rope suddenly went lax. The vines had stopped tugging, and had suddenly gone limp. As he reeled in the rope, the grappling hook stripped off the outer layer from a vine and it recoiled. Reagan heard a sound, like an animal when it yelps in pain.

Reeling in the rope from a safe distance, Reagan noticed that some of the green plant residue was caught on the grappling hook. He took a sample of it for later -- if there was a later. He then took a sample of both the marshy soil, and the water from the lake.

Reagan sat down to rest before planning his next move. Steam was rising from the lake. He'd been on the run for three hours straight, from reptiles, dragons, and even strange vines. He needed a few minutes to think. He cleared his throat.

Reagan knew the newly formed Corporate Alliance would think him dead. They would have seen his shuttle explode on their scanners, as would the GIB. The Corporate Alliance had proof that he had left in his shuttle, alive, and would claim that it was a tragic accident.

His question now was, how secure was his main ship? Did Lincoln still have control? Or had it been commandeered by the Corporate Alliance? He knew they would try to erase his report from the ship's computer.

Reagan stared at the lake, as if the answers he sought could be found there. He saw tiny tentacled creatures moving in the lake, as if they were swimming. A small swimming reptile scooped them up in its elongated mouth that had a rounded membrane on the front. The closest thing he could compare it to was a crocodylia from his own planet. He smiled at the reminder of home, and absentmindedly saw that partway across the lake were more ripples. *More little crocodylias,* he thought.

Reagan had his answer regarding the ship a few minutes later. As expected, if the ship had evaded notice or capture, the new remote shuttle cleared the cloud cover. He noticed the V pattern of ripples in the lake, but absently dismissed it as unimportant. His focus was on what was above him. He stood up, shading his eyes from the bright clouds, and watched as the shuttle drew closer.

With the shuttle hovered at a distance above him, one of the newly installed bots dropped a rope and harness for Reagan. Reagan attached his pack to a hook on the rope. As he was getting into the harness, he noticed what he had overlooked. The crocodylia swimming directly towards him wasn't like the other small, swimming reptile. It was considerably larger than the crocodylias from his home planet. As it got closer, Reagan started to realize how much larger it was.

Reagan urgently scrambled to get into the harness, and pulled the zipcord, just as the crocodylia was exiting the water. As Reagan rose on the retractable rope, he watched frantically as the five foot long mouth, full of sharp teeth, nearly closed on his legs. Reagan had quickly pulled his feet up so he was tucked in a ball. However, that didn't stop the crocodylia from slicing through the harness strap underneath him, halting the zipcord.

Reagan was slipping out of the harness, and trying desperately to hang on. His upper body wasn't harnessed, and he was hanging upside down, his head in range of the croc's mouth. The crocodylia's mouth was opening again. There was enough power in those jaws to easily snap him in half!

He feverishly pulled his upper body higher on the rope, while keeping his legs out of the fatal jaws. He grabbed onto the pack above him, climbing over it, while pulling the zipcord. When the jaws snapped shut, there were no souvenirs from Reagan's body in its mouth. The crocodylia remained below, watching its prey move further away. It stayed until Reagan had climbed up the ladder and was out of sight.

Once Reagan was in the shuttle, the door closed, and he removed what was left of his harness.

"Welcome, Governor," one of the bots inside the shuttle addressed him.

Reagan was coughing. "Connect me with Lincoln," ordered Reagan, barely able to speak between coughs.

"Cannot connect with Link-in, or will compromise location of ship and shuttle. Communications being tracked in this sector," replied the bot in a classic robotic voice.

"Ah, okay," said Reagan. So the main ship hadn't been commandeered as he'd feared. Reagan took the pilot's seat. He started coughing again.

"Status of main ship?" Reagan asked the bot. He still wasn't used to the newly implemented bots, but so far they had been very handy, even life-saving.

"Link-in saw shuttle explode, avoided capture. Then Link-in cloaked ship," answered the bot. Reagan breathed a sigh of relief, which turned into a cough.

"Playback from main ship, after I left," Reagan commanded. He watched the screen as one of the lesser directors demanded to board the ship. Instead of replying, there was a power surge, then a confirmation that the ship was cloaked. The corporate ship retreated and sped away in the direction of the alliance's convoy.

"So now they have lesser directors doing their dirty work," commented Reagan to himself.

"Funny how Lincoln used a power surge to emulate jumping to light speed, yet stayed in the same place, cloaked." Reagan laughed, but it turned into a forceful cough.

"Location of main ship," asked Reagan, searching for a bottle of water.

"16 h, -28 degrees, .01 light day. Hiding behind planet," responded the bot.

"Last known position of all other ships in Sector 5," ordered Reagan, taking a long drink of water. A star map jumped onto the screen, with various colors marking the ships. *Nice,* thought Reagan, *Lincoln labelled the different corporations.*

Reagan mapped out a safe route that would keep the shuttle hidden behind the planet until they reached the main ship. He put the shuttle on autopilot.

Reagan coughed and drank some more water. "Playback from planet," Reagan commanded. His suit had recorded his entire ordeal, as it was fitted with a 360 degree holographic recorder. He skipped through the recording, so he could tag sections with subtitles. Footage on the reptiles and dragons in the cave was fascinating. These were new species to him.

Playback of the reptiles pursuing him into the vegetation caused his jaw to drop. He had to watch the section twice to grasp it. While leaping through the area, he'd only had a quick glance behind him. In the recording he could see all the details.

Several enormous red jaws rose up from the ground and devoured each reptile easily. White liquid had been secreted in the pods, which turned to pinkish-red foam when mixed with the blood of the reptiles. Then the reptiles started to be absorbed. *No wonder the rest of the pack wouldn't enter that area,* thought Reagan. *They knew what was waiting at the perimeter.*

There was no giant monster attached to each set of jaws, Reagan realized, as he noted the thick green vines attached to each set. *And those weren't really teeth were they?* At least not animal teeth anyway. He hadn't seen any chewing involved. Instead they looked more like needles. Thousands of needles inside each mouth, strong enough to easily penetrate the hardened leathery skin of this pack of reptiles.

It was the vegetation. The plants had devoured the reptiles that had rushed headlong into the vegetation, because they'd been too obsessed with hunting him. The plants.

Reagan was coughing again. "Set quarantine procedures upon re-entry to the ship," commanded Reagan, as he coughed and cleared his throat. The entire shuttle would be quarantined and analyzed, since he and his gear had made contact with foreign entities. He would personally undergo quarantine procedures and be taken straight to the med bay until he was cleared by Lincoln.

QUARANTINE

CHAPTER FIVE

Changes in allegiance can completely shift the balance of power.

Deputy Governor Tarek Shaw, Galactic Investigations Bureau

Reagan went through decontamination and shed his clothes. He was encapsulated in a polycrylicarbonate tube, equipped with oxygen regulator, and wheeled by a bot to the med bay. There Lincoln would perform a series of tests on him. On the way there, Reagan began coughing up blood.

"Lincoln," started Reagan, as he entered the med bay, "I'm feeling irritation in my chest, and just coughed up blood." The bot returned to its post.

Lincoln secured Reagan under the scanner. "Scanning..." indicated the android. "Hmm..." The monitor was picking up a foreign object in Reagan's left lung.

By this time, Reagan was coughing more violently. He was coughing up more blood and his chest was in pain. The tube had automatically tilted his body to clear his lungs.

"An object in your lung is enlarging at a rapid pace. I need to operate on you before it becomes too large." The android sealed off the entire med bay as a quarantined area, and prepped for surgery. He opened up the sealed tube where Reagan was lying. By this time Reagan had coughed up a fair amount of blood and

was clutching his chest in pain. His eyes were rolling back in his head.

Lincoln put Reagan under general anesthetic and administered an epidural. He enlarged the object on the screen while the anesthesia took effect. The object was growing at an alarming rate. He put Reagan on a ventilator to ensure his other lung kept working during surgery.

Lincoln set the laser to make a six inch incision between Reagan's upper ribs on the left side. He inserted a tube to deflate the lung, clamped the muscles, and spread Reagan's upper ribs. The laser sliced into Reagan's lung. He then reached in with his gloved fingers to grasp the object.

He had the object between his forefinger and thumb, and pulled on it until it had been completely extracted. After rinsing off the blood, he could see it was plant-like. He sealed it in a vacuum container and ran another scan of Reagan's body to make sure there was no remaining residue.

Reagan's body was clear of any trace of the foreign object, Lincoln continued with the procedure. Reagan's left lung was repaired and reinflated. The android drained excess fluid from around the lung, placing a temporary valve to continue to drain fluid. Lincoln then sealed the wound with such precision that Reagan wouldn't have a scar or any indication of surgery.

As Lincoln was doing post-op cleanup, he glanced over at the vacuum tube. The plant's growth had slowed significantly. As he looked at the vacuum tube closely, he could see tendrils feeling their way along the polycrylicarbonate. Did it have sensory perception? He set the microscopic setting on the vacuum tube at forty times magnification. He found the original seed that had sprouted and saw that it could have easily been inhaled.

Another hour of rapid growth inside Reagan's lung would have been deadly for Reagan. Again, the new bot system had served its purpose by bringing Reagan home quickly. Reagan's tracker in his suit made him easy to find once he had left the rocky plateau. Until that time he had been undetectable. Maybe the type of rock had something to do with it?

Inside the vacuum tube, Lincoln took a slice of a cross section of the plant. It actually recoiled as if in pain! He watched as the organism actually moved backwards, away from where the laser scalpel had cut. He enhanced the microscopic setting to four hundred times magnification so he could examine the cross section. He wanted to get a good look at the cellular structure.

This organism was like nothing Lincoln had seen. There was no record of its cellular structure in any database he could find.

The cells had walls like those of a plant to retain its structure, but on the outer walls it also had tiny micro-hairs like cilia. This may be the way creature was feeling around its environment. Lincoln also saw that the cellular walls could remold and restructure themselves. This was why it could move, and why it had an elastic property.

Reagan felt like he was coming out of cryo-sleep all over again, except without the cold part. He tried to flex his muscles and there was a delay. His vision was blurry and his throat hurt. Not to mention the pain he was starting to feel in his chest. He tried to push himself up to sit, but then felt the searing pain in his chest.

"Governor, you must rest, at least until the general anesthetic has completely worn off. Besides, the IV drip hasn't finished yet. Humans aren't instantaneously healed like machines, regardless of how many advances in medicine we've made."

"Okay," said Reagan, gingerly lying back down with the android's help. "Status?" he asked.

"I removed some type of organism from your lung. It looks like you had inhaled a seed into your lung and it rapidly germinated," said Lincoln.

"My condition?" asked Reagan.

"Healing up nicely," reported Lincoln, looking up at the monitor. "Your lung looks healthy and was sealed perfectly with no surgical complications. You're free of the foreign object, and the drainage valve will dissolve in a few days. You'll feel like you've been bruised up for a while longer due to the muscle clamping and stretching of the ribs. Just don't do anything too strenuous until that valve has dissolved."

"Noted," said Reagan. "What about the organism?"

"Projecting now on upper screen." The visual from the vacuum tube was projected on the ceiling screen for Reagan.

"How big is it? Seriously, it wasn't that big when it was inside me?" Reagan's raised his eyebrows.

"Yes. It's stopped growing, for the most part."

"So two inches when in my lung then."

"Yes. It was pressing on your capillaries, perhaps even drawing nutrition from them. That's why you were in so much pain. It also accounts for the amount of blood you were coughing up. Another hour and it may have been too late for you."

The reference to time had Reagan suddenly thinking. "How long have I been under?"

"The procedure took an hour," reported Lincoln. "You've been out for a total of three hours. The organism's growth rate has slowed down on a gradual scale since I removed it."

Reagan could see the tiny tentacles feeling along the vacuum tube, as if exploring its environment.

"If that seed came from one of those aggressive giant plants from the surface, then it could become lethal if given the ideal habitat," said Reagan.

"I saw that in the video recorded from your suit," Lincoln said. "Quite vicious creatures, but they did, in a sense, save your life."

Reagan shivered. "Yes, by killing off the pursuing reptiles. But then those other vines tried to entangle me. I was fortunate that my step was so light and I had an extended stride due to gravity. Plus those jaws only seemed to be on the border between the vegetation and the rock."

"You might be surprised to find out then that the plants with the jaws and the entangling vines may actually be the same species," said Lincoln.

"What do you mean?"

"Well, take a look at the sample you inhaled, I'm assuming from the 'jaw plants', and compare it with the samples you took from the rope." Lincoln placed the cells side-by-side on Reagan's ceiling screen.

"The structure is the same," said Reagan. "Is there any chance that the seed came from the vines? Say, if it was a completely different species to the 'jaw plants'?"

"Well yes, but the jaws and vines seemed to act in unison when entrapping the reptiles. See, take a look at the video." The android played a brief video clip, highlighting the united motion to entrap. "However, we could cultivate this new plant to make sure." Lincoln projected the vacuum tube back onto the screen.

"Let's wait until we get back to the outpost with a proper quarantine section," said Reagan.

Reagan lay there with his thoughts. They needed to take every precaution with this creature. He'd seen what it could do first-

hand. He was glad of that, since they could now avoid making a fatal error.

By now he was able to move his arms without the delay. However, his legs were another story. He still felt the delay between his brain ordering his leg to move, and his leg actually moving. This was due to the epidural, or pain "block".

He thought he might be able to sit up now. Turning slightly to the left and pushing up with the right arm caused pain around his ribs. However, he managed to push himself up to a sitting position, without ripping out his IV. He leaned back on a pillow and pulled a computer console towards himself.

Reagan took a close look at their positioning. It was good to keep the planet between themselves and the Corporate Alliance. *What treachery,* he thought. With the bold attempt to dispose of him, the Aurora, Leo, and Asher Corporations had gained power over the smaller corporations. Those who weren't complicit from the start had been blindsided. There was no opportunity to run, and now they were in a very vulnerable position. Any of them could be destroyed on a whim, as the three largest corporations owned nearly the entire military force of the alliance. It seemed that the smaller corporations that had forced the Miners' Guild into a corner, were now in a corner themselves.

He vaguely wondered how the other five corporations had fared. They would have had time to make a stand or flee. Reagan hoped for their sakes they had fled. Reagan could use his legs now with minimal delay. He should be able to walk soon.

Reagan entered the bridge and sat in the captain's chair. He reflected back to his short time on the planet. "You said you weren't able to track my signal before I hit the vegetation on the planet. Why is that?" Reagan asked.

"It seems that the rocky substance made it impossible."

"Ah, okay. Any info on the sample I took on the planet?"

"Yes, I ran some initial scans and it seems to be a rare form of planitanium. This form is capable of deflecting or blocking signals."

"What?" Reagan raised his eyebrows in surprise. "There's an alloy that can do that?"

"Apparently there is."

"In the wrong hands that would be a disaster." Reagan started pacing, half-limping. "Imagine if someone built a military fleet using the alloy? They wouldn't be detectable on scanners. It would be as if they were cloaked, but able to move." Reagan was talking to himself.

"Speaking of being cloaked," said Lincoln, "we're unable to detect the corporate ships around the other side of the planet. The revolution of the planet will cause us to be within sensor range soon."

"Then we should uncloak and get out of here."

"As you wish, Governor." Lincoln complied. Reagan sat back down in his chair, carefully.

The ship uncloaked, and its thrusters began pushing the ship further behind the planet. They would move away from the planet, using it as cover so they wouldn't be detected.

Reagan hadn't decided what their next move should be against the corporations. He just needed to get back to base and debrief the team on what had transpired in the past twelve hours. He needed to inform them about the newly formed Corporate Alliance, treachery, and the samples from the planet.

Reagan tilted back in his chair, taking the pressure off his painful ribs. Until they had left Sector 5, he would take a much-needed nap.

Reagan was running. Running from hideous creatures, some reptilian, some half-reptile and half-plant. The reptilian creatures kept morphing from the Vitaari, to the lizards in the caves, to dragons, then to crocodylia with wings.

He kept seeing the giant plant creatures snap up the reptiles in pursuit of him. Then they were suddenly in the lake swimming like octopi with their giant brains in tow. He was running towards *her*. Warning Lady Cia to run, to get out of the way of the destruction to come. But she couldn't leave, because she was in chains, thick, heavy metal links that weighed her down. She was somehow enslaved by fate but he couldn't see how. He had to remove that chain from her neck before it became a noose.

He was hurtling towards the Z-Class planet, ejecting from his shuttle before it exploded in flames in the desert below, when he awoke startled.

Reagan's shuttle docked at the Galactic Investigations Bureau outpost. Reagan, trying to run but was half-limping as he did because of his ribs, had called an emergency meeting upon his arrival. The rest of the team were rushing to the boardroom to be debriefed by their governor. They knew he had been through some type of trying ordeal.

Deputy Governor Shaw pulled up a chair for Reagan, who was apparently injured. Reagan thanked him, and they sat down to discuss the status of the quadrant. Deputy Governor Shaw commenced the meeting.

Reagan had prepared his debriefing report upon entry back into Sector 2. He included video of his experiences so explanation and questions could be skipped. He showed clips of the reptiles with the dragons, the carnivorous plant, and the giant crocodylia to quickly sum up parts of his story. He also showed analyses results of some of the samples he took on the planet. The entire committee was riveted to every word Reagan said, and to every video on-screen or holographic projection they viewed.

His presentation gave info about the newly formed Corporate Alliance, which began with the attempt on his life. It also discussed the Corporate Alliance's plan to take over mining operations and portions of planets "legally". This all added up to one important fact. The newly formed Corporate Alliance now posed a huge threat to all those in Quadrant 3.

Another major issue was the potential military use of planitanium from the Z-Class Planet. The Corporate Alliance had the capability to mine and quickly process the alloy, if they discovered it.

Deputy Governor Shaw shook his head. "Director Finley's been a ticking time-bomb, just waiting to go off. But I'm surprised that he was able to get the leaders of the other corporations to agree with him on anything, especially the Leo and Asher Corporations. They've been at odds with each other for years, decades even."

Reagan commented, "During the conference meeting, it seemed that the other two powerful corporations, Leo and Asher, were in league with Aurora. My disposal was an example to all of the smaller corporations. If they would so easily dispose of me to take over this quadrant's colonist planets, then they would easily dispose of one of them.

"Once Leo and Asher decided to stand with Finley, then a corporate dictatorship naturally fell into place," said Reagan.

Deputy Governor Shaw nodded. "We had no warning that this was coming. The corporations as competitive entities have kept each other in check for years, even decades. Now they've merged, along with their militaries. They are a formidable power motivated by greed. They are apparently prepared to operate outside the law to get what they want. If they can get away with murder, the attempted murder of the governor in this case, and there are no repercussions, their power will stabilize even further. They will attract new allies who are motivated by greed and power. We're looking at lawlessness, chaos, and a change in the balance of power.

"General McKenna, what is the status of our military, if we are forced to act?" asked Shaw.

"We are prepared to respond as needed. However, we would need some serious strategic planning in order to go up against all three major military powers of the three most powerful corporations. In the past, we were prepared to face one at a time, if the need ever arose, but never all three at once," responded General McKenna. "I suggest we call an emergency military strategy meeting immediately after this, so we can prepare right away. We don't know what we may face in the upcoming days."

ESPIONAGE

CHAPTER SIX

Fear of discovery leads to mistakes, which then leads to discovery.

Secretary Jaylen Cohen, Galactic Investigations Bureau

Brady Nash knew he was involved in some pretty risky business, but he tried not to stress over it. He found it easy to justify his actions because to him, money spoke louder than any other language.

Although stationed at the Galactic Investigation Bureau's outpost, he had been on Director Finley's payroll for years. Nash's time to shine had finally come. Director Finley would see that his investment in him had been worth the cost.

The problem that Director Finley faced was that the GIB computers containing classified information were on a completely different grid than the outpost's other systems. Making it impossible to obtain that data through a hack from the outside. The only way it could be obtained was from within the station itself. That's where Nash came in.

Nash's task was simple. He was to provide information to Director Finley. Since he worked in the tech department, it had always been a cinch for him to nab a bit of information here and there. Well, this time it wouldn't be a cinch, since the files he was eyeing were on a computer in a glass-encased office in a well-lit area. Or would be shortly.

Nash's plan was to enter Secretary Cohen's office to place a decrypter and long-range transmitter, since the Secretary had just rushed out for an emergency meeting. All new data added to the computer would then automatically be transmitted to Finley after it was saved.

This would relieve Nash from having to stick his neck out to gather any more information in the future, lowering his risk of being caught. It was a one-time risk, for a good payoff. Finley never refused to pay generously when he gave him something good. He was sure that an emergency meeting would provide some very interesting information to start with.

Nash gathered his equipment together, placing a signal bypass transmitter, long-ranged transmission device, and acoustic decrypter in his tech bag underneath his tools. He also had a number of faked service orders. He put on his uniform, pulled his hat down low, and walked out of his quarters.

He quietly unscrewed the panel underneath the key card entry, then used the signal bypass transmitter to open the door to Wilson Karter's quarters. He saw Karter's tech bag, neatly placed beside his uniform on his dresser. Brady took the name tag, key card, and USB key out of the tech bag. The guy had been laid up in the med bay for twenty-four hours with a broken ankle, and it was the perfect disguise for Nash's current task. He pinned on Karter's nametag.

In one of the laboratories on the Galactic Investigations Bureau outpost, holograms of the "carnivorous plant" had just been shown, demonstrating the potential hazard of the creature they were dealing with.

"Wow." Jesse hesitantly opened the case that contained the vacuum tube, almost expecting a monster to jump out and eat him. Instead, he saw a two inch plant-like creature, with tendrils "walking" along the glass as though feeling its surface.

Jesse looked at the enlarged sample of the cross section that Lincoln had taken, and saw that it wasn't really a plant or animal. But it did look like a plant. "Alright, our job is to cultivate this plant-thingy *carefully*." Jesse was speaking to his lab assistant, Thrace. His lab assistant nodded. "So let's start by enlarging the tube, and flooding the bottom half with a nutrient compound, the equivalent of the soil it would normally grow in, based on the soil sample we have." Jesse's assistant inserted the tube ending into a module, typed instructions on a console, then a minute later, a clear gooey substance was injected into the vacuum tube.

"Setting atmospheric conditions and radiation levels based on the readings of the governor's spacesuit." Thrace made more adjustments on the console. "Adjusting lighting to recreate the five hour night and thirty-five hour day, based on the planet's axis rotation."

"Good, and let's carefully monitor its growth pattern. We've been asked to include projections regarding…" Jesse checked the order paper. "One, the rate of progression if it had been left inside the victim's body and been carried to another planet, and two, its potential threat to a planet if used as a weapon for biological warfare. Most importantly, we need to make sure the vacuum tube expands at a rate compatible with the creature to avoid it breaking through." Jesse's assistant typed more commands into the console.

"Wow, look at that." Jesse was fascinated. The creature looked like it was swimming in the nutrient goo.

"Is that thing really a plant?" asked Thrace.

"No, take a look at the cross section," suggested Jesse. "From the data that was collected, the organism contains plant-like qualities with animal-like responses. Plus, the cross section doesn't match anything in our databases. It could be that there was no clear division between plants and animals during planetary evolution. Instead, the division was skipped, and this organism retained the properties of both plant and animal." They watched as it swam around the vacuum tube in the nutrient goo.

Jesse watched as the numbers on the tube increased, showing that the organism's size was increasing, although imperceptible to the human eye. It did seem slightly bigger than it did before they added the nutrients and changed conditions to match its home planet.

Jesse's assistant was inquisitive. "Do you think the organism originated on the planet? Or did it come from somewhere else?"

"It's difficult to tell," said Jesse. "The other life forms on the planet, so far they are primarily reptilian: dragons, dromasaurs, and crocodylians. Some planets where humanoids evolved were inhabited primarily by reptiles millions of years ago. It's difficult to tell without analyzing a larger portion of the planet. There may be all types of organisms we are unaware of."

"I noticed on the video there wasn't a single insect visible in the cave with the rotting carcasses," said Thrace. "Must be broken down by microscopic organisms."

"Yes, insects would normally be attracted to that type of feast," said Jesse. "Look at that thing. I've never seen a creature that looked so much like a plant that could move like that, not even in a goo like this. There might be subtle changes in position of roots, but nothing like this."

"I know, right?" agreed Thrace.

"Hmm, here is a hypothesis so far regarding its origin. If these organisms evolved on this planet, then we wouldn't see reptiles, animals. We would see a conglomeration of animal/plant-like organisms like this little guy." Jesse gestured towards the vacuum tube.

"Also, it looks like the reptiles may be dying out, headed towards extinction. That's assuming the rest of the planet is similar. This type of aggressive plant-animal organism would have taken all available nutrients, killing off any plant life, which means eventual extinction of animals. That indicates an imbalanced ecosystem, without natural regulators.

"However, if the organism was brought to the planet... Was it brought accidentally or on purpose? And for what purpose?" asked Jesse. "And, which solar system has produced creatures similar to this one? None in our four quadrants."

"There are a lot of unanswered questions," started Thrace, thoughtfully. "If someone accidentally inhaled a seed, there's the issue of how long it takes to travel. Unless someone went into cryosleep, they would be dead within hours. And if they were showing symptoms like the governor, why wouldn't the scanners in the med bay detect the organism?"

"I think the most likely conclusion is that the organism was brought here deliberately," stated Jesse. "As to why, we can only speculate at this time."

"Hey look." Thrace gestured to the vacuum tube. Taking a closer look, Jesse noticed that the creature had stopped swimming, and saw a tiny leaf on a tentacle that had grown upwards out of the goo. It wasn't behaving like the other tentacles. Jesse thought it must be a sprout.

"Hmm, it looks like it has a leaf." Jesse was straining his eyes to see. "Could you enlarge that? I'd like a closer look." His assistant enlarged the area on the big screen in the lab. There was, in fact, a tiny heart-shaped leaf there.

As they watched, the heart-shaped leaf evolved into a tiny carnivorous trap. By this time, several other sprouts had formed, and more heart-shaped leaves were developing quickly. As more traps developed, the organism increased in size, as did the vacuum tube.

"Wow." Jesse gave a low whistle. "This means that all those traps on the video that attacked the lizards could actually be from one plant."

Then Jesse noticed something else interesting. The seed mass was growing, and with it, more tentacles above and below the goo. There were more sprouts, traveling along the top of the goo like vines. Those sprouts grew the heart-shaped leaves which became more traps, but further along the tube. The traps kept getting bigger and by this time had turned bright red. The seed mass kept enlarging, and more and more sprouts were extending from the seed mass.

By this time, the vacuum capsule had enlarged quite a bit, keeping up with the organism's growth. It had started at eight inches long and four inches high, and had now expanded to two feet long and one foot high, with over a dozen traps inside.

The creature continued to grow, and the polycrylicarbonate tube stayed in sync with that growth.

"You know what the implications of that many traps are?" Jesse glanced at Thrace.

"What are you referring to?" asked Thrace.

"Well, in the video we saw several large traps demolish the reptiles. Imagine the amount of ground that a dozen would cover when full sized." Jesse was looking at the tube again, "And there are even more tiny heart-shaped leaves growing on the new shoots. It is possible that the entire area of vegetation that the governor saw from his parachute was actually one plant."

"Seriously?" asked his assistant.

"It's possible. Especially when you consider how 'in sync' the vines are. Take a look at this." Jesse showed Thrace a series of clips showing differently positioned vines working in tandem with each other, trying to seize Reagan.

Some new readings were showing up on the vacuum tube. "Whoa, look at this!" exclaimed Jesse. "Electrical impulses are traveling to and from the enlarged seed mass, causing chemicals to be released or withheld."

"Wait a minute," said Thrace. "You mean...it's functioning like a brain?" Thrace's speech was quiet and hesitant.

"Well, it definitely has been showing evidence of 'lower brain function', as we call it in animals. It was moving and swimming, could sense restriction of the vacuum tube, and could feel pain. These were some initial signs that something along those lines was developing. Now add in the electrical impulses and chemical releases. It's functioning like a very basic nervous system right now," said Jesse.

Thrace shook his head. Everything he'd learned about biology had been overturned in one day.

He and Jesse used the lab's robotic arms to move the tube and module from the table to the floor. The creature seemed to feel the little bump. It started to push forward, and the tube rocked slightly. It pushed forward harder with its tentacles, and the tube rocked again.

"Now now, none of that," chided Jesse. They placed some blocks in front and behind the tube so it could no longer move. "It definitely has intelligence, I'll give it that."

By the time the creature had expanded to eight feet long and four feet high, with thirty traps, Jesse and his assistant had most of the answers they needed.

"So, fully grown, would you say that the organism could go on for miles then?"

"It would seem so," replied Jesse. "It looks like we have our answer, regarding what could happen if this organism was brought to another planet. It's sufficient to say that it could take over an area of many sectars square, if it was on another planet with similar conditions.

"Let's remove the nutrient composition so it stops growing any larger. That way we can write up our nightly report without any worries," said Jesse. The governor had asked him to personally deliver the finished report to him. Jesse wanted to make sure he dotted all his i's and crossed all his t's.

Before they left for the night, as a precaution they had the robotic arms move the tube into the quarantined half of the lab, behind safety glass. They weren't taking any chances with this creature.

Technicians were needed regularly around the outpost, so it wasn't odd for Nash to be close to the Secretary of Bureau Investigations' office. He started doing routine nighttime maintenance of the other machines in the area so he could keep an eye on the office. Finally, when the traffic dipped, Brady Nash was ready to execute his plan.

Nash walked to the Secretary's office while pretending to check a fake service order form. He used Karter's key card to gain access to the office, then was about to install the acoustic decrypter and long-range transmission devices. However, that's when his nerves gave out.

At the last second, when he was about to unscrew the computer's casing to place the devices discreetly inside, he was hit by a wave of anxiety. Sweat was dripping down the back of his neck, under his collar, and down his back. His heart was pounding and his fingers started fumbling with the screwdriver. *Take a deep breath,* he told himself. He slowed down his breathing.

Brady had difficulty removing the casing, since he was right-handed, and the screws were on the left panel. He installed the long-range transmission device and acoustic decrypter in two of the unused ports. He used Karter's USB key, typed in a number of lines of code on the computer, and pulled out a piece of paper that had been concealed in the pocket of his tech bag. He then typed in the digits listed on the piece of paper to make sure the transmission got to the correct destination. Then he started to screw the casing back on.

He glanced up and saw a couple of men who would have been at the Secretary's meeting. They had returned to the area. *Oh no,* he started to panic. Brady started fumbling again with the screwdriver, and accidentally dropped the last two tiny screws on the carpet. He had no time left to lose. He had to get out of there. He put his screwdriver into his tech bag, got up, then bent his head as if reading a service order form, as he left the Secretary's office.

A minute later, just as Nash was exiting the area, he got a glimpse of Secretary Cohen as he walked through the outer door, and over to his office. Nash kept on going. He headed straight for the locker room, and placed Karter's name tag, key card, and USB key in a locker that was never used, but that could be accessed by anyone.

He walked down the corridor to another men's washroom, and tore up and disposed of the faked service orders. He hoped his scribbling wasn't recognizable if they were discovered. He took off his hat and his jacket and put them into his tech bag. Then he headed to his quarters.

Brady entered his quarters, where he took a shower and lay down with a book. His job was done, and with luck, no one would discover where the decrypter and transmitter were hidden.

Secretary Cohen sat down at the desk in his office. He was extremely troubled by the events that had transpired over the last twelve hours. It upset him that the young governor had been targeted. The corporations joining as an alliance, and their plans to steal land were also troubling. No one knew how far they planned to take their agenda eventually, and that was concerning, especially due to the size of their combined military.

He ran his hand through his short, jet black hair. He was a handsome gentleman with clear, dark skin. He looked at the picture of his family who had finally joined him on the outpost three years ago, and now wondered if it had been a wise decision to bring them here. Jack and Taylor were now fighter pilots on the outpost, and his beautiful wife was an instructor at the academy. The outpost hadn't faced a potential threat like this one in over eight decades.

The files from the two emergency meetings, one a debriefing by the governor, the other the military briefing, had been saved to his office computer. That way he could easily review them, send out the minutes, and forward changes or updates. Secretary Cohen had a meticulous sense of attention to detail.

As he edited the minutes of the meeting, he could feel something tiny against the bottom of the sole of his shoe. Glancing down, he saw that it was a tiny screw. He rolled his eyes. Technology wasn't his strong suit, but a screw on the floor was a sign that something needed to be fixed.

He spoke into his com device, "Send a tech to the office of the Secretary please." Then he continued editing the minutes.

A few minutes later, one of the techs on duty arrived at his office. The Secretary rose and stepped back from his desk. "Found a small screw on the floor, and was hoping you could give my machine a check."

The tech nodded and smiled. "Sure thing, Mr. Secretary." He set down his bag, and proceeded to check underneath the Secretary's machine.

"Well this is odd." The technician placed the tiny screw on the desk. "There are two missing screws on this side of the machine. Which means that they were both removed manually."

"What? For what purpose?" The Secretary looked alarmed. This day had already been trying enough, with the threat of the new Corporate Alliance looming before them.

"Let's take a look," said the technician from behind the computer, and removed the other two screws from the panel on the side of the machine.

The two men looked at the devices plugged into Port 6 and 8. The technician inhaled sharply.

"What is it?" asked the Secretary.

"It looks like an acoustic decrypter and long-range transmitter." The technician was breathing at a faster rate. He gulped out, "This is not good news."

Before he'd finished speaking, Secretary Cohen had already spoken over his com device, "Internal Affairs to the Secretary's office immediately."

There was a commotion in the hallway, as security and investigation staff dropped what they were doing. The Secretary walked out of his office. "Stay here and don't move," he ordered the technician. The technician looked like he was about to have a panic attack.

"There's been a security breach," said the Secretary to the men in uniform. "Decrypter and long-range transmitter on my computer."

Internal Affairs moved in to carefully go over the room, to see if any evidence had been left behind that would identify the perpetrator.

"What about this guy?" One of them was pointing to the technician, who was kneeling on the floor with his hands up, eyes closed.

"He's the one who discovered it. Remove him from the office as soon as you can. You can interview him later. I have some vital questions for him." The Secretary looked straight at the technician, who clearly thought he was in trouble.

Internal Affairs had the technician point at exactly what he had done and touched from the time he had entered the room. They removed him from the room. They asked the Secretary the same question regarding his movements in the office. Then they started processing the room for evidence.

The Secretary, the Sergeant of Internal Affairs, and another three officers sat opposite the technician in the conference room further down the hall. They could see the processing team going over the office, but five sets of penetrating eyes were focused on the man sitting in front of them.

"What is your name?" asked the Sergeant in a formal voice.

The technician looked white as a sheet, like he was going to be sick. "Estevan Dixon, Sir, but my friends call me Steve." One of the officers wrote something on his notepad.

"Alright, Steve. We're going to ask you some questions and we'll walk you through the process." The Sergeant attempted to put Steve at ease. "You're not under any suspicion. We're hoping to glean as much information as possible from you to understand the situation better."

Steve nodded. He could still feel his heart racing, but his breathing began to slow a bit.

"What were your initial observations regarding the devices attached to the Secretary's computer?"

"At first glance, they looked like an acoustic decrypter and long-range transmitter," said Steve slowly.

"Anything you can tell us about the devices that will help in our investigation?" asked the Sergeant.

"Well," said Steve thoughtfully, now that his heart rate was slowing. "The transmitter is the type that can be purchased at any space station, by anyone. This model is used to provide easy video communication between two computers, up to a quadrant in distance. It looked new, too. Not like some of our transmitters which have been transferred from one computer to another. Come to think of it, it didn't have any dust on it either.

"However, this type of acoustic decrypter is rarely used, since it has to be in close range in order to be effective. It's old tech, and usually only available as a teaching tool to show how acoustic decryption used to be done. We would only have a few in storage for the academy's use, if any at all."

"Tell us about the installation of these devices. How difficult would it be to install them?" asked the Sergeant.

"It would just take a screwdriver, and to know they needed to be plugged into the ports. However, to set up the devices so they know what to do, someone would either need the Secretary's password or a USB key from the Tech Department. Then they would have to *one*," Steve tallied the steps on his fingers, "enter lines of code to activate the decryption device, and *two*, tell the transmitter where to send specific information. Someone would need a good understanding of code."

"So we're most likely looking at someone who works in the Tech Department, or at least has good tech abilities." It was both a statement and a question. Unbeknownst to Steve, the Sergeant was transmitting some sentences through his com to the Internal Affairs Team.

"Yes, an amateur wouldn't know how to access the protected operating system files, or where to enter the lines of code as commands. But unless they used the Secretary's password, you'll be able to identify the person by the USB ID number in the log." Steve brightened visibly. "Or what about the key card used to access the office?"

The Sergeant nodded slowly. He'd already been fed the card owner's identity, the card that accessed the office after the Secretary. They were currently trying to locate him, since he hadn't used his card in two days. At the same time they were investigating the USB ID in the log and the lines of code on the computer.

IA had already interviewed witnesses who had seen a technician inside or entering the Secretary's office thirty minutes earlier. They had viewed surveillance footage, which confirmed the same. They were currently changing the level of access to the Secretary's computer, so only a Master USB Key could be used. Those keys were held by the three supervisors in the Tech Department. The Internal Affairs division was fast and thorough.

"Tell me what you know about Wilson Karter," said the Sergeant, leaning forward.

At breakfast, Steve shared his recounting of the night before with his friends. Once he had calmed down a bit, he'd realized he was a sort of hero.

"...and then they asked me about Wil!" he exclaimed.

"Wil Karter's been laid up in the med bay for a couple of days," said one of the guys at the table. "Plus, they placed a cast on his ankle right after surgery, and he's been using crutches. So it would be hard to miss him, if he could actually pull off something like that in his condition."

"I think the most relevant question here is 'Who has access to Wil's quarters, or possibly his locker.' They've obviously zoned in on him because of something that's identified him, such as a key card," suggested another man at the table.

"Yeah, I bet it was stolen," speculated another man, who was sipping cava.

Steve noticed that his coworker, Brady, was sulking. There had always been a sense of competition between them, even back at the academy. He figured Brady was upset he hadn't been the one to uncover a plot to steal classified information. He never even entertained the idea that Brady was the one responsible.

Brady was having a miserable morning. He couldn't believe that a couple of tiny screws had given it away. *Yeah, I literally "screwed up".*

He kept going over the question in his mind, *Did I cover my tracks well enough?* As the morning went on and he pondered the question, his anxiety level rose.

It rose to an even higher level when he found out everyone in the Tech Department was being interviewed and asked for alibis. He had expected this, but nonetheless, he was feeling even more anxious.

This is what it must feel like to be hunted, he thought. *Always looking over your shoulder, afraid to be caught.* It was anxiety-provoking, but it was also somewhat exciting. Brady still wasn't sure if he liked the feeling or not.

He hoped any information Director Finley had received before discovery was valuable. If so, it would garner himself a good payday. He also didn't want to stick his neck out again for a while. This time things had been too close for comfort. There was no way he would attempt to return to the scene of the crime to do a repeat. Security had been tightened, and everyone was alert.

Brady had found out there had also been an emergency military meeting. It would have been decrypted and transmitted as well. That meant the info from both meetings should now be in Director Finley's hands.

Director Finley sat in video conference with the directors of the Leo and Asher Corporations, and all three generals. They were discussing the info they had just received from the GIB outpost, via Director Finley's "sleeper".

The video and documentation from the Z-Class Planet, they were now calling "Planet Z", had been riveting. They all had to admit that Governor Reagan Vasilios was a "gutsy kid", and had gained their respect. To go through what he did and survive was astonishing.

Military info from the second meeting outlined the GIB's troop numbers, deployment, and strength. It also showed possible defensive formations should they be under attack.

It had been agreed by the three corporations that elimination of the GIB outpost was in their best interest. It would give them free reign in the quadrant, where they could then pursue their interests uncontested.

They had the current deployment info of the GIB, which showed scattered forces. Currently they were lacking a full defense. Based on this, it was unanimous that attacking sooner rather than later was the best plan.

The generals agreed to have the Aurora Corporation's general, General Parker Channing, promoted to Military General of the Fleet. He would lead their combined forces for the attack on the outpost. He was well respected by the other two generals, General Eiden and General Maveral. The Aurora Corporation also had a larger and better trained military.

They agreed that mining the metal alloy on Planet Z was the priority after the outpost was destroyed, and after the prisoners had been dealt with. They were acutely aware they'd need a strong military presence for the mining operation, due to the dangers. General Channing also had a personal interest in the life forms discovered on Planet Z. His mind was moving towards weaponizing them in the future.

All in all, the information obtained from the GIB outpost had been incredibly valuable. Director Finley's informant had returned his weight in gold many times over with this information.

There was a lot of planning to be done in a short period of time. The military would focus on attack strategy, while the corporations dealt with any planetary agreements. Promise of a percentage of this new alloy should keep them off their backs as they attacked the GIB outpost.

Colonel Alan Campbell, overseer of the Red and Green Squadrons, was in Sector 8 with the Vodyanyov and Kitsuine, when he got the message to return to the outpost. The GIB's presence there was a deterrent to war, and they were also there to intervene. They had been asked by both the Vodyanov and Kitsuine to mediate discussions between them.

Colonel Campbell ordered all ships to return to base, and asked the mediators on the surface if they would like to continue or return to the outpost.

"I think we're finally making progress with the two sides. The Kitsuine are more eager to settle things formally, whereas the Vodyanyov are reluctant and difficult. However, the talks are going in a good direction. It will just take time," reported Kristina, one of the mediators on the surface of Kitsuina. "I'd like to stay to continue mediating discussions, as would the other mediators."

The colonel's ship set coordinates to return to the outpost. They would pass through the southern part of Sector 4, in order to avoid the Corporate Alliance situated in Sector 5.

One of the laboratories at the GIB was getting a lot of traffic, people curious to see the creature that had been cultivated. "I hear it's a newly discovered plant-animal hybrid -- amazing!", "I wonder if it's as dangerous as I've heard?", and "Yeah, I heard there's a video of a larger one, demolishing a large animal," were some of the comments.

As the onlookers admired the hybrid creature, its smaller tendrils had been sweeping the entirety of the enclosed tube, searching for something. It was now focused on the right end of the tube, where it felt variations in the plastic, as well as another rigid substance, metal. Some of the newer tendrils twirled together and twisted, until there were several tiny ends as thin as hairs merged together. The creature inserted this group of hair-width tendrils into a circular crevice that was surrounded by metal. Then as it pushed against it, with each small victory stretching the metal outwards, it sent thicker tendrils inside the crevice to repeat the motion.

After a number of hours, the creature had stretched out the metal enough to get a larger tendril through. It felt its way around the valve. It gave a huge yank on the metal plug that surrounded the valve, and the nutrient goo started slowly flowing back into the tube. The creature basked in it.

The onlookers thought it was fascinating how the tendrils seemed to "swim" in the tube, and put pressure on the outer wall of the tube itself. "Look at that, it can feel the inside of the tube," one onlooker said. "It looks a lot bigger than it was earlier today," another onlooker said. "Umm, is it supposed to be that big? It's running out of room," was another comment.

Jesse ran as fast as he could down the corridor. He had just been paged that there was an emergency at the lab. He skidded to a stop inside, and could see that behind the safety glass, the organism was twice as big as it was last night. It was tipping its tube back and forth. Once in a while it pressed outwards with its largest vines, hitting the polycrylicarbonate tube as though trying to break through. The seed mass was over a foot in diameter now.

Jesse's assistant was already there, but riveted to the spot. "Thrace, hit the incinerate button!" Jesse had to push him out of the way, because he stood there, frozen. Jesse hit the control for the vacuum tube. "Initiating incineration," a woman's voice said.

Jesse knew something was wrong when he heard a loud wail. The creature smashed through the polycrylicarbonate of the vacuum tube, shooting into the quarantine room. Jesse heard screaming, and saw its tentacles waving wildly, some fully engulfed in flames. Tentacles shot into the door mechanism of the quarantine room, and the door flew open.

"Fire protocol initiated," a woman's voice said, as foam started pouring from the ceiling of the laboratory. The flames were so hot in the tube, that once the door was open, they'd set off the laboratory fire alarm. Foam came down in the quarantine room to put out the fire, since quarantine mode was disabled when the door was opened.

Tentacles with a trap attached had snaked over to where Jesse's assistant was standing, frozen to the spot. Thrace suddenly woke up and backed away, tripping over some of the thick vines behind him. As he fell, the trap snapped down on his leg, and he screamed in pain, as a white foamy substance was secreted around his leg.

"It's burning, it's burning!" Thrace screamed in agony.

Jesse rushed over to the fire extinguisher and grabbed the axe. He didn't know if it would be strong enough to cut through the bigger vines, but he would try. By this time the foamy ooze had turned pink, an unknown chemical now mixed with the blood of his colleague.

Jesse hacked at the vine that was attached to the trap. Suddenly the creature dropped Jesse's assistant and recoiled. Jesse hacked at more of the vines. He *had* to get the creature back into the quarantine room. The creature continued to recoil, until it was behind the door, still writhing. Jesse slammed the door and locked it, then hit the "freeze" button. *Anything that was in the room should be frozen,* he thought.

Jesse ran over to Thrace, to see how he was doing. "Oh no." Jesse was dismayed. It looked like alkaline fluid had melted away the flesh on the leg. In places, the periosteum on the bone had eroded away, and the bone was partly disintegrated. The blood vessels above the area had been cauterized.

"Medical emergency in laboratory number three," Jesse yelled over his com.

"Dispatching unit immediately," was the response. Jesse hoped they would get there quickly.

Lord Bartholomew Sullivan had just made an agreement with the five corporations who weren't associated with the Corporate Alliance, to secretly take them into his fleet, as traders. As they were "wanted" by the alliance, there was no way for them to safely continue to work along the colonists in the Antares system. Their ships were to be rebranded, and their directors to be kept out of sight.

WARNING

CHAPTER SEVEN

The passst and the future are the sssame. They are one continuousss cccycle that repeatedly turns. When we focusss only on amassssing wealth in the present, we lose our connections to our passst, and our relationship with the future.

Chief Elder N'kaam Dastoyl of the Vitaari

The Vitaari were not happy with Director Finley's proposal. The Vitaari Council was in a conference call with him.

"We, the Vitaari, have a claim to Planet Azram," stated the Chairman of the Council.

Azram? That planet has a name? Director Finley was surprised anyone had taken an interest in the planet before now. "How is that?" He felt unsure of himself.

"Before the Hashain came, our ancccessstors lived on the planet. Azram is the Vitaari planet of origin," the Vitaari explained.

Hashain? What is he talking about? Director Finley asked himself.

"So what would it take to satisfy the Vitaari? We'd be doing all the work, mining and processing the alloy." Director Finley hoped it wouldn't cost too much to placate these creatures.

"30% of all profitsss," answered the Vitaari.

"What?" Director Finley's eyes nearly popped out of his head. "How can you demand that much? You aren't even inhabiting the planet."

"Our relatives are currently inhabiting the planet," the Vitaari said slyly. "Tra*ccc*e our DNA and you'll *sss*ee the link between us*ss*."

"5% of all profits," said Director Finley. One of the Vitaari guffawed, another one snorted, the others sneered.

"That will NOT do." The Vitaari's voice was harsh. He was clearly offended. "There are many who would cons*ss*sider your mining operation to be a des*ss*ecration of an important Vitaari landmark."

"Then 15%," said Director Finley, gritting his teeth.

"Make it 20% and we have a deal." The Vitaari attempted to smile but instead flashed a wicked grimace. "For that amount, we should be able to pers*ss*suade the other Vitaari to overlook the des*ss*ecration of their homeland."

"Fine." Director Finley spoke petulantly. "20% of profits will go to the Vitaari. Would you rather have it in the form of funds or the alloy itself?"

"We'll *sss*tart with the alloy, then let you know once we finish our tes*ss*st*sss* on it," said the Chairman.

Paying the Vitaari with the alloy was preferable to Director Finley. They would just strip the planet bare, without worrying about trading for the funds. And it would be easier to fudge the numbers since they had a commodity of unknown value.

"20% paid in alloy. We'll even deliver it to you to save you the trip to the processing plant. In return, radio silence as we pass through your airspace to attack the outpost tonight, and no assistance rendered to the GIB," said Director Finley.

"Agreed," replied the Vitaari.

"The alloy won't be mined right away, as we'll be delivering prisoners from the outpost first," said Director Finley. "We'll keep you posted on the status."

The Vitaari nodded.

"Communication end," said Director Finley. He smiled. Although it was more than he had expected to pay, they could manage it.

It wasn't a practice of Lady Cia's to eavesdrop at other's doors. However, she had learned during a recent ordeal, that listening and observing had great value. She rapidly walked down the hallway to Isla's rooms, but Isla wasn't there. She set off to find her.

Cia found her sister in the study with K'Vaal, having cava.

"We have a *ssspecial guessst* who's *jussst* arrived, Lady Isla," he was saying. "One of the Vitaari Coun*ccc*il is currently *ssstaying* at the *ess*state. He's currently freshening up in his rooms and taking care of *ss*some business*ss*s."

Lady Isla could see that something was troubling her sister. "Come and sit with us, Cia," beckoned Lady Isla. Lady Cia nodded, closed the door to the study, and walked over to a lounge chair covered in teal green courdoroy.

Lady Cia said to K'vaal as she sat down, "I did just notice one of the Vitaari, in D-wing. Will he be staying long?"

"Not long," answered K'vaal. "But it'*sss* a privilege to have him, one of our Vitaari Coun*ccc*il, under this*ss* roof."

"Lord K'vaal, could you tell me about Azram?" she asked cautiously.

K'vaal suddenly became still. He took on a serious tone. "The planet Azram is *sss*acred to the Vitaari, as we originated there.

Sssomeday we will return to our homeland. Why do you a*sss*k?" His eyes narrowed sharply.

Cia knew now that she could trust K'vaal to act on the information she was about to share. "Lord K'vaal, I have discovered information about the planet Azram that may be important to you."

Quietly she outlined, "The Vitaari Council has made a deal with the corporations regarding mining on Azram." K'vaal's face hardened. "The Vitaari will receive 20% of the profits because of their claim, and under three other conditions.

"Firstly, it is a payoff for the Corporate Alliance's use of Vitaari airspace tonight as they approach the GIB outpost to destroy it. Secondly, it buys radio silence. Thirdly, it buys their loyalty, meaning that the Vitaari Council has agreed to not support the GIB if they survive." K'vaal was gritting his teeth by the time she had finished. Although he could be motivated by greed at times, he considered Azram to be sacred ground, off limits, apparently.

"Attacking the Galactic Investigations Bureau? Why that would be disastrous," whispered Lady Isla. She spoke, facing K'vaal, "They are the ones keeping lawlessness from ruling this sector. The corporations must be stopped somehow."

K'vaal had to agree with her, although his motivation was torn. If open lawlessness was the new standard, covert illegal agreements would no longer provide profit for the Vitaari. Millions of Vitaari businesses would be affected, since their society thrived on illegal negotiations.

"Someone *must* warn the GIB outpost," said Lady Cia.

"All transmissions are being monitored if they've reque*sss*ted radio *sss*ilen*ccc*e." K'vaal spoke in a miserable tone of voice.

"Monitored by both the corporations and the Vitaari Councccil. I mus*sst* gather the Elders together for a meeting."

"But the GIB needs to be warned right away. Don't you see, Lord K'vaal? They will stand between the corporations and Azram on behalf of the Vitaari. That is why they are in this quadrant, for situations like these," insisted Lady Cia.

K'vahl looked at Lady Cia, then dropped his head down. "I'd never cons*ss*idered they might be of value to the Vitaari in that way. I've only ever *ss*seen them as a nuis*ss*ance, and an opportunity. By not allowing open lawles*sss*nes*sss* it has given us*ss* a market for our underground operations." He reluctantly admitted his motivation was not noble. He had been exposed, and for the first time felt ashamed, so much that he couldn't look at Lady Isla.

"Lord K'vaal, I can go and warn them," announced Cia, boldly. "I'll stay close to the border of Sectors 4 and 5."

K'vaal thought hard for a minute about all the variables in play, his personal and business interests, and those of the Vitaari in general. Lastly, he thought of Lady Isla and what would please her most.

"Lady Isla, would you be kind enough to entertain our gue*ss*st, while Lady *Ccc*ia goes out for the evening and I meet with *sss*ome old friends?" K'vaal asked.

"Since we can assume they know our strength and our new deployment strategy, we should change things up." General McKenna was in a meeting with the other department heads.

"I agree," nodded Reagan. "We need a new defensive strategy. All leaks are now looked after?" he asked the Secretary.

"Yes. However, we haven't discovered who planted the transmitter yet," answered the Secretary. "But we've tightened security everywhere on the outpost, and we've emphasized confidentiality with all those under our command."

"I'd also like to suggest that we go to Code Yellow," said the General. The other men nodded. Having everyone in a state of readiness would put them in a much better position if they were attacked.

"So what are your ideas for military strategy, General McKenna?" asked Reagan.

General McKenna connected his USB drive and a number of new formations came up on the holographic emitter. "Here are some ideas," he said.

K'vaal's smallest shuttle was about to take a trip to the GIB outpost. Lady Isla hugged her sister then kissed her on the cheek. "Take care, Cia. I'll set the autopilot to stay close to the outskirts of Sector 5 so you won't be discovered. Be safe."

"Goodbye, Isla," she held Isla's hands in her own, then threw her arms around her older sister's neck. "I love you."

Isla embraced her. "Let's get you into the shuttle and off the ground," she said, passing the few remaining supplies to Cia. K'vaal kept the shuttle in good repair and well-stocked, so the girls didn't have to worry about equipment, just personal items that Cia would need for the journey, especially since she had no idea how long she would be gone for.

Lady Isla sent one of K'vaal's household bots with Cia, in case of emergency. She was worried about her sister, but knew this was the path she was destined to take.

Cia started the engines, and the bot guided the shuttle out of the landing port. Then she was off to warn Reagan of this important development.

Once she was off-world and the electromagnetic drive kicked in, she gave a sigh of relief. She hadn't been stopped or followed. The trip should be fairly straightforward from this point.

Four hours later, when she was in range of the GIB outpost, she hailed them. She had no passcodes, but asked for permission to land. The outpost was at Code Yellow.

"I'm sorry my lady. However, no one is permitted to land without passcodes during a Code Yellow alert," said the Chief of Operations.

"Please, I must speak to the Governor. It's an emergency. I have important classified information that I must discuss in person," said Cia, urgently.

The Chief of Operations had an officer do a search for Reagan. He was notified, and he asked to be patched through to Lady Cia immediately.

"Lady Cia." Reagan was surprised to see her in a space suit, asking to land a shuttle.

"I must speak with you, Governor. It's urgent."

"Let her land," said Reagan. He rushed to meet her at the shuttle bay.

The urgency of the situation had overtaken Lady Cia. She spent no time in greeting.

"I overheard a conference call between the Vitaari Council and Director Finley." She inhaled sharply. "The Corporate Alliance intends to attack. Tonight. Before you have a chance to fortify yourselves. They were monitoring communications, or I would have transmitted the message to give you more warning."

"Thank you, Cia."

They rushed to the briefing room, while Reagan instructed the other officers to meet them there. Cia was still in her spacesuit.

Reagan introduced Lady Cia to the committee, and she debriefed the council.

"The Vitaari are joining with the Corporate Alliance?" asked General McKenna.

"No, the corporations intend to attack tonight. The Vitaari have been paid to look the other way. However, some Vitaari may take a different position in the future. There may be some political wrangling," she said.

"Was there anything else?" asked General McKenna.

"There was a lot of discussion about a valuable alloy on a planet named Azram. The Vitaari Chairman said Azram was their ancient home planet. Many Vitaari may have issue with the alliance mining on Azram. They also said something about a group they called the Hashain. The Vitaari lived on Azram until the Hashain arrived," said Lady Cia.

"So we were right to assume they had the report on the Z-Class planet and they knew our original military strategy," said Reagan. "Azram is it?"

"Another thing. The corporations are planning on taking prisoners, I don't know what for. Director Finley said they would be delivering them somewhere."

"Lady Cia observed this conversation herself," stated Reagan to the council. "Thank you, Lady Cia, for risking your life to fly here to warn us. Do you intend to return or to stay with us?" Reagan was looking into her eyes with concern.

"I intend to stay, Governor," said Lady Cia, softly. She left the room. She was escorted to the crew quarters.

After Lady Cia left their presence, a Code Orange went into effect as the meeting continued.

After the meeting, Reagan found Lady Cia in the crew quarters. She had changed into a rich purple dress that brought out her eyes.

"Reagan," she whispered and put her arms around him to greet him with a squeeze. He winced from the pain, but put his arms around her gingerly. "I wasn't sure what had happened when I hadn't heard from you."

Reagan told Cia the main points of what had occurred over the last thirty-six hours. He didn't want to risk contacting her upon arrival at the outpost, as it may have put her in danger.

"I understand. You've been through a terrible ordeal. That and the surgery must have taken a toll on you. Not to mention the stress of the news I've brought with me tonight."

"To be honest, I'm sore, exhausted, and living off of adrenaline. But I can't allow myself to rest. The outpost is at stake. Tonight I'll be on the bridge with the other officers and military." Reagan said in a serious tone, "Cia, I'd like you to stay close by in case anything happens. That way I can get to you quickly."

"I'll stay here in my quarters," said Lady Cia, searching Reagan's face. "You don't think the outpost can withstand this attack," she asked and stated at the same time.

"We have far less resources to draw on than they do," Reagan said slowly. "However, General McKenna does have some defensive tactics we may be able to use." Cia nodded.

They kissed each other tenderly on the lips, then Reagan made his way to the bridge.

K'vaal had called on the Elders. They met in the Elders' council room, a remote cavern, far from the hustle and bustle of the Vitaari cities.

"The Vitaari Coun*ccc*il has ac*ccc*epted a deal with the Corporate Allian*ccc*e," K'vaal announced.

"What deal is that?" asked one of the Elders, four times K'vaal's size.

"The Corporate Alliance will mine on Azram, and the Vitaari Council will re*ccc*eive 20% of the profit*sss*."

The Elders sat forward, some of them jerking upright, shocked and outraged about this news. They were all talking at once.

"Children, children," said the oldest and largest of the Elders. "*Sss*ettle down. Let u*sss* have dis*ss*cussion."

K'vaal looked at the Vitaari, eight times his size, seated in a stone chair that was made for him. K'vaal bowed, as he had said his piece. It was now up to the elders to decide how to proceed.

"The Corporate Allian*ccc*e is ignorant of our plan to return to our homeland. They do not know the depth of our his*ss*tory with Azram. Their *sss*ights are *sss*et on the present, and how they can amas*sss* wealth. Not the pas*sss*t nor the future.

"Too many Vitaari have forgotten their connections to the pas*ss*t, and no longer look to the future. They have been corrupted and are motivated by greed," stated the Chief Elder. "Isn't that right, K'vaal?" The Chief had a knowing look on his face.

K'vaal bowed. "I was on*ccc*e corrupted by greed, and am *sss*till *sss*ometimes driven that way. Purchas*ss*ing Elanis*ss*e as *sss*laves at a great pri*ccc*e to display my power is eviden*ccc*e of that corruption."

"Yet you have elevated them in your hous*ss*ehold to positions of res*ss*pect, and let one go," stated the Elder.

K'vaal startled slightly. He hadn't realized he'd been under surveillance.

"There has been a change in you, K'vaal."

K'vaal nodded and looked down.

"This*ss* shows that the Vitaari are not los*sst* to us*ss*. *Ssseek* out those who follow the old ways," ordered the Chief Elder. "We will bring them together with one purpos*sse* and *ssstop* this nons*ssenssse*."

K'vaal was speaking again. "Are we talking *ccc*ivil war?" he asked, anxiously.

"No, just taking back Azram," the Chief Elder replied.

"If we go down that route it will mean war with the Corporate Allian*ccc*e," insisted K'vaal.

"We will work underground for now," replied the Chief Elder, "gathering those together of like mind and gathering intel. When we are ready, we will reach out to diss*sc*over who will ally thems*ss*elves with us*ss* agains*sst* the Corporate Allian*ccc*e. Until then we won't make a move."

K'vaal bowed, relieved.

"For five hundred years, I've lived on Vitaaria," said the Chief Elder. "Many of you left your homes at the *sss*ame time, when the Hashain *sss*ought to des*ss*troy our ra*ccc*e by making our planet uninhabitable. Please, share your news with us*ss*, Elder E'oghan."

The Elder stood. "After *ccc*enturies of res*ss*earch, we have finally found a *sss*olution. We are now able to take back Azram from these creatures with minimal los*sss* of life. This*ss* means that we als*sso* can fight the Hashain if they return to our quadrant with the same biological weapon."

The Chief Elder gave assignments to the other Elders.

When he was done, he stretched out and unfurled a pair of wings on his back.

He was a dragon.

WAR

CHAPTER EIGHT

Many wars have been fought in our universe over eons of time. Why do these wars start? No one remembers the real reasons, since it's only the victors who write our history. Will they cause any lasting change? The change is but one star in an endless galaxy full of stars.

Magistrate Kian Anderson, Galactic Investigations Bureau

The Corporate Alliance had crossed into Sector 2, where the Galactic Investigations Bureau was located. They were close to the outpost, and assumed they had the element of surprise on their side.

As ships encroached on the outpost the unexpected happened. The surrounding area was littered with booby traps. The front line had it the worst.

A ship on the right flank exploded, whereas another on the left disappeared. One of the bigger ships in the middle broke apart as half of it disappeared.

"Halt! Mines and phase shifters!" yelled General Channing. "Regiment B, do a magnetic sweep of the area!"

The fleet halted, but not before several more carrier ships were destroyed.

Regiment B shot magnetic mines out long-range, in order to attract the defensive booby traps. They were far enough out so the attacking fleet wasn't affected by the explosions. The general hoped the defenders would see the explosions and assume they had destroyed a significant portion of the attacking fleet.

"Front line cloak!" ordered Channing. As the mines exploded, the front two lines cloaked themselves. As the other ships moved passed them, they now became an invisible rear guard.

On the GIB outpost, there was an element of optimism, as they watched the explosions from the bridge.

"Looks like we took out a lot of their oncoming force with the mines and phase shifters," commented Corporal Lennox.

"Right and bottom flanks breaking off. I wonder what they're intending," said Seargeant Trevana.

"Keep a close eye on both, and note any changes in formation," ordered General McKenna. He moved the battle from screen to holographic projection.

Corporal Lennox and Sergeant Trevana each kept an eye on the holographic projection of the two groups and saw them merging together below them to the right. They swept in close to the outpost, and launched a series of smaller fighter ships. The smaller ships weren't as easy to target and could do damage to the outpost close up.

In response, the GIB outpost launched a squadron as a countermeasure. "Yellow Squadron's up to bat," said General McKenna. They watched the squadron split, half in pursuit of the larger Corporate Alliance ships, doing damage yet staying out of range of their powerful canons.

Taylor Cohen's adrenaline was pumping as she spun her fighter ship into a roll to evade incoming fire, while fluidly circling around so she was now on her attacker's tail. It was important that their squadron take out the ships to her right before they could do significant damage to the outpost.

She fixed on the other ship, forcing it out of range of the outpost, and swung around to catch another fighter as the first one exploded. She liked to be systematic like her father, eliminating one opponent at a time, but that didn't mean she wasn't good at improvising.

After the first few kills, it was apparent to Taylor that the opposition wasn't as well trained as her squadron. If they kept the pressure on, they should come out of this okay.

Taylor unexpectedly made a swoop below an oncoming ship to evade it as it fired on her, circled around and sat on its tail. She was relentless.

She heard her brother's voice on the com channel, "This is Yellow Squadron Leader. Keep the pressure on." She smiled. They would compare scores later, she thought as she took out another opponent. They were depleting the ships quickly.

"Cue up the remote mine-carriers, Regiment B," ordered Military General Channing. "Launch Squadron A, and allow the mine-carriers to go in together. We don't want the mine-carriers targeted. Let them blend in with the regular fighter ships."

Now that the main force had pulled in closer, more squadrons could be launched from the Corporate Alliance's ships. Squadron A and the mine-carriers were launched from their own right flank, and banked in a wave towards the middle of the outpost. They intended to swarm the midsection. The GIB in return shot down a number of the incoming ships.

Once the mine-carriers were in close, Squadron A pulled back, and the remote mine-carriers crashed into the outpost's launching pads, taking away the GIB's ability to launch any more squadrons, and apparently splitting the outpost in two.

The shaking on the outpost was like an earthquake. At first there were small tremors, areas of the ship being targeted, shields holding most of the time, and then there was one large tremor after another.

"They've taken out the launching bays," said Corporal Lennox. "We can't launch any more squadrons."

"Let them keep thinking that, and we'll give them a surprise later," said General McKenna.

"We detached the launching bays before they caused significant damage to the ship. We're now operating in tandem with Outpost B," said Sergeant Trevana.

"Outpost B, move into an echelon position behind us. Have our other ships move behind us in echelon formation, and protect those damaged. Keep all guns focused on their larger ships, the carriers," said General McKenna. "Especially the ones that haven't launched any fighter ships yet. That way we either take out their squadrons in one shot, or disable the carriers from launching ships."

By this time, the GIB had fighter ships all over the Corporate Alliance, targeting their guns and launching bays, doing serious damage. Things were looking up for them, and they realized there was a chance they could defeat the Corporate Alliance in this battle, giving them time to regroup and reinforce.

Blue Squadron Leader Abigail Hawking had just destroyed the cannons on one of the Corporate Alliance carriers. They were now going for the launching bay, to disable their squadrons. Suddenly, a fighter ship shot out from the launching bay. One of

Abigail's pilots fired and the ship exploded, but too far away from the carrier to do significant damage.

One of the pilots banked to the left, and fired on the launching bay, hoping to catch a ship in the process. No such luck.

This time as Abigail approached she was being shot at, so she knew there was a ship in the bay. If she could only destroy it...

Suddenly there was an explosion, and Abigail circled around just in time to avoid the blast. Blue Squadron had destroyed another one of the launching bays.

General Channing couldn't figure out where all the GIB Squadron ships were coming from.

Then he inhaled sharply, while swearing an oath under his breath. He ordered, "Take a shot below the bottom of the front outpost, on the left side."

"But there's nothing there, Sir," replied a young corporal.

"Just do it," ordered Channing.

The corporal shot in the direction he was ordered to. They both saw a shield light up quickly, then disappear.

"Just as I thought," said General Channing. "Their carriers are cloaked and near the bottom, see? That's where their squadrons are coming from."

"Take out the carriers at the bottom of the outpost," ordered General Channing.

Although most of the smaller fighter ships had already been launched, the cloaked ship was targeted. To avoid damage, it uncloaked and moved up between the two outpost halves, so the first one was shielding it. Channing gritted his teeth in frustration.

The GIB was much more successful with their use of small fighter ships. They were rendering the larger corporation ships useless by taking out weapons and launching bays through repeated wave attacks. They were also an effective countermeasure against the small fighters and mine-carriers.

General Channing realized that right now, his greatest asset was his larger warships, those that hadn't been disabled yet. He gave orders to pull all capable large ships back to feign a retreat, leaving all disabled ships in front. They would provide some cover for now, obscuring what he was about to do, and the GIB would assume that their thrusters had been damaged.

"Are they really retreating?" Corporal Lennox sounded excited.

"I'm not sure," said General McKenna slowly, while evaluating the situation. "But it looks like we have more firepower left than they do. See how many disabled ships they have? They aren't being very effective due to our countermeasures, so maybe they've recognized that. Still, I'd prefer to be cautious. Let's pull back the rest of our fleet into a protective position behind the outpost."

All GIB fighter ships were pulled back into a defensive position, as they waited to see what the Corporate Alliance's next move would be.

As soon as his ships were all in position, General Channing gave the order. A dozen warships uncloaked, ones assumed destroyed by the booby traps planted by the GIB, and the full fleet of remaining warships flew straight at the outpost in two lines, firing. They moved upwards then backwards in a wave, so the next ship could fire then rejoin the line of attacking ships.

They took minimal damage with this formation keeping the pressure on the outpost with their continuous assault.

"We have no other good options," shouted General McKenna. "If what the Lady Cia says is accurate, then the corporations intend to take prisoners, and won't immediately execute our personnel." As a family man, with a wife and daughter on the outpost, he wouldn't be making this decision unless it was absolutely necessary.

The noise was deafening, and the outpost was shaking under the pressure of the attack. "Shields and weapons are down," yelled Sergeant Trevana. "Fires occurring all over the outpost."

"Eject stations, authorization 5264, Bravo, Echo," shouted General McKenna.

Suddenly, the outpost halves fragmented, separating into many sections, then some of those sections divided into smaller segments shooting out in all different directions. Nearly all fires were extinguished. Some of the largest sections were shaped like ships.

Seconds later, those large ships and the carriers jumped to light speed, all in different directions. Most smaller sections had thrust, and began spreading out from the battleground. A dispersal tactic, but also a survival tactic. The GIB outpost was no longer a threat to the Corporate Alliance, so there was no longer any reason for them to attack. By dispersing, there were multiple targets, more difficult to kill or capture.

The Corporate Alliance started bringing in their heavy transport ships that hadn't entered the battle area yet.

Janine Cohen, wife of the Secretary of Bureau Investigations, walked through the flexible plastic tube with those caught in the family quarters. They entered the cargo hold of a Corporate Alliance ship. They were being evacuated under guard to who-knows-where.

She stood in the cargo hold, with a courageous and stately air, in a light grey dress that complimented her dark skin. She must

stay strong for those around her and not give in to despair trusting that those who loved them would find a way to rescue them.

That was...if the plan was to keep them alive. Janine didn't allow her mind to go down that path, the fate that numerous civilizations had faced in the past -- complete annihilation. But she knew that was a definite possibility. She shivered, both with cold and the dread she was feeling.

Why keep them alive then? The answer was simple. They wanted to salvage anything from the GIB outpost that may be of value. They needed survivors cleared out.

Outwardly, she smiled at the others in the cargo hold, squeezed a shoulder, patted a child on the head. She reassured her people. Through that reassurance she gave them hope.

A group of guards came and handed out blankets to the newcomers. "It's taking a while for the cargo hold to warm up," one of them said to the group of prisoners, sympathetically.

"Thank you," Janine said with a smile, as one of the guards handed her a blanket.

"You're welcome, Ma'am," he responded. His face was unreadable.

After General Channing ordered a halt to the attack, he contacted Director Finley.

"The outpost is disabled as a defensive weapon. It fragmented to keep the personnel alive, and hasn't been completely destroyed, which means your follow-up plan can be executed effectively. The total number of prisoners is estimated at 35,000. We estimate that 15,000 GIB troops were destroyed, and 30,000 escaped from the outpost." reported Channing. "Which planets would you like the first prisoners transferred to?"

"Have one of your generals transport them to the three colony planets in Sector 5 behind Planet Z. We'll take the mining operations, saying the colonists reneged on their contracts, then evac the colonists several hundred sectars away," said Director Finley.

"Then start amassing troops at the mining locations. Our troops will evade notice since they will be spread out across the planets. The rest of the prisoners can go to the mining operations in the Alniyat solar system."

Director Finley raised his glass, "Great work today, Parker. Since we have so many prisoners, it solves the lack of workforce for the takeover of the colony planets. Thank you for following through with that. A toast to many more profitable endeavors."

"A solid long-term solution," agreed Military General Channing. "Ground patrol will keep the prisoners under control while accumulating forces for the next step of the plan." Channing raised his glass of water in a return toast, "To you and I, Rowan. It's a pleasure working with someone who's on the same page, focused on efficient solutions and on the future."

Two soldiers from the Corporate Alliance hooked up a plastic tube to one of the floating compartments of the GIB outpost. They were prepared to evacuate and take prisoners.

They heard movement inside the fragment, likely prisoners scurrying to hide from them. They pried open the door that was jammed shut, and raised their weapons. Visibility was limited, due to a mist with red lights blinking, reflecting through it.

Suddenly, one of the soldier's ankles was pulled from under him, he fell, and was yanked along the floor. The other soldier, hearing his screams and a gurgling noise, kept his weapon up, pointing in all directions. He was alert and wide-eyed, but unable to locate the enemy. He also kept an eye on the floor, since his companion had been yanked by the ankle. He jumped backwards as he felt something slithering over his feet.

The soldier started stepping backwards into the plastic tube, and was planning to make a run for it and detach the tube. However, as soon as he stepped back onto his ship, green tentacles shot towards him. Some grabbed onto beams inside the cargo bay, and others grabbed his arms, yanking him forward towards what looked like giant, hungry jaws.

Colonel Alan Campbell and the Red and Green Squadrons had travelled through Sector 4, into Sector 1, and were about to cross into Sector 2. He saw a ship on the scanner. As he drew closer, he recognized it to be one of the larger segments of the outpost. It was signalling his ship by flashing its lights, indicating that radio silence was necessary. He knew that something must have gone terribly wrong.

The ship docked beside the colonel's ship, and he was met by General McKenna and Governor Vasilios.

"General, Governor," said Colonel Campbell with surprise.

The General debriefed the colonel on the night's events, and gave an accounting of those troops he estimated to have escaped.

"We'd like to do some recon, to see if it's safe for us to return to rescue those left behind," said General McKenna. "However, we have to maintain complete radio silence. The last thing we want is a big fire-fight where the survivors are."

"There were a number of fighter ships left in the area, before we jumped to light speed," said Reagan. "Perhaps if we sent a single pilot in, he would go unnoticed," he suggested.

"A good suggestion, Governor," said General McKenna.

"I'll dispatch a pilot right away," said the Lieutenant. He signalled one of his officers to follow through.

"In the meantime, there may be other ships in the vicinity. They all scattered from the battle site," said General McKenna.

"We'll do a long distance sweep, see if we can detect anyone travelling away from the battle site, and offer assistance," said Colonel Campbell.

Although the outpost had fragmented and the GIB had scattered, there was a rendezvous point, known only to those high in the chain of command. The place they would be regrouping was in Sector 3, the Paikahale system, behind the second moon of Planet Neo Terrene, named Calderra.

In the meantime, General McKenna and Colonel Campbell had calculated how far away those who had fled would be. They would make several arc sweeps until there were less Corporate Alliance troops at the battle site. The pilot sent for recon had returned with an estimate. Too many warships for them to safely take on without collateral damage to survivors.

As they covered the area with arc sweeps, they were able to pick up survivors. Stranded fighter ships entered the landing bay of the large carrier ship. They made several arc sweeps, with long range scanners engaged, before sending out another pilot for recon at the battle area.

This time, the area was clear of most Corporate Alliance's ships. No ship remained that was engaged in salvage or transport. They assumed any remaining alliance ships were disabled. The two GIB ships entered the vicinity.

As the crew of the two large ships scanned visually, they suddenly saw lights flashing SOS on outpost fragments. They dispatched shuttles for rescue. They also conducted a careful scan for life signs based on heat signatures.

Many of the individual escape pods hadn't been picked up by the Corporate Alliance's ships. The alliance had focused on taking large groups of people, leaving the individual pods behind. Those in the pods were rescued quickly, before they faced danger of suffocation.

The scanners also picked up pilots who had ejected from their fighter ships during the battle. However, some of them were in bad shape. The oxygen in their suits had diminished. Many of them were taken to the med bays where they would be given extra oxygen and looked after.

Once the rescue operation was complete, crews quickly salvaged anything of value they could. Many small, complete sections of the outpost were stored in the large cargo bays, along with retrieved supplies.

Many of those rescued had to double up in quarters, but they didn't mind. They were thankful to be alive.

After the rescue and salvage, the two ships hurriedly jumped to post-light speed to proceed to the rendezvous point, before any of the Corporate Alliance ships returned to the area.

Janine breathed a sigh of relief. Their group had been journeying for a while and hadn't been "spaced", ejected from the cargo hold. Perhaps the Corporate Alliance was not going to eliminate them.

The room was warming up, and the soldiers brought water for the prisoners. "Thank you," smiled Janine, as she was given bottled water to hand out. The soldier nodded.

Although she was uncertain where they were headed, she knew they would survive. They would make the best of the situation, and at some point fight back.

RETRIEVAL

CHAPTER NINE

The things we place value on show who we are.

Delaney Walker, Alpha Team Leader

The Corporate Alliance's retrieval ships landed on five different rocky plateaus, while military ships circled around armed and ready. The alliance was not taking any chances while mining the priceless planitanium.

The terrain of the planet had been mapped out easily. Any terrain "undetectable" pointed to the metal alloy. The vast remaining sections were assumed to be areas of vegetation, land, and water. Those areas held no interest for the retrieval teams.

The three leaders of the Corporate Alliance had made an agreement with the smaller corporations. Assist with the mining campaign and the new military fleet would serve to protect them. Since they were now part of the allied work effort there would also be considerable compensation in the deal. The value of the alloy was beyond estimation, and a percentage would be sold, the profits split.

Together, the smaller corporations made a powerful workforce that would man half the operation. However, they felt pressured to follow the lead corporations without question. To stand alone in opposition meant being annihilated. Director Finley had demonstrated that.

At "Site A", the area Reagan had discovered, the retrieval ship landed lightly on the rocky plateau. Twenty retrieval teams emptied from the ship, each with their own role, carrying equipment. Transporting their equipment was an easy task, due to the lack of gravity.

The teams were anchoring equipment to the rock. They were using powerful drills that could penetrate some of the hardest substances known to man. However, piercing the planitanium with drills to anchor the equipment with bolts wasn't easy.

"Look how hard this stuff is," said Davis Cooper, leader of the Epsilon Team.

"I've never seen anything like it," his coworker replied in awe. "We're going to be rich." He grinned ear to ear. Thanks to the Aurora Corporation he already lived with a handsome income. There was sure to be a bonus for this job, plus substantial hazard pay. They were aware of some of the dangers, thanks to the stolen GIB reports.

After seeing the video of the governor's ordeal, many of the workers secretly admired Reagan. However, they knew there may be additional dangers out there they were unaware of. Even with that possibility, they weren't worried, since the military was close by.

Team Epsilon was in charge of one of the drills. They would be drilling for more samples, and to determine the depth of the rock. Other teams were going for straight extraction, removing and retrieving as much alloy as possible. There were also standby medical teams in case of injury.

The employees knew that the financial operation was two-fold. The alloy would be used to sell to the highest bidder, and to coat the outer hull of a new military fleet. Being with the Corporate

Alliance gave them access to both wealth, and protection of that wealth.

Team Epsilon was eager to get started, and they set the decibel reduction on their ear buds. Tiny microphones were embedded in their work uniforms, and a special antenna was up at the main ship. If they stayed outside the caves they could communicate with other teams and the command center. The command center could dispatch the military or med teams if necessary.

After Davis double-checked the stability of the drill and was given the "go ahead" by the command center, they started.

Team Alpha was in charge of explosives. They had been told to collapse the caves first, to block any "unwanted visitors" from joining the party. Everyone had seen video of the reptiles and dragons, and knew to avoid the vegetation. All three were lethal.

Alpha could already hear the military firing to the south. They could hear howling, almost bellowing coming from there, but knew the military was in control. The carnivorous reptiles now known as "dromasaurs" lived in or across the desert, but they seemed to have migrated onto the plateau.

The team climbed partway up the small mountain to where they would drill and insert explosives. Thanks to the governor's map of the cave system in the stolen files they knew exactly where to drill to have the greatest impact.

After putting in their earbuds, something caught their eye. Further up near the peak, they could see a couple of dragons flying around frantically, as if enraged. They were charging at the military heliplanes hovering above.

The heliplanes were attempting to evade the dragons, while at the same time shooting at them. They seemed to only have succeeded in making the dragons more angry. Those scales were so thick they were deflecting the bullets easily.

Alpha Team went back to work, and drilled with difficulty into the alloy. They inserted explosives at the seams of the cave walls to bring down the lower part of the mountain safely.

After detonating the explosives, Team Omaga moved in to load the alloy, and transport it to the first cargo shuttle. Team Alpha would now move to another area marked on their map.

As they skipped over to the right one of the team members turned his head. One of the dragons had swiped a heliplane with its tail, shattering the rotors and hitting it downwards towards the mountain.

"Look out!" he yelled, running and diving for cover. The heliplane hit the mountain where their original explosion had been, creating another explosion right above where Team Omega was working. A secondary explosion occurred as some of their machinery exploded as well.

"Is everyone okay?" yelled Alpha Team leader, Delaney Walker.

"Oh man, Del, I think Marty's gone." Marty's friend, Liam, lay there shaking. They weren't close enough to be caught in the explosion, but Marty hit his head as he was thrown forward. Blood was pooling slowly in front of his face from a gash underneath that Liam couldn't see. Marty's eyes were wide open, and his expression was one of surprise. His death had been instantaneous.

Delaney rushed over to Marty to verify. There was no pulse. He managed to peer under his head crooked on the rocks, without moving him. He realized his skull had been crushed on the side. He closed Marty's eyes and sighed.

"Alpha Team reporting. Our team has a man down, confirmed deceased. Team Omega was directly underneath that

explosion and may be in imminent danger," Delaney spoke into his mic.

"Copy," said the command center operator. "Sending in equipment operators, medical team, and secondary loading team, Team Gamma."

Delaney knew there wasn't much hope finding Team Omega alive if they were down there. However, if they hadn't been caught up directly in the explosion, they would need evacuating before they suffocated.

"Team Omega reporting," shouted their leader. "Two men were at the site, two of us were loading the shuttle. One man with minor injury enroute between explosion site and shuttle."

"Team Gamma about to merge with Team Omega. The last explosion widened the retrieval area, so we'll work together."

"Copy Omega and Gamma," said the operator.

"Machine operators, Delta Team, headed to the explosion site to clear debris and recover two missing Omega men," said Delta Team Leader.

Alpha leader Delaney knew now there would be a large, fast efficient retrieval team. If anyone was alive down there, they would be out soon. That second explosion caused by the dragon had brought that whole section of the mountain down. While ultimately it helped the speed of the operation, they had likely lost two more men, he thought sorrowfully.

Three casualties in their retrieval operation alone, including one of his own team, plus the two military guys that went down in their heliplane if they hadn't ejected in time. That was more deaths than he'd seen in the last three years as an employee of the Aurora Corporation.

Then there was the rest of his team. He quickly started to evaluate them. Liam was dazed and in shock, and another a ways back from them wasn't moving. Del thought it best for his team to withdraw from the mountain. The retrieval teams had enough to work on, without needing another controlled explosion for now. Even with corporate pressure from up top on this operation, Delaney wouldn't risk the health of his men.

"Alpha Team here. Two men injured, need medical assistance. Possible concussion, second unknown status."

"Copy. Sending medical Team Beta," said the operator.

Delaney's team would wait for assistance, and he would do what he could until then.

"You okay?" Delaney yelled at a man with no apparent injuries.

"Yeah, let me give you a hand," Rhys Copelan, his other team member, called back.

Rhys grabbed the med-kit from his pack. "I'll assess Cameron. He looked like he was in rough shape." Rhys ran back to where Cameron was lying.

Delaney knelt beside Liam to examine him. Liam was stumbling over his words, racing so barely intelligible. Delaney picked up a few words here and there.

"Liam, look at me," said Delaney. Liam looked up, and Delaney could see that one of his pupils was more dilated than the other. "I want you to breathe slowly. Follow me. Breathe in. Now breathe out." Delaney walked Liam through until his breathing slowed down, all the time taking his pulse. There was no need to even count. Liam's heart was racing.

"I can't feel my legs." Liam had fear in his eyes.

"It's okay. Calm down, you're just in shock," reassured Delaney, but he checked for evidence of a spinal injury. "I'm going to lay you down so we can elevate your feet." Delaney lay Liam on the flat outcropping of rock and put his feet up on his pack. He covered him with a blanket, and blocked his view of Marty.

Suddenly Liam started to vomit. Delaney flipped him quickly onto his left side, so he wouldn't choke. Delaney grabbed the bottle of water hooked onto Liam's pack and rinsed his mouth.

"Del!" called Rhys. "I need your help."

"Liam, I'm going to give Rhys a hand with Cameron. Stay lying on your side. I'm just a few feet away." Liam nodded.

Delaney dashed over to where Rhys was kneeling beside Cameron. "How's Cam?" Delaney asked.

"Not good," reported Rhys. "He's breathing, but his heart beat's erratic. He's lost a lot of blood."

Rhys had cut Cameron's soaked, bloody pants up to the hip, and Delaney groaned at what he saw. There was embedded shrapnel, Cam's left leg was split open and his tibia was sticking out, and Del could see that parts of the fibula had shattered. Rhys was placing a temporary tourniquet around his leg to stop the blood loss.

"Okay, let's keep him stable until the med team arrives," Del said. He monitored Cameron's vitals. "I sure hope he doesn't lose his leg," whispered Rhys to Delaney, shaking his head.

The arterial bleeding had stopped. Rhys cleaned up the wounds as best he could, and Delaney covered them with a polyacrylnet sheath.

"Del!" They heard Liam calling over.

"I'll check on Liam, shout if you need me," said Delaney.

Delaney rushed back over to Liam, who was now sitting up. Liam looked over at him, then pointed to the south.

From their vantage point, Delaney could see hundreds of reptiles racing across the plateau towards them. The military heliplanes were there in full force, trying to take them down. Once in a while, a reptile would break the line, and was taken out by the powerful guns on the main retrieval ship.

"It's okay, Liam, it looks like they have things under control." Del was more worried about the dragons near the mountain top. To him, they seemed to be the greater threat. However, there was a possibility that a reptile could make it to their position, so he decided to group.

"Here, come on, I'll help you over to the rest of the team." Delaney gathered their supplies, helped Liam up, then over the rock face to the other two men.

"Liam, Cam is in pretty bad shape, but he's doing okay. Just stay calm. I need to stay close by to assist with his care, and we thought you might feel a bit lonely over there." He smiled at Liam, as he lay him back down.

Cameron's breathing was no longer shallow. "I administered pain blockers and antibiotics," Rhys quietly said to Delaney.

"Good," said Del. He reached into his bag and pulled out a firearm. "This is just a precaution," he said to Liam. "It looks like the military has things under control, but just in case we encounter a stray reptile, we have protection." Liam nodded. Delaney explained the situation to the south in detail to Rhys, speaking in low tones, so as not to alarm Liam.

"Beta med team should be here any minute now," said Del to Liam, with a smile.

At that moment, Del saw them come into view. His team would now be taken care of.

Director Finley was pleased with how the operation was going. Although there had been casualties, the first delivery shuttles had docked at the processing plant with their precious cargo.

"A toast to Director Finley, and his success bringing our first alliance operation together," said the leader of the Asher Corporation.

The directors in the elaborate banquet room on the Aurora Corporation's main ship were all smiles as they toasted. Director Finley saw anxiety behind the smaller corporation leaders' eyes. They knew what they were losing down on the planet, people and resources. It was best that he remind them of what they were gaining.

"A toast to the abundance of wealth we are about to gain from this operation, and to our new alliance." Director Finley held up his glass. "I have before me, the contract I promised to draft up, which is ready to be signed and ratified." He could see the impact this reassurance had on the smaller corporate leaders' demeanors. They seemed much more relaxed.

"Would you like the honor of reading the contract?" He motioned to the leader of the Leo Corporation.

"Absolutely," he smiled.

The contract dictated the division of the alloy between the new military fleet, and sales. It had a profit distribution chart with all percentages listed. The largest corporations had made the largest investments of personnel and resources to the retrieval operation. Their returns would be highest. But even the smallest corporations were in a position to benefit greatly. Everyone was about to become extremely wealthy. The corporate heads were all calculating numbers mentally as they were signing the documents. There was a feeling of anticipation in the room.

With every hour that ticked by, more potential profits were being deposited at the processing factories.

General Parker Channing knew that from the state of things, they might soon have to retreat, regroup, and rethink their strategy. Right now, he was just buying time for the retrieval operation. There were too many dromasaurs, far more than were anticipated, and no end to them. They were going to run out of ammunition before they ran out of reptiles.

His main force was south of the mountain on Site A, the rocky plateau. He had several troops working on the dragons, to evade and keep them distracted. The tactic was to tire them out.

Perhaps that would be a viable option for these dromasaurs, he thought. *Have them chase a few heliplanes around instead of taking a purely defensive stance.* That might give them a few minutes of breathing room.

He barked out the orders, and four heliplanes left the main group, swooped down low to the dromasaurs but out of jumping range, and tried to draw them back towards the desert. Good, some were following, but many were still coming at them. They were climbing over the other motionless dromas, racing towards the main sources of noise and vibration. Or maybe it was that they smelled the workers. They could definitely see the commotion, as they had binocular vision. He wasn't sure if they also hunted by smell or by sound, as the dromas' records weren't clear on that point.

This job was important to him. Not only would this be one major paycheck, but this new alloy they were calling planitanium would revolutionize his military power. He saw it as his own personal military power, since Director Finley had given him free reign with military matters. It didn't matter to Finley "how" he got the job done, as long as it was done. They had an unspoken loyalty, quite an effective partnership. They both benefited from each other and neither of them got in the other's way. It was a match made in heaven.

General Channing *would* get this job done, no matter what it took. It just might take more time than was originally thought. These reptiles had amazing strength and defensive capabilities. If only he could weaponize them and use them in battle, that would give him a formidable land force. If he could weaponize the dragons, he would have an air force as well. It definitely was something worth giving some thought to, weaponizing creatures from this hardened planet.

The machine shipyard had been given orders to relocate to new coordinates. Although the rate of travel had been slow, Kalisanna saw they were almost at their destination.

They were being hailed.

"On screen," said Kalisanna. An image of Director Finley at some type of celebration popped on screen. "Oh, Director Finley. We're nearly in position."

"Yes, our first shipment of the processed alloy is on its way to you now," said Director Finley.

"I'm excited to see its properties with a larger sample. Strength and ability to avoid detection are two incredibly desired properties for those involved in ship building." Kalisanna was enthusiastic. "By the way, several ships are ready for the fusion to the hull, and we are about to start production of a full fleet as you ordered," reported Kalisanna.

"Wonderful." Director Finley laughed heartily. He was trying to stay above the hubbub in the background. "Some new ships are to be used to interest potential alloy purchasers, and the others are to supplement our fleet."

"However..." said Kalisanna.

"What is it?" The director's demeanor changed abruptly and his eyes narrowed.

"Well, after analyzing that small sample, we discovered that the melting temperature is much different than that of our hulls," she replied in a conclusive manner.

"Go on," said Director Finley.

Did she have to spell it out for him? Although the director was shrewd, he might be lacking a bit. Or maybe he'd just had too much to drink. Yes, that was likely it.

"It seems that the coating can be removed from the hull, upon heating to 400 degrees. If the melting is carefully controlled so as not to melt the actual hull's metal, then the coating will slide off. Then it can be reused on another newer ship."

The director was very interested now, showing that his full concentration was on what she was saying.

"In other words, you can coat the current fleet instead of waiting for the new fleet. Then exchange the older ships for the newer ships, one by one." Kalisanna was clearly excited.

"Plus that means the value of the substance will shoot even higher, since it's reusable," exclaimed Director Finley. "Kali, if you were here right now, I'd kiss you. As it is, I'll be adding a sizeable bonus to your next payment for this discovery. Anything else?"

"Yes, another property I determined from this small sample is that the alloy has shape memory. This means instead of coating the hulls, we could look at making reusable "sleeves". I'll keep thinking of other ways it could be used. Hopefully, now that I'll have a larger sample to work with I'll be able to make more conclusions about the alloy."

"Well, please inform me of any other discoveries you make in the future, regarding this substance," Director Finley smiled, wine glass in hand.

"Yes, Director Finley," Kali responded.

"Communication end," said Director Finley.

This night was just getting better and better.

Med Team Beta finally reached the position of Team Alpha.

"He's in rough shape." Rhys was debriefing the med team on what had transpired up until the time they arrived.

"Will you be able to save his leg?" asked Alpha leader Delaney.

"At this point I can't say," said the Beta Team leader. "We need to get him to a proper facility asap for treatment."

Beta Team worked quickly and had Cameron strapped to a backboard in no time.

"Medical extraction needed. Southwest side of mountain," said the Beta leader into his com device.

One of the team had been trying to talk with Liam, at the same time he was examining him. He walked over to Delaney and the med team. "This guy needs an emergency evac as well. He may have a brain bleed," he said quietly. "We'll need to use a decompression chamber due to evac altitude issues."

Beta leader asked, "You guys okay to get down the side of the mountain and back to the area around the main ship? I hope you understand, but we can't have those explosives on board."

"Yeah, I think we're good to go," said Rhys. "You good?" he asked Delaney.

"Absolutely. Let's get this gear and these explosives down. Thanks for looking after our guys, Doc." Delaney hesitated and lowered his voice to a near-whisper. "The other member of our team is about twenty feet left of our current position. No vital signs on impact."

"Okay, we'll make sure he's retrieved. You guys look beat. We'll meet you down at the shuttle."

Delaney and Rhys headed down the southwestern side of the mountain, while keeping an eye on the reptile situation to the south. Halfway down, they saw a heliplane headed towards their previous position.

Their teammates were going to be alright.

From the southern desert and across the rocky plateau, the dromasaurs kept coming. There seemed no end to them.

General Parker Channing had been able to draw them off for a while with the heliplane diversion, but they were too smart to keep running after them. They wanted something they could hunt. And eat.

The dragons had finally settled down in their cave at the top of the mountain. General Channing would have ordered the heliplanes to cause a cave in to lock them in, but he wanted to eventually retrieve the babies from the nest.

Now that the dragons were settled down, he would have those heliplanes as reinforcements. They would be arriving soon.

But it wasn't soon enough.

Three of the reptiles had used their powerful legs to propel themselves over the growing mess of reptiles lying on the ground. The military was able to shoot two of them down, but lost sight of the third, an abnormally large droma.

The creature was likely in a cave, or they'd have a clear view of it. The general called it in.

"One reptile's forced its way through on the south side. No visual on it."

He reluctantly turned back to the south to fight the others off, while the remaining heliplanes from the mountaintop joined the line.

General Channing hated the fact that one had made it through on his watch. He liked a clean kill zone, nice and tidy.

Delaney and Rhys were on their way down a precarious part of the mountainside when they heard the loud whirring of the heliplanes. They slid down until they were on a rock ledge.

"What about the dragons?" asked Rhys, trying to see above, but not able to see the mountain top.

"Maybe they cornered and trapped them?" suggested Delaney.

They got to their feet and dusted themselves off, still looking upwards, shading their eyes with their hands.

"Yeah, looks like..." Rhys didn't have a chance to finish his sentence. Out of nowhere, a lizard with its front claws extended landed on his back, gripping him, and ripping his back to shreds. His scream was agonizing.

The droma balanced itself on one back leg, and it was about to slash with the other leg's sickle claw. Suddenly there was a bang, and its head jerked sharply backwards.

Delaney stood, facing the droma in a shooting stance, as the reptile's enraged gaze settled on him. Del shot again, and the reptile lost its balance for a moment. He kept shooting, and emptied his clip, until the reptile finally keeled over. However, its claws were still in Rhys' back, twisting him onto his side.

Delaney rushed over to Rhys. "Man down, need med team and extraction immediately. Also need heavy cutting device. Claws of dead droma still in man's back. I repeat, we need to cut off the claws or legs to transport him."

"Copy," said the operator hesitantly, before sending out the request for assistance to the other teams.

"Alpha Team leader, this is General Channing. I'll be sending a heliplane immediately to extract both the creature and the injured." Delaney heard the general's voice over his com.

"Thank you, General Channing," Delaney said, relieved. "This droma is too large for one of the heliplanes though.

"No worries, Alpha Team leader. That creature broke through our line. A large heliplane is on the way with medical personnel immediately available to assist." Delaney breathed a sigh of relief.

The heliplane was so quick to respond that Delaney felt the breeze a couple of minutes later. It hovered above him and sent down a lift usually used to haul cargo. There were six military men on the lift who managed to get the reptile and injured man onto it. Delaney went with them and could hear Rhys moaning as the lift ascended.

In the heliplane they gave Rhys an injection and he settled down. They started an IV drip with antibiotics and fluids right away.

But most surprisingly, they had injected something into the reptile first.

"What was that for?" asked Delaney.

"A lot of these creatures have been stunned with bullets instead of killed. We want to make sure it's tranquilized as a precaution," explained the military doctor.

Delaney imagined what would happen if the droma woke up. None of them would be alive for more than a minute.

"Good call." Delaney was trembling a bit. He felt shaky, and his knees started to buckle.

"Hey, you okay?" asked one of the doctor's assistants with alarm, as Delaney slumped to the floor.

"I think I'm okay. Just feeling lightheaded," said Delaney. The assistant grabbed him a bottle of water.

The heliplane had stopped and was hovering again. The cargo lift lowered, and Delaney saw a hatch open in a space jet. Once they were in, four of the military men detached the corner cables of the cargo lift, the heliplane ascended as the hatch closed, and they were on their way.

"Alright, we're on the way to the military base to see that your friend gets the best treatment possible," explained one of the military men.

The doctors had been doing scans to determine the best way to detach the animal with the least amount of damage to Rhys' internal organs. Its front claws had barely missed his heart, and had punctured a lung.

Not only that, but the weight of the dromasaur had snapped right through the back of Rhys' rib cage.

Delaney felt better and got up to see how Rhys was faring and how bad the damage was.

"Notice how it used its front claws to clamp on?" the doctor was addressing Delaney. "This droma generally balances on one leg and does the major damage with the other. The front claws keep its prey close, yet at arms reach. You stopped the droma from killing your friend by shooting at it and throwing off its balance," said the doctor. He seemed to know a lot about the dromas.

"Can't you cut the claws off so they're more easily removed?" asked Delaney.

"We have strict orders to keep the droma intact, no matter the cost," one of the military men said to Delaney. His eyes were piercing.

Delaney's eyes widened as he realized the implications. "But..." he started.

"Please step back so the doctors can do their work. They are trying to save your friend," ordered the military man.

Delaney nodded while staring at Rhys and stepping back. The inside of the spacejet started spinning, his eyes rolled backwards in his head, and he crumpled to the floor.

Team Epsilon was drilling at fifty feet below the surface, when suddenly all resistance to the drill disappeared.

"It seems we've encountered some type of cavernous opening," said one of the Epsilon members.

"Okay, let's measure the depth of the cave," said Epsilon leader Davis Cooper.

"Alrighty." They restarted the drill.

Suddenly the drill stopped.

"That's strange," said Davis "It's like the drill can't twist anymore, like it's been tangled up in something. Let's reverse the drill and pull it up a bit."

They put the drill in reverse, but surprisingly the drill wouldn't move.

"Oh boy, it must have really tangled itself up. Let's turn it off for now, and take a short break to figure this out," said Davis.

The team stepped back from the drill and its console. Suddenly, the drill started shaking, and they heard the sound of crushing metal.

"What the...?" Davis turned back around. He stood by watching, not sure what to think.

The drill disappeared as if sucked down. Davis knew the amount of force it would have taken to yank that thing down. The outer casing would have needed to be crushed so the drill would fit in the borehole.

"What is it?" asked his teammate.

"I don't know," answered Davis. "But this place is starting to give me the creeps." He stepped forward slightly to look at the hole. Scrap metal was all around it, left over from the drill.

Suddenly, something green shot out of the hole.

"Get back!" Davis yelled. A green vine about four inches in diameter slithered over the rock, as though it was searching for something to entangle.

Davis threw a large metal bar at it. It suddenly snapped around the bar, squeezing and twisting, until it bent it into a ripple pattern.

"Get out of here, now!" yelled Davis.

"Some type of green tentacle just shot out of our borehole, after yanking the drill into an underground cavern. It bent an iron bar by itself with no effort. Team Epsilon is headed back towards the main ship."

"Copy," said the operator.

"This is General Channing here, all civilians keep away from the plants and vines. Let us deal with them."

The tentacles were shooting out of the caves, forcing themselves between rocks and debris blocking the openings. They were searching, grabbing, and destroying anything they touched.

Heliplanes were being pulled to the ground by six inch thick vines. However, thanks to the rotors, most of the heliplanes were spared, as the thinner vines were easily sliced through. When rotors cut the vines they recoiled as if in pain.

"Retreat!" yelled General Channing. "Operation is over for today at Site A. Let's get back to base."

"Everyone to the main ship. Now!" yelled the operator.

Everyone dropped what they were doing and scrambled to the main ship. No one wanted to be left behind. Time was of the essence, because the vines would eventually discover the main ship and start working on it.

The fleet of spacejets approached. One by one, the heliplanes were loaded to be flown back to the military base. General Channing ensured that civilians who hadn't made it back to the main ship were evacuated by spacejet. Most of the equipment was left behind.

As the last heliplane was being loaded, the vines snapped around it.

"Let it go," barked General Channing. "Evacuate the pilot and any personnel."

The last spacejet rose above the planet to return to base, with the pilot and co-pilot from the heliplane on a tether. The general watched as the heliplane was crushed in a matter of seconds.

"We need a more effective way to deal with the dromas," asserted General Channing. "Tomorrow we try flamethrowers." He was in a conference call with Director Finley, and the directors of the Leo and Asher Corporations.

Reports had come in from the other sites that the dromas were an issue. The bullets were stunning them most of the time, instead of penetrating the skin. They were also very agile, and difficult to target. Then there were the vines. Yes, flamethrowers were a good option to try.

General Channing thought it was a shame they hadn't been able to retrieve more dromas for his new "project". The sudden appearance of the vines had prevented that. He would have to wait. At least they could start testing on the droma that the civilian had captured. That was a huge score.

"Whatever you think is best to get the job done," said Director Finley, in good spirits. "Great job out there today, by the way, Parker. We are very pleased with the overall results so far. Equipment and workers can be replaced easily, and what we mined far exceeds the value of anything lost today." The other two directors nodded in agreement.

"Until tomorrow then," said the general.

"Until tomorrow." The three directors raised their glasses.

"Communication end." General Channing's screen went blank.

The day had gone well fiscally, but the general had wanted a better result. More captured dromas and annihilation of those remaining, to make the ongoing operation easier to manage. He liked to win. Tomorrow he would.

Cyber-plant technology was a newer area of study, but if she correctly understood what General Channing was saying, Dr. Elena Harlowe had just heard the best news of her career.

Dr. Harlowe was an expert in both biotech and botany, and had experimented on many types of plants. Never one with such rapid animal-like responses as described by the general though.

The tentacles that had attacked the crew at Site A were assumed to be of the same species as the creatures on the northern side of the plateau.

If that was true, well, she had viewed stolen data from the governor's brief excursion on the planet. She felt a thrill of excitement running through her body.

She prepared the lab for tomorrow, when the first samples would hopefully come in.

What she really wanted was a seed. She hoped the general could deliver.

Delaney woke up in a quarantine bed, and discovered he was being monitored. Medical personnel were wearing protective suits.

He sat up, alarmed. "What's wrong with me? Why am I being quarantined?"

"It's just a precaution. You passed out. We had to verify you hadn't been infected in any way," said one of the men in a yellow hazmat suit.

"Infected? By what?"

"Well, it's a newly discovered ecosystem," explained Mr. Yellow Suit. "We haven't mapped it out completely, so have to be cautious. We can get you out of here now though. I think the strain of the day was just too much for you."

The protective covering was unzipped, and Delaney emerged from the quarantine area.

"You're all clear, according to the scans."

Delaney thought of the stress of working with explosives, the dangers the uncontrolled explosions had posed, the death of Marty, Liam and Cameron's conditions, and now Rhys. Yes, today was too overwhelming for him to process.

"Well, that's at least *some* good news in the course of a horrific day," muttered Delaney, staring at the floor. He looked up. "Can I see Rhys?"

"He's in surgery at the moment, and it's complicated, obviously," said Mr. Yellow Suit.

"Mind if I have some water? And not to be troublesome, but is there anywhere to get something to eat? My stomach feels like there's a hole in it." Delaney rubbed his abdomen.

One of the military personnel stationed in the room came up to Delaney. "Of course. Let me take you to the mess hall and get

you something to eat," he grinned. "Sergeant Monroe, nice to meet you." He shook Delaney's hand.

On the way to the mess hall they passed another division on the base. Delaney read, "BioTech" on the signs. Two armed guards stood in front of the door, smiling and nodding as they walked by.

"Everyone's talking about you," mentioned Delaney's escort, smiling. "Capturing that droma has made the general a very happy man."

"I was just trying to save a man's life," Delaney replied softly.

"Yes, but at the same time you took down one of the larger dromasaurs, which we now will be able to study."

The realization suddenly hit him. "So it's still alive then?" Delaney gripped the other man's elbow, facing him with wide eyes, in alarm.

"Yup. Its vitals are strong. But it's heavily tranquilized and there's a full military team in the surgery suite. Don't worry about your friend," reassured the sergeant.

Delaney started walking again, his hands in his pockets, looking down.

"I hear your friend's doing well, too. We have the best docs here. He's going to be okay."

Delaney nodded. "Thanks," he said.

They walked into the mess hall and grabbed a couple of trays. Delaney felt like a hundred sets of eyes were following him in the lineup.

"We don't usually have civilians here. Plus with the story going around, you're a bit of a celebrity," Sergeant Monroe smiled.

Delaney wasn't feeling like a celebrity. He was feeling anxious about his team. Especially his friend still attached to that monster in the operating room.

He accepted the food handed to him. He needed to eat something or he might pass out again.

Sergeant Monroe led Delaney to a table and made introductions. The soldiers were keen on hearing Del's story about the droma. He wasn't keen on telling it, but he indulged them, answering their questions. He hated the sense that everyone seemed to be more interested in the droma than his friend's life.

After eating enough to ease the hollowness inside his stomach, Del and Sergeant Monroe headed back to the med bay. Rhys was out of surgery, and would be okay. Delaney breathed a sigh of relief.

The following day in the Intensive Care Unit, Delaney was lying on his side on a low couch to chat with Rhys who lay on his front, his face in a donut-shaped contraption. Sergeant Monroe rushed in excitedly.

"You've got to see this!" he exclaimed quietly.

"I'll be back later, Rhys," smiled Delaney, at the quizzical look on Rhys' face.

"What's going on?" Del directed in a low voice to Sergeant Monroe as he was led away.

"The droma's awake and kicking," he said as they started down the main corridor. "You've been given clearance to see it, since you're the one who caught it." Delaney wasn't sure he *wanted* to see it again.

The guards at the "BioTech" door let them through. They walked down a long corridor, until they reached a woman with mid-length, reddish-brown hair, carrying a clipboard and wearing a white lab coat.

"Dr. Elena Harlowe." She shook Delaney's hand. "I run the BioTech Division."

"Nice to meet you," Del responded politely.

"I wanted to thank you in person for capturing the creature." She sounded grateful.

Delaney felt embarrassed and mumbled something, as she led him and Monroe to a room to the left. They walked into a viewing area, and suddenly a very large dromasaur leaped towards them. Delaney startled and felt his adrenaline pumping from sheer panic.

The droma's claws had tightened around the thick bars of the room-sized metal cage where it had landed. It lowered one scaly foot to the ground as it growled and snapped at them.

"As you can see, it's now fully awake," said Dr. Harlowe. Delaney was trying to slow his breathing so his heart rate would drop. He hadn't remembered the droma being so large.

A big man in fatigues walked into the room, and Sergeant Monroe snapped to attention in a salute.

"General," said the doctor in a pleasant voice.

A very pleased General Channing directed, "At ease," to the sergeant, and introduced himself to Delaney.

"It's good to hear that your friend is going to be okay" said the general to Delaney.

"Thank you, Sir. I'm relieved that the surgery went well," said Delaney.

"As for this big guy," the general cocked his head in the direction of the droma, "we have him, thanks to your quick action." The droma was snarling at them and started barking, viciously.

General Channing laughed. "Not very happy, is he? We've determined he's an alpha male, one of the leaders of the packs. That's why he doesn't like me." Channing was amused.

"It was interesting to see these creatures working together yesterday. Normally, more than one alpha male in the vicinity would mean a vicious territorial battle. I guess they saw us as the real threat this time," said General Channing. "Well, I'm on my way to take another run at these things today. This time we're better prepared. Nice to meet you, Delaney." The general walked back down the corridor.

After the general left, Delaney asked Dr. Harlowe, "So what do you plan on doing with this one?"

"Studying him to start with, so we understand the species better. The general would eventually like to capture more," she answered.

"But why?" asked Delaney. "The risk involved..." he shook his head at his recollection of yesterday's attack.

"Well," said Dr. Harlowe, "the general sees these creatures as efficient killing machines."

"But there's no way you could control them?" Delaney both asked and commented at the same time.

"Well, that's where biotech comes in," she smiled. *She has a pretty smile*, Delaney thought. "And if we aren't able to control them through tech, they still have practical applications for war," she said slowly, looking straight into Delaney's eyes.

Delaney grasped what she was referring to. The complete annihilation of everything in their path, with no regard for type of life form or variables such as age. Just 100% killers. Delaney shook his head.

"We're also aiming to get one of the younger dragons, and that plant-like creature sounds amazing. Both the general and I are excited about the possibilities," her eyes lit up.

"Well, nice to meet you, Dr. Harlowe," Delaney said, shaking her hand. "I'm going to check on my friend."

"Oh yes, your friend who was in surgery with the droma. I'm glad he's okay. We weren't sure how much to use to tranq the droma, but it worked out," she smiled.

"It worked out?" asked Delaney, suddenly turning around to face her. "There was a chance that monster could have woken up during the surgery?" Delaney's voice was rising.

"Calm down," Dr. Harlowe motioned with her hands, realizing she had made an error. "The chances of it waking up were remote. Besides we had a tactical team in the room in case there was an incident," she insisted.

"An 'incident'?" Delaney asked incredulously. "Its claws were in my friend's back. If that *thing* had awakened, my friend wouldn't have had a chance. At the very least, his spinal cord would have been snapped!

"I can't believe you people." Delaney choked out. He marched back to the med bay with long strides, so quickly Sergeant Monroe had difficulty keeping up with him. Monroe was trying to talk to him, but Delaney was too upset to listen.

If it wasn't for Rhys, he would have picked up and left the military base, and broken ties with the Aurora Corporation.

ANNIHILATION

CHAPTER TEN

Although we may watch from a distance, tragedy is only real when we experience it.

Lady Isla of Elanissia

General Channing was enjoying himself as he watched the flamethrowers damage the dromasaurs. Many of them had gone back towards the desert. At some point he intended to find where they lived and seize their young. Eventually, they would make a deadly killing army for special ops.

The one regret he had was that the family of dragons had deserted their cave. Although it meant not having to deal with them during their operation, he wanted those infants. He would have to find a new nest.

He had seen that the flamethrowers had an unexpected effect on the vines. It looked like they actually felt pain as they were blackened by the flames which caused the other vines in the area to go into a frenzy. What this meant was that the vines over the entire area came from one creature. It was difficult to imagine its size. As long as they were consistent, they could keep the vines back while the workers did their jobs.

Today they had encountered the red jaws secreting the liquid that absorbed flesh and bone. Attached to vines, the jaws had surprisingly shot across the plateau. His soldiers were able to get a

sample of the liquid, which would be taken to the lab for Dr. Harlowe to analyze. After that, they used flamethrowers and fried the suckers.

The operation was going much better today, and they used less troops. That was a good sign, since more troops were needed on Aleph. After a long day, General Channing returned to base. He was going through daily reports. The remaining alliance ships that had been disabled during the battle and had lost thrusters were being repaired in Sector 2.

"We think that prisoners may have taken one of the carriers, since there is no response on the coms. When we send men in to investigate, they are attacked, and don't return," read one of the reports.

General Channing wrote his instructions on screen with his stylus. They were to tow the carrier in close to the military base, and a tactical unit would deal with it.

On three, signaled the leader of the tactical team. *One, two, three.*

The team detached the plastic tubing, disconnecting it from an outpost fragment and the carrier. Both outside airlock doors automatically shut. They advanced from their shuttle door to the left, and put a decoder by the key panel. The lock was decoded, they passed through the airlock, and swept the fragment room, weapons up.

"All clear. It's some kind of lab," said the tactical leader into his com. There were large pieces of broken polycrylicarbonate on the floor along with some type of pinkish fluid. "Glass to the quarantine room must have broken during the battle. Don't touch the fluid. Clay, take a sample of it, and send it to the lab." Clay did as he was instructed.

"Checking the carrier now," the tactical leader commented through his helmet com as he left the lab. "Careful, it's a bit of a leap." The team members glided over, one by one, to the entrance to the cargo hold. They held onto the handles on the side of the ship while their leader typed the entrance code into the yellow lighted keypad.

The door to the airlock opened. The team floated inside and the door closed. They prepared to open the door to the cargo hold.

"Heat signatures, Jan?" he asked Corporal Janerra, who was scanning the ship from the bridge.

"None. Darn thing must be malfunctioning," she said, clearly irritated.

He turned to Dru, "Scan each room as we move forward."

Corporal Janerra had all helmet cams on screen, arranged according to their formation, so she could get a panoramic view of what they were seeing.

"No heat signs yet," reported Dru. The door was opened and they advanced through, weapons ready. It felt chilly inside.

"What the...?" The team leader passed through the door to the cargo hold. "Pink fluid is completely covering the floor. And vines, some one feet in diameter... Abort!" he barked as his widespread arms backed his team out. The door closed just in time, as vines shot out and hit the airlock door, denting it.

The shuttle flew back to base, and the tactical team leader headed to the bridge immediately. General Channing had been called, and was just arriving.

"Jan, scan for organic matter on the ship." She did as the tactical leader directed. They could see the outline of the plant covering every part of the ship. "Holy. Look at the size of that thing. It came from the tiny quarantine fragment though."

General Channing remarked, "From the data we retrieved, the creature has an alarming growth rate when provided with the nutrients it needs. This must be the plant that grew in the governor's lung," he said thoughtfully.

Dr. Elena Harlowe rushed in. She shook hands with General Channing, and took a look at the screen. Her eyes opened wide.

"Elena, I'm about to conduct an experiment," stated the general. "I'd like you to record and document the information."

"Yes, yes," she nodded vigorously. "Anything you need."

"Good. Corporal Janerra, call someone who's good with tech up here," said the general. "There are a few things we need to prepare for the experiment." He called Director Finley to fill him in on the details.

"Rowan! Nice to see you," said General Channing.

"Parker." Director Finley nodded in greeting on screen. "What's up?"

"We've captured one of those giant plant creatures. I'd like to let it spread on Bethel, where there's an anonymous population," said General Channing. "In addition to the experiment, the outbreak would serve as a future deterrent, when we are ready to claim responsibility for it."

"Interesting," said Director Finley, elbows on his desk, fingertips together. "You think this would be a strategic move for us?"

"I think this will serve as an excellent deterrent to disobedience, since it's an example of what we are capable of doing," said Channing. "However, leaked too early it could have the opposite effect. People rising up to oppose us. We have to keep it under wraps for now, until we've taken Aleph, I'm guessing."

"Alright, go ahead. I won't inform anyone on my side," said the director, curious to see both the immediate outbreak and its political effects later.

"We don't know whether the creature will take over several sectars, several hundred sectars, or more. But the more, the better deterrent it will be," said General Channing.

"Sounds good. Keep me posted."

They signed off after agreeing to get together for dinner that evening to watch the "show".

Brady Nash had been asked to put together a remote control system for a carrier. He had been picked up by the Corporate Alliance immediately after the battle and taken to Aurora's military division, once Director Finley verified who he was.

"As soon as it lands, I want all outer doors to open automatically," said General Channing, "but not before then. Not even to test the doors."

"Sure, that's not a problem." It was a good way to synchronize troop movement, so they all advanced at the same time after landing. Brady had no clue why the general was so adamant about no testing though. Some people were so finicky.

After he had finished putting together the remote flight system, Brady made it possible to remotely access cameras on the outer hull.

General Channing and Dr. Harlowe went to a private viewing room with several large screens preset to specific channels. The views projected were from the carrier, the satellites orbiting the planet, and from an organic matter scan.

All cameras were pointed at Planet Bethel.

As the alliance military stationed on Bethel left the planet, the carrier ship descended, and landed in a remote area. Its doors opened automatically.

"I wanted to give this a test run, and Bethel is the perfect planet to experiment on," said General Channing. "I need to get an idea of how fast this spreads, and the amount of area it will eventually occupy."

They could see from the ship's cameras that the creature was starting to spread out its tentacles. They were actively seeking something. Some vines went into the soil, while others kept slithering away from the creature's center, its large traps ready to catch the unwary.

Dr. Harlowe was watching the readouts of the organic matter map and making notations on her tablet. She could see huge amounts in what she thought must be a city full of people. She switched the console from using organic matter to heat signatures. Yes, they both matched. She switched back to watching the organic matter grow.

General Channing had to leave to meet with the director for dinner, and left the project with Dr. Harlowe. He looked thoughtful. Inside, he was very pleased at the fast and thorough progress the creature was making. He and Director Finley would patch into the viewing room from Rowan's private suite.

On Planet Bethel, all hell had broken loose. People were acting out of sheer panic.

Some jumped into zoomcars to race far away from the creature, but that created its own issues. With speeds out of control and too many risks taken due to panic, there were accidents everywhere.

Others just ran as fast as they could away from the creature, which wasn't fast enough. There was pink foam liquifying in spots all over the ground and on floors inside buildings.

Connor and Mia were in City Hall when the vines broke in. Connor didn't hesitate. He grabbed Mia's hand and tugged her along as she glanced backwards, wondering what was happening. After seeing people wrapped up in vines that were six inches in diameter, she ran as fast as her legs could carry her. The vines were advancing everywhere, feeling their way along.

By the time they had run a block, they had seen firsthand the endgame, hungry red jaws and their ability to absorb people. Vines tried to entangle them as they ran, but they stayed a step ahead. They jumped into their zoomcar and flew low with caution, since most panicking drivers were in the higher airspace.

Dr. Harlowe had taken notes late into the night and had fallen asleep. She jerked awake and stared at the screen, trying to make sense of it.

There were no heat signatures left in the city, just organic matter. The creature had completely wiped out all colonists there, or they had fled. She yawned and made notations as she watched the creature continue to grow.

The military on Bethel had mobilized into action. They found fire was somewhat effective, but sent the tentacles into a frenzy, making them attack more viciously. They could hear the creature wail as though it was in pain. Cutting vines or blowing up parts of the creature had the same effect. They kept trying different ways to deal with it.

Connor and Mia travelled south by zoomcar until they found a military camp preparing for the creature's arrival.

News came in that freezing slowed the tentacles down, and made them go dormant. Once they discovered that, they were able to slow its spread. After the news was broadcast globally, there was a huge migration of people from the northwest hemisphere to the coldest parts of the planet.

The military was able to engage in split tasks after the creature slowed down. They transported civilians to camps in the coldest regions. Relief tents that could block the cold and withstand the wind were set up.

Governments from the northwest had relocated to colder regions and were broadcasting from there, urging their people to relocate.

Connor and Mia traveled by military shuttle to one of the refugee camps. They were allotted cots in a large communal tent and provided with warm clothes, blankets and water. They were reassured that it was temporary, until other shelter was built.

"What can we do to help?" Connor asked a soldier.

"You're welcome to help us set up more tents," he replied. Connor and Mia spent hours assisting, then returned to their tent. They were both exhausted and sat together huddled under blankets on the bottom cot.

Connor held Mia in his arms in the dim light. He could see others in the tent, including restless children. Across the tent a baby was crying.

"It's okay, we'll get through this." Connor kissed the top of Mia's head. She snuggled up to him. After a few minutes of cuddling together, they crawled onto their bunks for the night.

General Channing walked into the private viewing room, and Dr. Harlowe startled awake.

"How is it progressing this morning, Dr. Harlowe?" he asked.

"Well, as you can see, it's taken out a segment of the northwestern hemisphere, and most life with it," she said. "However, some of the heat signatures have been migrating. It will be interesting to see where they go. What would you like me to do with the data when I'm done recording and analyzing it?"

"Send all your observations as well as the recordings you're making in both organic and heat modes to my office," said General Channing.

"Will do," replied Dr. Harlowe, and started making notes again on the data.

In the morning, Connor and Mia walked over to the mess hall. They were served hot oats and cava, and sat on the floor to eat their breakfast. Tables and benches would be set up eventually, but the priority was to get everyone transported in, fed, and sheltered. Connor recognized people from the shuttle ride and they exchanged nods.

He could tell some had lost loved ones. They were in shock and having difficulty functioning. One woman was sobbing quietly.

Connor reached over to Mia, put his arm around her, and pulled her close to his side.

Mia looked at him inquisitively. "Just relieved we both made it together safely," he whispered. She kissed him softly on the cheek.

PRISONERS

CHAPTER ELEVEN

*The moon could shift, causing the tides to turn at any moment.
There is no time to dwell on misfortune, or we could miss the
turning of the tides. Our action is what causes the moon to shift.*

Professor Janine Cohen, Galactic Investigations Bureau

Janine Cohen had been working in the mines on Planet Gamuel for three days now. The prisoners were under guard in the mines, and patrols circulated around the dilapidated houses where they slept. Janine was exhausted, but needed to stay strong for her people, keep up their hopes and will.

She shared a house with others caught in the family quarters when the outpost was attacked. Among those was her friend Marian, whom she had been visiting at the time of the assault. Janine had some disappointing news to deliver to the group that sat circling a lantern in the large room. Voices were kept low, since guards were patrolling outside.

"We haven't been able to locate any colonists nearby, so we haven't been able to ask for assistance. They must have been transported far away," Janine whispered to the others in the circle. Shoulders slumped, heads looked down, Janine could see the dejection in the group.

"But although the colonists are a dead end, we need to stay strong, look after each other, and keep thinking of other options.

"

We need to get to know the planet better and where the different settlements are. We will likely find more of our people where the other mining colonies are located."

"I can point out the rough locations of the mining colonies from memory," whispered Nolan.

"So our next step is to make contact with other groups of prisoners?" asked Marian.

"Yes, to assess their situations, and to help each other overturn our captors. Many of our own people are military and have hidden that, and others have specialized skills. We could work together to seize their weapons."

"Any ideas on how we could go about that?" asked Marian.

"We need to keep a count of their military, and stay on top of any changes," suggested Janine.

"I've noticed they've been bringing in more soldiers every day," said Corporal Lucas Kim. "They have far more than they need to look after a small group of prisoners. I think they're planning something big."

"We could send out someone to scout for other mining colonies, a fast runner with stealth, and extreme survival skills. And in the meantime, map out this whole area to show how the military has deployed," suggested Nolan.

"I'd like to volunteer to be the scout," said Lucas. "I'm fast on my feet, stealthy, and used to rough terrain."

"Let's gather what Lucas needs during the day then. A pack, rations, supplies, a silent weapon," said Janine. "He can slip out under cover of night and search for the closest prisoners to us."

"I can map out the local area," volunteered Nolan.

"Good," smiled Janine. She saw that the group was looking more alert and hopeful. "The rest of us need to hang on and spread the word to others about the plan." It would take some time, but they would break free, eventually.

Nolan removed a large rock in the mine, and climbed through a small opening that led to the outside. He then climbed up the rocky incline, until he found the sheltered opening where he could start drawing. The military camp surrounded their housing to the east. He saw no sign of settlements or cities in any direction, through the binoculars he had stolen for Lucas.

Nolan drew the area, scale and directions, and the estimated number of troops. He added the locations of the closest mining colonies and cities from memory. When he was done, he climbed back down, slipped back through the hole, and got back to work.

That night everyone laid what they had scavenged in the center of the circle. Lucas took the pack and filled it halfway with the rations, compass, knife, cooking pot, string, water bottle, binoculars, torch, and blanket. Nolan laid out the map to show Lucas the patrol positions, and point out prisoner locations. The closest mining colony was 450 sectars away. Nolan gave him the map, then turned down the lantern. After quietly whispering his goodbyes, Lucas put on his warm coat, then snuck out into the night.

The icy hail stung his cheeks as he crouched beside the door, waiting for an opportunity to run to his next position. The weather was on his side, since it lessened visibility. Once the closest patrol had walked by, he dashed into the open for a few seconds before reaching cover at the next house.

Lucas made his way back to the mine, which was unguarded. Inside the mine, guided by the torch, he reached the hole Nolan had told him about. He put his pack through the hole, then crawled out. Once he was out he rushed to a cluster of rocks where he took cover. He had made it out of the area. He was headed south towards a mountain range, the closest colony.

Once he was completely out of visual range, he set a comfortable pace and jogged to the south. He had good endurance, and knew he could keep this pace for a few hours. After dawn broke, he used stealth again.

The nights were hard when the temperature dropped, since his blanket was inadequate. There was limited cover in the tundra terrain he was traversing. Lucas dared not start a fire at night until he was a few days out, so his nights were long and cold. The only shelter he had was from large rocks that would cut the wind from one direction.

When he was finally in the clear, he'd warm up by the fire, take breaks to eat, and lay snares at night. Once in a while, he would find a frozen puddle of water, and boil the ice for use.

When he was close to the mountain range, he stopped lighting fires at night, and kept them low during the day. He would start doing recon soon.

As he came closer, even while elevated and with binoculars, he couldn't see signs of prisoners. He saw a large modern city, with no alliance military presence. This must be one of the mining settlements that had dealings outside the Corporate Alliance.

On the evening Lucas entered the city seeking help, the leadership of the colony called the council to an emergency meeting.

"Although the City of Aeaqualis has been left alone by the Corporate Alliance, we know what their forced presence on our planet means." Lady Cadrius of the Aeaqualis Council was chairing the meeting. "As your Governor Vasilios pointed out to us during his visit, once the corporations have a foothold, they can bring in as many troops as they wish. That doesn't bode well for those of us who enjoy our freedom. How many troops are at your location?"

"A few thousand to guard our small group, and more coming every day," reported Corporal Lucas Kim.

"Ah, that illustrates my point. They aren't just here to guard prisoners," said Lady Cadrius. The others on the council nodded.

"We will send out word to the other governments around the planet to notify them of what is happening, and ask for their assistance with overturning the military while their presence here is small. It won't matter if our message is intercepted, as long as it gets out.

"Corporal Kim, are you ready to travel back to your people with some support to help you fight back?"

Lucas thought of the nine day trek on foot he had just experienced. "Yes, I'm willing to do that."

"Good. You, Phalasat, and a group of warriors can quickly travel back by megaceratops. Although we don't have a lot of metal fighting power, we have some heavy ground troops," said Lady Cadrius, smiling. "General Milen, could you gather your officers and plan your strategy? Then you can leave first thing in the morning."

Lucas felt things were looking up.

Lucas stared up at the megaceratop that he and the other scout were going to ride. It had hoofed feet and strong legs accustomed to running, a muscular body, and two horns on the front of its head. It's eyes were large, and it had a slightly beaked mouth. The colonists put shoes on the bottom of its hooves, and it was used to carrying them over long distances. But the most surprising characteristic about the megaceratop was its size. It was so large, that Lucas had to use a ladder to mount it.

Phalasat and Lucas started ahead of the rest of the unit. Lucas was to sneak in and update his people, and then Phalasat was to report any new info to his unit.

The trip back to the mining settlement took less than half the amount of time. Lucas and Phalasat snuck back in the way Lucas had left, using the hole in the wall of the mine. Then they made their way carefully to the house where Janine was staying.

They snuck inside, and Lucas whispered as the residents woke up, "Janine, I'm back, with help."

Janine and the group made a circle in the middle of the floor with the lantern turned low. "Good to have you back, buddy," whispered Nolan.

"Thanks," replied Lucas. "This is Phalasat. He'll be reporting back to the troops that are on the way."

"Nice to meet you," said Phalasat.

Lucas and Phalasat debriefed them. Janine let them know that another thousand troops had arrived during the two weeks Lucas was gone.

"The unit from Aeaqualis should be here the night after tomorrow," Lucas said.

"Then we will be ready," said Janine. "Let's put a plan together on the inside, to make their job easier."

Nolan helped draft out a strategy, taking into account the guards' night patrols. By this time he had a detailed map of the military camp. They would prepare their people over the next two days and let them know what their roles were.

Phalasat snuck back out to inform the army of the change in troop numbers and of the plan the prisoners were going to execute.

One of the perimeter guards thought he heard a yelp, and looked to the northwest. If it was anything significant, the patrols would be on it. The prisoners hadn't been any trouble. Their military numbers far outweighed the prisoners, plus they had weapons, so there were no concerns. He watched the nearby patrols doing their rounds in the prisoners' camp.

Corporals Sayan and Vinay quietly dragged two unconscious bodies into the mine. Another group stripped them of clothes and weapons, tied and gagged them, and carried them down a tunnel. That totaled twelve patrolmen taken and hidden in houses or the mine. Two of the men quickly put on the discarded clothes, took the weapons, and walked out of the mine as though on patrol.

The hole Nolan discovered had come in handy. After circling to the west and hiding behind the rock, Phalasat had shown the squad the way into the mine. They had spread into the camp, replacing patrolmen by incapacitating them with taserbeams. It was shift change, and the group started again with the new patrolmen.

There was a low rumbling, coming from the south. At first, perimeter guards thought it was a storm moving in. They looked towards the sound, but weren't able to see anything in the darkness. As the rumbling became louder, they called for a spotlight.

With the spotlight, it looked like a wave was drawing near, and they were about to encounter a desert storm. However, they weren't in the desert. They sounded the alarm bell. One guard looked through his binoculars, yelling "Stampede!". The sea of grey wasn't a storm drawing near. The guards from the south started firing their weapons into the herd.

Soldiers were on their feet within seconds, and rushing to the arms locker.

"What the...??? What kind of practical joke is this?" The officer with the keys was furious. The locker had a heavy lock latched to it in addition to the regular lock. "Grab me bolt cutters, a hacksaw or blowtorch, NOW!" she yelled.

"Equipment locker, too!" yelled another soldier. They were scrambling to find a toolbox in one of the tents, when all-out chaos hit.

The nine feet tall megaceratops were charging, their riders turning their taserlances on right before impact. They took out the entire southern flank. Soldiers and tents went flying everywhere.

The soldiers had finally found a saw and were about to open the weapons locker, when another group of soldiers with weapons forced them back.

"What are you doing?" yelled one of the soldiers.

Lucas, Nolan, and the other "soldiers" blocking the locker didn't answer. One soldier pulled out a service weapon and aimed it at Nolan. He was taken down by a taserlance.

Lucas grabbed the hacksaw, and ran towards the prisoners' camp as the rest of the soldiers by the locker were taken down with taserlances.

As soon as the megaceratops had attacked, prisoners had fled into the mine. Those who could fight took tools from the mines, pickaxes, hammers, and sharp spikes. The plan was to guard the mine until the children and civilians had been completely evacuated. The alliance soldiers would assume the prisoners were hiding from the attacking cavalry, and were trapped in the mine. The soldiers would have no idea they were using the hole to escape. Instead of pursuing them, they would focus on defending themselves against their opponents.

The next wave of attackers viciously attacked the soldiers' camp on the east side. Mesarchyds, giant dog-like creatures six feet tall, were snapping at the soldiers with their sharp teeth. Their riders were taking down soldiers everywhere with taserlances. The megaceratops and mesarchyds were pushing the soldiers north.

Nolan saw it was now safe enough to start grabbing weapons for their group. He rushed back to the arms locker with military-trained prisoners. He found the keys on the fallen officer who had been shocked by a taserlance, and unlocked the first lock. Nolan pulled out the key to the larger lock, and they emptied the locker and distributed the weapons quickly.

Next, Nolan unlocked the large transport ship in the military camp, and the pilots readied it. Some of the soldiers were fighting to get back to the camp once they saw it take off, but they were held back by their opponents. The ship landed south of the mine, so the prisoners could file onto it with cover.

More megaceratops, these ones pulling empty carts, strolled into the military camp and were loaded up with weapons and communication equipment. Nolan unlocked the heliplanes for more pilots.

By the time everything was loaded up, the remaining few soldiers had surrendered, and were kneeling on the ground with their hands behind their heads. They were surrounded by the Aeaqualis. They had been hit hard and fast. As the sun rose, they could see that the ground was littered with soldiers, some stunned, some dead.

The victors from the GIB travelled to the City of Aeaqualis. The transport and heliplanes would return to bring back the

Aeaqualis soldiers and equipment. Nolan and Lucas hoped the alliance soldiers would be too focused on looking after their people and finding rations to make the nine day journey after them.

After General Milen had made his report to the council, Lady Cadrius met with Janine Cohen, who had been appointed as the GIB representative.

"During the last week, the governments around the planet decided to take action. Now is the time to remove the Corporate Alliance's military, before its presence gets too much for us to handle. Reports have come in that three other groups of prisoners have been saved through joint efforts."

"Are there any other groups of prisoners that need rescue?" asked Janine.

"Yes, it's been reported that three other mines also have prisoners, but rescue missions are on their way," reported Lady Cadrius.

"That's good to hear," said Janine, relieved.

"Let your people settle in the city. It may be some time before you are reunited with your families. We've made arrangements for your care while you are here."

"Thank you, Lady Cadrius. It is much appreciated," said Janine, grateful that her people were safe and would be looked after until rescue came. However, she was worried about her family, her husband, and Jack and Taylor.

Director Finley had just learned they'd lost contact with their troops on Gamuel. The planet's governments had issued a warning to the Corporate Alliance, that any alliance ship attempting to enter their airspace would be shot down. Although

this made Director Finley grit his teeth, he decided to leave it alone. With the mining of the alloy, and the ships transporting prisoners to Alniyat, their military was spread too thin.

Instead they would reinforce their troops on Aleph, and consider Gamuel lost. For now.

He wondered if he and General Channing had been too ambitious, going for three colonist planets at once. Finley wanted Aleph for the new Corporate Alliance headquarters, close to their long-term mining operation on Planet Z.

Bethel provided a buffer for them and was supposed to be a deterrent to future resistance. Well, it would be when they publicly claimed responsibility for the destruction there. But right now the last thing they needed was a united uprising. Until they were ready, they had spread rumors of natural disasters and epidemics on Bethel. They'd also spread rumors of a quarantine of the planet, so no one would look too closely. Perhaps going for Gamuel had been overreaching.

Soon, they would have enough troops on Aleph to dominate the cities and declare them as their own, pushing some of the colonists out. They had been gradually bringing in troops to "their" land, so as not to cause any alarm. After taking over the first city, they would bring in their main force. It was just a matter of deciding which city to take. Finley had narrowed it down to two.

He put a call through to General Channing. "Parker, when will we be ready to take over the first city on Aleph?" he asked.

"We currently have over 50,000 troops scattered around the planet and another 18,000 arriving today. We can converge on any major city when you're ready to claim it for headquarters and go from there. Just let us know the coordinates. I'm giving orders to take the areas with minimal damage.

Director Finning looked at his split screen, showing rotating images of the cities on the left, and maps on the right.

"I'm liking Belhandelar. The way their city radiates out from a central tower in the shape of a tall prism, appeals to me. The water outside the inner circle of buildings, flowing downriver, gives an extra means of transportation, and outside the second circle of buildings there is room to keep our military fleet. The inner circle would be for the Corporate Alliance, and the second circle could be for military housing and operations. The outer circle would be used for the colonists and their trade."

"Alright, Belhandelar it is then. We'll commence our attack shortly," replied General Channing.

Director Finley smiled as he leaned back in his chair, pressing his fingertips together.

CALDERRA

CHAPTER TWELVE

To hope is to hang onto the light, even during the darkest of days.

Lady Cia of Elanissia

The Galactic Investigations Bureau ships had been gathering for days behind the moon, Calderra. For some, the one week trip from the Antares system had taken longer than others, as they tried to evade capture. The plan was to keep the ships out of sight at all times, between the planet and moon, while setting up base on the moon itself.

Calderra was chosen because it was inhabitable, and because the planets in the Paikahale system held no interest for the corporations. This meant there was no reason for the alliance to travel to the solar system. It was also good positioning, far enough from the Corporate Alliance's main fleet, yet close enough to respond eventually. The GIB could communicate with Isidore in the Shaula system without interception by the alliance.

Officers Slate Beckett and Marshall Jennings were on the other side of the moon, scouting for the most suitable area for a hidden base. A group of soldiers had been sent with them to ensure their safety.

Several potential sites had been suggested, based on maps in the database. However, they had discovered a hidden network of lava tubes during their detailed scans of the planet.

The tubes were leftover from a low volcanic range that was active several hundred years before. It now contained many large caverns, all connected. It looked ideal for their purposes. There was a large lake on the top of the range from a collapsed volcano, a couple of smaller lakes nearby, and an expansive sea not far to the west.

Officer Slate Beckett was exploring one of the tubes, when he found something interesting. "Marshall! Come here!" On a lower level of the tube system, Slate had found some tubes with water flowing freely through them.

Marshall, placed a device in the water. He then pulled it out and checked the reading. "We're in luck!" Marshall couldn't wait to share info on this mountain range with the rest of the temporary council.

Three days later, General McKenna and Colonel Campbell's ships arrived at the rendezvous point. The excess people were being distributed among the other ships.

During the previous month, Reagan had gained a lot of admirers, after the holographic footage of his journey to Azram was publicized. Since the Corporate Alliance already had the information, there was no reason to keep it classified. Reagan had attracted a lot of young followers in particular, who liked to follow him around the ship. Lady Cia found this to be amusing.

Pilot Taylor Cohen had been picked up in the search for survivors, and although her oxygen had been depleted, she recovered well. However, she had been more concerned about her mother, since she wasn't on any of the military ships. For that reason, she was both anxious and relieved when they reached Calderra.

After searching through the list of those at the rendezvous point, there was no sign of her mother. She went in person to thoroughly check and still no sign.

"I'm telling you, Jack, she's not here," she insisted to her brother. They had both been sure their mother would have found her way to Calderra.

"She's got to be alive," he stated. "Either stranded or maybe taken prisoner by the alliance. Don't worry, we'll find her," said Jack. "Dad will send out a recon mission then a rescue, once we find her." His sister nodded. She suddenly seemed so small.

Jack took her in his arms and rocked her, "We'll find her, I know we will." He thought it best they both take their minds off it for now. "Now let's go see this new base."

Jack and Taylor took a large cargo shuttle to transport equipment from a carrier to the surface. Colonel Campbell's team had salvaged many of the outpost compartments, and they were reconstructing sections of the outpost on the ground. The interlocking sections would be rebuilt beside the mountains along with a new launch pad and docking bay. Some solitary sections would be dismantled and reassembled within the caverns, or their parts used for construction.

Teams had been working tirelessly to make the caves liveable. When Taylor and Jack arrived they found a clean tunnel system with power, water, and sanitation. Some sleeping quarters had been constructed.

There had been drilling into the sides of the tunnels and caverns to widen them or create new caverns. There were also indentations for extra sleeping areas, and built in desks for working areas. Everything had been done carefully, under the supervision of a structural engineer.

Some of the larger caverns were being set up as eating quarters. The plan was to start moving in those not involved in ship-based operations, as soon as possible.

On their next run, while the equipment was being unloaded, Jack and Taylor explored the area around the main entrance. Jack's jaw dropped open when he saw a man coming towards them, riding a giant cat. It looked just like a tigras from Isidore, but much larger. The man slipped off its back and patted it through its thick fur.

At that moment, Taylor turned around, saw the tigras and jumped backwards with a yelp. "What...what...how?" she stammered.

"It's okay, she's quite friendly," said the the good-looking young man with bright blue eyes and brown hair. Taylor was absentmindedly smoothing her own hair, suddenly feeling shy. "Hi, I'm Jesse, one of the biologists. I've been taking teams to explore the local plantlife and wildlife."

"Nice to meet you, Jesse," replied Jack assertively, holding out his hand, which Jesse grasped firmly. Jesse shook Taylor's hand, and it felt like an electrical shock was running through her body. She blushed.

"Would you like a quick tour of what we've discovered?" asked Jesse.

"We would love that," replied Jack, enthusiastically. He noticed that his sister was uncharacteristically quiet and wondered what was up.

Jesse, with the tigras walking on one side of him, took them south. They saw samples of plant life, laid out on a large flat rock and labelled.

"Some of these species of plants will be great as a food source, others not so much," Jesse commentated. "Currently, one of the

biggest chores is to figure out a long-term, sustainable plan for our new 'colony'. Running across Paega here was a great find. Don't worry you're not food," he said, affectionately. The tigras rubbed Jesse's hand with her head upon hearing her name.

They walked east around the range. "Over here, we have some fun little critters," said Jesse. "These little guys aren't being sourced for food, either. They are quick and intelligent, and have a mischievous streak." What looked like tiny monkeys were swinging back and forth above them, in the trees. Taylor looked closely, and saw that one had a pouch with a baby monkey in it.

One of the monkeys reached down to touch Taylor's curly hair, and got its hand tangled in it. It was trying frantically to get its hand out, but the more it pulled, the more it became entangled.

"Owwww!" yelled Taylor. Jesse quickly came to the rescue and untangled the little guy, who then scampered off. It peeked back at them from behind a leaf. Taylor ran her fingers through her hair to try to untangle it. Jack tried to help, but Taylor was flustered and gently slapped his hand away.

"Here, this is more suitable for your hair than that little guy," Jesse picked up a beautiful crimson flower with mauve highlights and placed it in her hair. "Much better."

This time Jack saw his sister blush. He became amused.

"Over here, we have a few animals that we're looking at as possible livestock." Jesse directed them to the northeastern route and to a cleared and fenced area. There was a cow, some walking birds, and a few woolly animals that Taylor didn't know the name of. Behind the fenced area, there was an entrance to a cavern.

"We have a makeshift door in behind the cavern, to keep the animals from wandering into the tunnels, but shelter is an absolute necessity. There are some vicious night storms. They aren't common, but when they come, they destroy everything in their path."

Jesse took them east, away from the edge of the mountains, and pointed out an area in the distance where they may eventually plant crops. However, it was a difficult dilemma since some storms could destroy an entire crop in a flash. Most of the trees had a certain amount of flexibility, enough to bend and survive the storms, but they would still take damage.

"...so we're still trying to decide what to do about crops. Building clear enclosures for the plants may be our best option, but we need the materials to do so." Taylor looked up at Jesse with big eyes and nodded. "However, we may need to experience a storm first to know what we're up against."

"I need to check on the shuttle and see if it's ready to take up for another load," remarked Jack. Then he said quickly, "But Taylor, maybe you could stay here and assist the doctor. Taylor always had a knack for biology back on Isidore."

"Oh, but I couldn't..." Taylor started, giving Jack a look when she saw how amused he was.

Jesse encouraged Taylor to stay. "You're welcome to stay here for the afternoon. In fact, I could use an assistant to help me catalogue some of the plants we've discovered."

Jack waved, as he walked off. "Catch you later, Taylor. Nice meeting you, Jesse," he smiled.

Jesse seemed like an interesting guy, someone who might be good for Taylor to spend time with. Jack chuckled to himself as he thought of his sister blushing. At least he would keep her on her toes.

Lady Cia had been formally accepted by the GIB Council as the Ambassador to the Elanisse. They'd sent out a distress call to both Isidore and Elanissia two weeks before. The two planets were now aware of what had transpired in Quadrant 3. They were sending reinforcements to Calderra, but wouldn't arrive for another two weeks.

"Our sources say that the prisoners on Aleph, Bethel, and Gamuel are being forced to work the mines under threat of execution," said Officer Marshall Jennings. "Similar things are likely happening in the Alniyat solar system, but they are too far away right now for us to intervene. We anticipate we have people imprisoned in both systems."

"This is exactly the type of thing the GIB was placed here to prevent," said Secretary Cohen bitterly. He held onto the hope his wife was still alive, but dreaded the thought of her working as a slave for the Corporate Alliance. Knowing they would be able to mount a successful rescue attempt in a few weeks was not a comfort to him.

"We need to get word out to the GIB outpost in Quadrant 4, since they are closer to Alniyat. They would be of great assistance there," said Reagan. "However, transmissions sent in that direction are all intercepted."

"You're forgetting the reports about the alliance shipyard, Governor Vasilios. Their ships are being repaired and new ones built, and they now have the alloy to evade sensors. For all we know, they could have taken out the other outpost by now," said the Secretary.

"Actually, we would have heard of a large fleet of alliance ships crossing towards Dschubba in Quadrant 4 by now if that was their immediate intention. No, it seems they are working to rebuild their fleet and reinforce themselves," said Magistrate Kian Anderson.

"You're right. I apologize, I let emotion overrule my logic," said Secretary Cohen.

"Understandable under the circumstances, Jay," General McKenna put a hand on the Secretary's shoulder, "but let's try to keep logic and facts before anything else. We will mount a rescue mission, but we want to be thoroughly prepared with reinforcements from the Shaula system first," Reagan and Lady Cia nodded at the mention of their home solar system.

"Let's move on," said Deputy Governor Shaw. "Officers Beckett and Jennings, tell us about the new base on Calderra."

Officer Slate Beckett took the floor, "We found the ideal place for a base. A lengthy underground tube system in a mountain range with large caverns. There are water sources both inside and outside the tube system, and a mountain range for cover of our ships. There are multiple ways out of the tunnels, so we wouldn't be trapped underground if we were attacked. A gravitational turbine energy recycling system can be set up, using the lake above, for long-term power."

He continued, "The local plant life is consistent with our nutritional needs, and there is potential livestock to produce eggs, milk, and wool. The main issue to contend with is the occurrence of super-storms which can suddenly appear with minimal warning. Thankfully, we haven't had to face one of those yet. However, that will make growing large amounts of crops difficult, since they might need to be kept under cover. It's a matter of being able to produce the material needed. Once that's established, then food sourced from crops would be abundant."

Since they were all eager to take a look at the new base and surrounding area, the meeting closed quickly without further discussion.

The council took a shuttle to the surface, where they went their separate ways.

Reagan held Cia's hand as they slowly explored the grassy fields on the southwest side of the mountain range that led to the sea. Reagan thought Cia was breathtaking in her white dress with opal sheen. Her hair was up, although some dark blonde ringlets had escaped. She wore a matching hat with dark pink ribbon.

Cia slipped on the uneven ground, and Reagan caught her. He took her left hand with his left, so he could put his right arm around her shoulders and stabilize her as they walked. Reagan could feel her relax.

After a few minutes, they stopped walking, to take in the view. Mountains on one side and the sea on the other. Cia smiled up at Reagan and he tried to kiss her, but her hat kept getting in the way. She giggled.

Cia flipped her hat backwards over her head so it hung, draped over her back, held on by another ribbon. Reagan gently put his finger under her chin and tilted her head up for a kiss. Her long eyelashes framed her beautiful eyes. He bent down to touch Cia's lips with his as their eyes closed.

Cia was swept away in the moment, and her hands moved to Reagan's shoulders as her arms draped down his back. They held each other closely as their kiss became deeper and more passionate.

After a few minutes, Cia came up for air. She rubbed her cheek against Reagan's in affection.

They walked towards the shore, where they discovered a thick strip of sand. They both took off their shoes and walked along the beach, hand in hand. Cia was enjoying the feeling of sand between her toes.

"It's so beautiful here," she remarked, as she breathed in the cool air.

"It is," smiled Reagan. "This is the perfect place for our people to settle, with housing protected from the storms, and sources of water and food. It solves the problem of not having enough room to house everyone comfortably on the ships."

"Now that we've made it to this sector, we could discuss Reimus 5 again with the council," Cia said, glancing at Reagan as she walked beside him.

Reagan looked towards her worriedly. "You know I don't like the idea of you going on the mission."

Cia spoke with resolve, "I'm the only one who knows where the records are and what to look for."

"I know," said Reagan, "but I'm still worried for your safety."

"I'll stay close to you, so you can keep an eye on me. Like you are now." Cia wore an impish grin.

"I'm serious, Cia," he responded.

"It will be fine," she insisted. "As long as we have a good plan, things will go smoothly. Besides, I'll be with the legendary hero who survived Azram," she teased him.

"You're not going to let me talk you out of this, are you?" he asked, with a side glance at her.

"Of course not. You know me by now," she said.

Reagan sighed. They continued walking along the beach in silence. Then Reagan took Cia into his arms.

"I don't want to lose you," he said, kissing the top of her head.

Jesse and Taylor had been working tirelessly, cataloguing plants and animals on Calderra. Jesse was grateful for Taylor's assistance. Each biologist had a different area to cover. Taylor saw on the virtual holographic map that Jesse's area was a rectangular strip that stretched to the east. The location of each species was marked on the map, and she could zoom in to see what it looked like. Paega was found at the east end.

The sun was warming, yet there was a cool breeze at the same time. As they moved further east, methodically, they discovered more unique food sources. Paega was munching on some plants, which the analysis found to be protein-rich. These details were entered on the computer pad with their new alpha-numeric identity. They were automatically added to the virtual holographic map.

"Okay, let's end here for the day. Would you like to join us for dinner?" he asked Taylor.

Sure," she said, with a smile. She had thoroughly enjoyed the afternoon working alongside Jesse. It was fascinating work, discovering new species. She didn't mind the cataloguing part. The virtual map made things easy, and she was a fast typist.

They climbed up on Paega, who was excited to have them on her back. So excited that she took off in a run before Taylor had a chance to ask Jesse how to hold on. She grabbed onto Jesse's waist before she lost her balance.

The experience was exhilarating, as much as flying a fighter ship. But having the air whip by felt amazing. It was as if she herself was flying. Taylor's long, curly hair streamed behind her as they were taken back to base, riding this beautiful animal. She laughed, just enjoying the ride.

When the got back to base, the food station had been set up outside. Local plants had been used to supplement their freeze-dried rations, which was a nice change.

"Would you like to assist again tomorrow?" asked Jesse as they ate together. "Having you with me made the cataloguing easy and even fun," he smiled.

Taylor really wanted to, but instead she said reluctantly, "It depends if my brother needs a co-pilot for the cargo shuttle tomorrow. I'd love to stay and help though. I'll ask him after dinner."

She reached Jack after they had done eating, and he said he'd already found someone. There were so many idle pilots that all the positions had been filled.

"Just enjoy yourself, Taylor," he said in an amused tone.

"You do know I *am* working, right?" Taylor sounded defensive.

"Of course I do. I meant that there are so many interesting *things* to explore down there," he laughed.

She gritted her teeth as she turned off her com. She hated being teased by her big brother.

Taylor walked over to Jesse and let him know she was available to assist him as long as needed. His face brightened to match his eyes, and he took her by the hand to get set up for the night.

Taylor was led through the twisting tunnels to a cavern that had sleeping quarters. Metal bunk beds were neatly in rows, and there were light grey lockers bordering the room.

Jesse had her assigned to the top bunk across from his and showed her which locker was hers. She placed her things in her locker, then walked with him down another tunnel. They arrived at a room with tables.

"This is one of the mess halls," he explained. "But we eat outside when the weather's nice." Taylor saw that there was a stack of games on a table, and a group was enjoying a game of dice. "Would you like to play something?" he asked.

A sly smile appeared on her lips. "I think I should warn you that I'm very competitive."

"Oh really?" He smiled back at Taylor. "I can be pretty competitive myself."

They picked a card game and started to play. Partway through, a man Jesse's age came up to them. "Hey Jesse. How's Thrace doing?"

Jesse's face turned grave. "He's doing fine, but he lost his leg."

"Who's Thrace?" asked Taylor.

"Jesse's lab assistant," answered the other man. "Hi, I'm Kyler, and you are?" he held out his hand to shake hers.

"I'm Taylor. Was your assistant hurt during the battle?" she asked Jesse.

"No, we were working with a life form in the lab. We knew it had intelligence, but didn't anticipate it would break free." Jesse told Taylor the story of what happened in the lab that day.

"That must have been terrible," said Taylor with compassion.

"My adrenaline was pumping. All I could think of was getting that thing off him and back into the quarantine room. Then I pushed the freeze button. After that we were in the med bay. Thrace has recovered well," Jesse brightened a bit. "He's walking on his new leg now and it's responding well. It was just a really bad situation."

"Understandably," said Taylor.

"Mind dealing me in?" asked Kyler.

The three of them played for some time, laughing and joking around. Taylor had the most wins, and Jesse challenged her to another game the following night to regain his honor.

They headed down the corridor, and quietly crawled into their bunks. Taylor lay there silently for a few minutes. Then she turned over to face Jesse.

"Jesse?" she whispered. He opened his eyes.

"Yeah?"

"Thanks for a great day. I needed that," she said.

"No problem," he said.

They both lay in their bunks, looking across at each other. Neither of them could sleep. After a few minutes, Jesse pointed to her, then himself, and then made it look like his fingers were walking. Taylor nodded her head.

The two of them slipped out of their bunks, and headed outside. They nodded to those on security detail and walked along the side of the mountain until they reached the flat rock where Jesse's samples lay hours earlier. They sat down together, and looked up at the stars.

Antares was hidden from them, due to their position. In the opposite direction, they could see Weixiuer and Xamidimura.

"Such a contrast to them, Weixiuer's orange and Xamidimura's blue," said Taylor, gazing upwards.

"True, but at the same time, they compliment each other," remarked Jesse.

Taylor looked at Jesse then leaned sideways into him. He put his arm around her and pulled her close.

"You can even see Shaula from here," Jesse said, pointing to another star.

"Reinforcements should be here from Shaula in a couple weeks. Then we can jump back into our rescue efforts," Taylor said. "My mom is still out there somewhere."

Jesse gave Taylor's shoulders a squeeze. "I'm sure you'll find her."

"Thank you," she whispered.

ETHICS

CHAPTER THIRTEEN

A hero is someone who has great courage in the face of adversity.

Delaney Walker, Alpha Team Leader

Delaney had decided to leave the Aurora Corporation. Now that Rhys was healing well, he wanted to get off the military base. He felt they had their priorities upside down. How could they believe a vicious animal was worth more than a man's life?

He said goodbye to Rhys, and made his way to the docking bay. He wasn't sure where he was off to, but thought maybe Kitsuana would be a good choice for now. The Kitsuine were hospitable to strangers, and he needed some hospitality right now. He decided to make the journey there.

Delaney paid for passage on a military cargo ship that was traveling to Gamuel. He would then hire a military shuttle to take him to Kitsuana.

Delaney slept during the journey, then was startled awake when they landed. Although it was dark, there were reflections of flashing light inside the ship. He looked outside and saw a fleet of the planet's military ships firing, trying to corner the Corporate Alliance's troops. Suddenly, he realized he was a target, and scrambled to get out of the ship as fast as he could.

"

Delaney ran from the ship and hit the ground hard when it exploded. He lay there, stunned. After an unknown amount of time had floated by, he was found by the planet's military.

"This one isn't in army fatigues," he heard them say. "Looks like a civilian."

Then someone was leaning over him, talking to him, but he wasn't able to respond. The next thing he remembered was waking up in a white room in some type of medical facility.

"Where am I?" Delaney asked a nurse.

"You're in Laetus, the capital of Corusco," she replied. "How are you feeling?"

Delaney's head was hurting. "My head feels like there's a knife stuck in it."

"Well, you took quite a blow to your head. I heard that a ship exploded, and you were thrown to the ground. You'll have quite a story to tell your friends back home," the nurse said, smiling.

She offered him some water and something for the pain.

"We have some information to fill out on your chart. We never did get your name," she said, taking the clipboard from the base of his hospital bed. Together they filled out the form with Delaney's information.

"Would you like to borrow a tablet?" the nurse asked. "You can contact your family and friends to let them know how you're doing."

"Sure, I'd like that," said Delaney.

After Delaney sent his messages, he checked the news. The battlefield he had inadvertently ended up at was a camp for prisoners from the GIB outpost, who had been forced to work the mines. *That's crazy,* thought Delaney. He scrolled down and there was a breaking story. The Aeaqualis had made public a copy of the report they'd received from Governor Reagan Vasilios before he went missing.

Delaney watched as the deception was revealed. The Corporate Alliance hadn't followed through with their contracts, and was seizing land and declaring it legal. They had been building up their military on the land they had seized. But each of the military base camps had now been destroyed, and the planet's governments wouldn't be allowing any more troops from the alliance on Gamuel.

Again he felt admiration for the governor, just like he did after viewing the video of his excursion. Governor Vasilios wouldn't back down from telling the truth. Delaney had now seen his courage displayed twice. He wondered if the Aeaqualis had access to his whereabouts, if he was still alive.

The more he thought about it, the more he felt compelled to meet the governor, or at least learn more about who he had been.

Scrolling further, he saw that the holographic recording of the governor's excursion on Planet Z had been intercepted during an alliance transmission, and made public. From the comments, he could see that Reagan had a huge following, and had become a hero to many of the colonists. He had gained the respect of the entire planet, for the same reasons why Delaney respected him.

He also noticed there was an article on a mysterious epidemic that had been sweeping Bethel. He hoped he wouldn't be exposed to anything like it during his stay on Gamuel.

A couple of days later, when Delaney was feeling better and he was steady on his feet, he was ready to travel to the City of Aeaqualis to find out if they knew how to contact Reagan.

He was taken by a shuttle to Aeaqualis, where he asked to meet with someone on the council. He posed his question, and was referred to Janine, wife of the Secretary of Bureau

Investigations. That night he had dinner with Janine and several others.

"So you mentioned that you're interested in contacting the governor," said Janine.

"Yes, I saw a video of him on the Z-Class Planet, and I also saw what he was trying to reveal with his report. I admire his courage very much. I've been with a company with poor ethical standards that has been cheating and stealing from people for years. I didn't realize what I was involved in until now, but felt something was 'off' when I saw their priorities were upside down."

Janine nodded.

"I left the Aurora Corporation, and after learning about the governor's report on the mismanaged contracts, I see I made the right decision," stated Delaney.

Janine felt Delaney was being truthful, and not just sharing a rehearsed story to get access to the governor for malicious reasons.

"We do expect them to attempt a 'rescue mission' at some point," said Janine. "Until then, we're unaware of his location. But he was alive at the time the outpost fragmented."

Delaney nodded, thoughtfully. "I think I'll stay in Aeaqualis, if you don't mind. I'd like to get to know this governor when he appears, and I do have some important info to pass on to your government and military." Delaney was thinking of the dromasaur and the plans to weaponize dragons and the plant-like creature. The results could be disastrous if General Channing's designs worked out.

"That would be our pleasure," said Janine, smiling. "We have a great group of people, really nice to get to know, and our ethics align with the governor's."

Director Finley had been working on gaining new allies, and had some hopeful contacts. Right now he was focusing on the Vodyanyov. He felt that with the right persuasion, they could enter into a beneficial relationship. They weren't always the most pleasant of creatures to deal with up close, due to their frog-like forms and questionable hygiene. However, the Corporate Alliance needed more troops and finances in order to expand their holdings.

A call was coming through from General Channing. "Rowan, the city has been taken, with no resistance. We've cleared the inner circle of civilians. You can start sending your people down to settle in."

"Ah, thank you, Parker. Good to hear. I'll start sending crews down immediately to prepare things for us," said Director Finley, smiling. "Feel free to take other key areas as military bases."

He gave the order for crews to head to the surface to set up communications and other important systems. He then called the other key players in the alliance to let them know what was happening. They were also very pleased to hear what had transpired. They would send their people down immediately to get settled into their new homes and offices.

All over Aleph, major cities were being taken over by the alliance military. Anyone who resisted was shot, and this was shown over their satellite network as a deterrent to any resistance. Colonists were to continue with "business as usual", but now the Corporate Alliance would be charging a tax, amounting to 50% of their profits.

Although they thought they were making good progress, the mediators were disappointed when the Vodyanyov withdrew from mediation with the Kitsuine. They then became a closed door, unreachable.

Something must have happened, thought Kristina, as she disappointedly packed up her files. The Kitsuine had invited their team to stay as long as was needed, since they had been left behind by the GIB ship.

"We are very sorry that negotiations seemed to have failed." Kristina was addressing the Kitsuine who had come to the meeting. The three seats for the Vodyanyov sat empty across from them.

"It is disappointing that the Vodyanyov do not want to continue," said Lady Liska, the leader of the Kitsuine. She had beautiful large green eyes and lashes that complimented her silky golden fur.

"They've shut themselves off from every type of communication, and we're unable to reach them," said Kristina. "Something must have happened."

"Do you think it's related to the takeover of Aleph?" asked Liska.

"Possibly," remarked Kristina. "The timing may be more than a coincidence."

There was a knock at the door. "Come," said Liska.

A courier stood in the doorframe. "News, my Lady," he announced. He passed a drive to Lady Liska, and she plugged it in. It was a holographic news report from Gamuel. It contained the details of how the Corporate Alliance illegally commandeered land, their dirty work on the Colonists' Planets, and Aleph's takeover. Gamuel expected an invasion any day soon.

"We must assist them," stated Lady Liska. "The Corporate Alliance is growing too powerful and lawless. I don't like the idea of them amassing forces on the planet next to ours, if Gamuel should fall."

"I agree," said her Second-in-Command, Vulpes. "It would be too risky having them so close, and they clearly have no qualms against invading. It's been a slippery slope for them, according to the way they approached these contracts, and now they've stepped over the line. Twice."

"The GIB would definitely assist if they were here. However, we are no longer aware of their presence in this sector," said Kristina. "They may have fled, and if they have, they will reinforce then return."

"We must operate on the assumption that the Galactic Investigations Bureau is no longer able to assist," said Liska, sadly. She didn't mention the possibility they all had on their minds, that the GIB was no more. They all knew the carrier had been recalled due to a threat to the outpost, and the outpost hadn't been seen for some time.

"Let's meet with the leaders of Gamuel and see what we can do. Their main challenge is with fighting an air battle. Their ground troops are excellent," assessed Vulpes. "Having GIB mediators at the meeting would help greatly. That way they know no treachery is afoot."

"Would you be willing to assist with this?" Lady Liska asked the mediators.

The three mediators nodded.

"We would be happy to assist," said Kristina.

The Kitsuine and GIB mediators had requested a meeting with the government leaders of Gamuel. The meeting was to take place on Gamuel, in the Capital City Laetus of the Province of Corusco.

Janine Cohen had been invited to the meeting as one of Lady Cadrius' guests, and her eyes widened as she saw the mediators from the GIB. Perhaps they would have news of her family!

"We welcome you to our planet, Lady Liska, and other guests," announced Lord Ehzen who was chairing the meeting. "Lady Liska and the Galactic Investigations Bureau mediators have called this meeting. We shall let them proceed."

Lady Liska smoothed her light pink skirt as she stood.

"The Kitsuine received a copy of one of your broadcasts, regarding the Corporate Alliance's illegal moves against the colonists on all three planets. We also acknowledge that there is a high risk of invasion of your planet, since they've taken over one of the colonists' planets already.

"It is important to the Kitsuine that Gamuel remains autonomous. The first reason is its proximity to Kitsuana, and the second is because the Corporate Alliance is growing more powerful and will attract allies. If we don't intervene now, there may not be another opportunity.

"We would like to know if you require assistance, particularly air support." Lady Liska bowed slightly before she sat down.

Lady Maddy of Terelina was recognized by the chair.

"We are very pleased with this offer and feel very honored, Lady Liska. Do you have any terms?" she asked.

Lady Liska was recognized.

"We would ask the same in return. This morning, the Vodyanyov pulled out of discussions suddenly, and are unreachable. For what reason, we do not know. Although they haven't threatened or made any aggressive posturing towards us, there is concern that may change. Aleph and Bethel next to you, Vodyanyov beside us, and the two of our planets in the center."

She gestured the positioning with her dainty paws. "I suggest that we ally in case one of us is invaded."

There were nods around the table.

The chair recognized Lady Kiara from Corusco.

"From what we understand, Bethel has undergone a series of natural disasters or some kind of epidemic. We're not clear on the details as of yet, but whole cities have been emptied over the last two weeks." There were a couple of surprised looks in the room.

The chair recognized Lady Cadrius of the Aeaqualis.

"What type of assistance were you thinking of, Lady Liska?" she asked.

"We have good air support, but not a lot of ground support if they are able to deploy soldiers. We could use some help there, since the Vodyanyov have very strong ground troops," said Lady Liska.

There were more nods around the table.

"If we help each other, we can better balance our forces to face whichever strategy our enemies attempt. They know our weaknesses. I suggest we fix those weaknesses with each other's assistance," Lady Liska said.

The chair recognized Lord Brendan from Obsanitale.

"From what I understand, we have been strengthening our air force since the last attempt at an invasion," he said.

The chair recognized Lady Kiara from Corusco.

"We are working on strengthening it, but it will take us at least another month until there is a significant boost in our air support. Our mechanics are working around the clock," she said.

The chair recognized Lady Liska of the Kitsuine.

"There was already an attempt at invasion?" she asked, surprised. "How did you defend yourselves successfully?" she asked.

The chair recognized Lady Cadrius of the Aeaqualis.

"Thanks to a warning from the prisoners taken from the Galactic Investigations Bureau after the outpost fragmented, we were able to devise a plan early enough to respond." Kristina startled at the news Lady Cadrius had just shared about the outpost fragmenting.

"The Corporate Alliance was amassing troops at its location, and we received that information before they had a chance to grow big enough to strike. Instead, we struck first. Then we sent out a communicae to all the government leaders on Gamuel. We informed them of the threat the Corporate Alliance posed, and provided them with the report that exposed the alliance's cover-up, received from Governor Vasilios, before he went missing.

"As an aside, we've also heard from Janine Cohen, wife of the Secretary of Bureau Investigations of the GIB, that the governor *did* make it back to the outpost alive before it fragmented," said Lady Cadrius.

The chair recognized Lady Liska.

"Then I would also propose a motion that we share any early intelligence gathered. It was crucial to avoid invasion on your planet. We could work together on that," said Lady Liska.

"I second the motion," said Lady Cadrius.

"Motion passed," recorded the chair. "Lady Liska and Lady Cadrius will form a committee to share intel. The representatives will report back to their governments. I'd also suggest someone from the GIB be on the committee."

"I propose a motion that we share military resources with each other to fill in the gaps," said Lady Kiara of Corusco.

"I second that motion," said Vulpes of the Kitsuine.

The meeting drew to an end, and both Janine and Nolan were asked to serve on the intel committee.

When Delaney heard an intel committee had been formed and that Janine was on it, he shared the info he had found out while in the biotech lab at the Aurora's military base. The general was planning on weaponizing the creatures found on Planet Z. Janine passed on this information right away. Because of their proximity to the planet, it was a concern. They would need to come up with countermeasures.

Nolan drew maps from memory, of Aleph and Bethel, realizing that the people would have shifted by now. This would be due to military enforcement on Aleph, and due to the epidemic that had occurred on Bethel. But he still marked the settlements and major cities for them, and any land-markers he could think of.

Vulpes helped with the calculation of ground troops needed on Kitsuana, and Lord Ehzen delivered the calculations for the colonists. Those numbers were passed to the militaries of both planets, to help them prepare.

There were also rumors shared that the Vitaari may be supporting the Corporate Alliance, and that some of the prisoners may have been taken to the Alniyat system, so those items would need to be investigated.

Kristina met with Janine later on. They both needed a hot cup of cava. Although Kristina had no news of Janine's family, she had questions about the fragmenting of the outpost. Finding out that large pieces of the outpost in the form of ships had escaped was a relief. Kristina knew the GIB would regroup and call for reinforcements from Shaula if possible.

Lord Bartholomew Sullivan was aware the alliance had moved to Aleph. He was still hiding the directors of the five corporations who were wanted by the Corporate Alliance. The alliance had the attitude: "If you aren't with us, then you're against us." That was their reasoning for targeting the five of them.

However, Bartholomew, as a trader between quadrants, was able to get away with not publicly picking a side. That meant he could travel where he wanted to and without concern. No one interfered with him. Right now, he was approaching Sector 3 to trade in the Paikahale system.

"Is there anything we can do to help ease the situation on the colonists' planets?" asked one of the directors. He was concerned about the colonists he had done business with.

"Aleph is now ruled by the Corporate Alliance, but we could assist the others, if Barholomew was willing to risk it," remarked a second director.

"How would we be able to assist, though?" asked a third.

"Providing info, money, weapons, supplies, equipment?" commented the second director. "It would have to be significant though, considering the risk involved. But we're now a week away from the Antares system."

The others nodded. For now there was nothing they could do, but they would think on it for the future.

SLAVERY

CHAPTER FOURTEEN

Public opinion controls the ebbs and flows of trade and can make or break a company. Unethical practices can be stopped, if courageous people stand up to them.

Lady Cia of Elanissia

Somari was working as he had every day, since he had been sold to the Caviena Company on Reimus 5, one month ago. Every day, from dawn to dusk, he would work on the plantation, picking cava beans. Slavery had become a more popular way to cut costs, and now that the GIB outpost had been destroyed, it had become open practice on Reimus 5. Increasingly more kidnap victims were being transported in each day.

The owners of the plantations lived offplanet turning a blind eye to the way their contractors treated the workers and where they got them from. As a result, the slaves were treated poorly by those with a "heavy hand".

Although Somari was a cava bean picker, there were many other jobs that needed to be done on the plantation and mill in order to prepare the cava beans for trading. Other slaves filled these positions as well. The finished products sold by the Caviena Company were bags of cava beans, ready to brew.

However, not all slaves were being purchased by cava bean plantations. Some were purchased to work in households or even to be trained as fighters for the sport of the crowd. All purchases had been through an underground network in the past at great risk, but slave auctioneers had now arisen, and the trade was thriving on Reimus 5. Some celebrated the destruction of the GIB outpost since it meant they could trade openly and expand their trade.

Today, the slave auction in town was full of buyers and sellers waiting for the auction to start. The outdoor square smelled like sweat and unwashed bodies, in addition to the muddiness surrounding the Vodyanyov in their grey, rumpled garments.

"Both the hospitality and the quality of the merchandise has rapidly been downgraded," remarked one purchaser in sateen robes to another as they left the viewing area. "I personally prefer private sales in better company. There's nothing I want here. Let us take our leave."

The two men walked down a flight of stairs around a bend to the right, then up another flight of stairs to the left. They passed by two pointy-hooded characters in short layered khaki and beige belted cloaks with dark tights, who had been carefully watching the crowd from a distance. They looked to be from Ezio Prime from the way they were dressed.

The two characters were standing in the shade of a building, keeping their faces hidden. After getting the gist of what was occurring in the square, they left on the heels of the other men. The other men quickened their pace, glancing back at the cloaked ones following behind them. They visibly looked relieved when, at the next bend, the strangers turned in the opposite direction, heading out of the city.

The strangers kept walking out of the ancient stone city, and a few minutes later turned right, scampering behind a thicket in a large grove of trees.

"What did you find out?" asked Jack, who had piloted the shuttle.

Reagan and Cia flipped back their hoods. "It's very different than it was when I was here," commented Cia. "For one, they would never have dared auction off slaves in the town square. All sales made were in secret to private audiences, people with immense wealth. These new auctioneers are bold. These slaves today are obviously to be forced into hard labor.

"The best chance we have of finding her is to check the record books inside the Merchants' Hall. It is tricky to get in and out without notice, but now is the best time, when the Record Keepers are focused on the auction in the square," remarked Lady Cia.

"I don't want you taking any risks," Reagan said to Cia.

"Out of all of us here, I'm the only one who knows what the book looks like and where it's kept," replied Cia. Reagan saw that stubborn look on her face again. He thought it best to get it over with while the town was occupied elsewhere, instead of arguing a losing battle.

"Alright, but I'm not letting you out of my sight," said Reagan. Cia nodded. "Sam and Leighton, stand guard once we get there. I'll go inside with Cia to find the book." Samay and Leighton nodded.

The four of them backtracked to where Reagan and Cia had parted ways with the two merchants in the sateen robes. They went in the direction the two men had headed. After several turns through alleyways and up several flights of stairs on the way they were in a nicer area of the city.

The Tower of Records was made of white polished stone, unlike the rest of the inner city. As it was one of the main attractions on Reimus 5, the four of them were not out of place when they walked in. However, they could not just stroll into the Merchants' Hall as travelers from Ezio Prime.

The tower was actually made up of three towers joined together, shaped like cylinders. The largest tower was in the middle. Looking up, they could see the round white balconies which made up floor after floor of one of the smaller towers. There was intricately patterned masonwork, and scrollwork that had been etched into the stone. At the very top, there was stained glass in a conical shape. Vibrant colors shone down on them, and mirrors had been placed so the light would brighten up the balconies and reflect off the polished white stone.

"Ah, visitors from Ezio Prime. Is there anything I can assist you with?" asked a tall man who had approached them upon entry. His face had been powdered white, and he wore a rippled collar around his neck. His robes were also white, and he wore a colorful, conical hat, giving the overall illusion that he himself was a miniature tower.

"We'd like to see the records on Ezio Prime, please," said Cia, careful to keep her hood forward enough to cover her ears. It would not do to announce that there was one of the Elanisse on this planet.

"Why certainly," the keeper replied. He led them up a winding staircase, took them to the third level of the library, and directed them to the records on Ezio Prime.

"Were you looking for anything specific?" the guide asked.

"Yes, all records for the last five years on trade with Reimus 5," replied Leighton.

"We have many, many books filled with those records. What specifically are you looking for?" asked the keeper.

"We're doing a comparison of the types of trade and analyzing the economic trends," answered Samay.

"Oh, then I'll leave you to search out what you need. Please remember, we have a strict policy that the books remain in this room. All records are the property of this library. If you need assistance, or wish to move to another room, please let one of the keepers know." He descended the stairs to go back to his post, while Leighton placed two large record books on the table.

"Okay." Leighton spoke in a low tone of voice. "If any keepers ascend the stairs, we'll distract them by asking for assistance," he said.

Reagan nodded. "We'll be as fast as we can."

Reagan and Cia alighted the stairs as quickly and quietly as they could. By the time they reached the tenth floor, they were completely out of breath.

"Three more floors to go," gasped Cia. They continued to the highest level in the public section of the library.

When they had made it to the thirteenth floor, Cia pointed and whispered, "There it is. A way into the largest tower."

Reagan looked up at a small aperture several feet above the floor. "That's it? But it's so small!"

"Give me a boost," she whispered.

Reagan boosted Cia up so she could slide through the small opening. She squeezed through so she was sitting on a tall cabinet, then quietly dropped to the floor on the other side.

Reagan put his hands on the aperture, jumped, and attempted to pull himself up. He was able to get his head through, but there was no way he could fit his body through the opening.

"Cia," he whispered, "let's try another way to get in. I can't fit through."

"There is no other way. I'll just be a minute." She ran quietly through the room, and out the door.

"Cia!" he whispered. She was already gone. He was kicking himself for going along with this plan.

As Cia entered the corridor, she heard voices. She ducked into a dark corner and made herself as small as she could.

Two men were walking down the spiral staircase, talking to each other. They passed from the floor above to the floor below.

Cia heard one of the men speak before he passed out of hearing range. "I'm telling you, what they're doing with these auctions is lowering the value of my own merchandise. All these slaves forced to work in the cava bean plantations. Owning a slave has become commonplace now. I don't like it."

When the coast was clear, Cia darted up the same staircase they had come down. She peeked around the corner into the Merchants' Hall, and saw no one was in the room. She dashed across the room and to a locked cabinet that was labeled "Acquisitions".

Cia pulled out a pick gun and used it on the lock. She found a slim book labeled "2240-2244", placed it on the lectern in front of the cabinet, and flipped through the pages quickly. She opened the top of the emerald encrusted ring on her middle finger, then turned it around her finger so the small lens was faced away from her palm. When she found what she was looking for, she snapped pictures with her mini camera, using the thumb depression button.

She was ready to head back, but then she paused for a minute when she saw the book labelled "2245". The book was already three inches thick.

Cia made an impulsive decision, pulled out the book, placed it on the lectern, and started flipping through the pages quickly while taking photos of the lists. She was so focused on getting the info quickly, that she didn't hear the footsteps on the spiral staircase outside the room.

"I'm telling you, Ellis, I don't like what Gibbs is proposing. It leaves us out in the open," the man said as he entered the room. "It will also bring all kinds of rabble to our planet. No, I'd prefer to go back to the way we were conducting business."

"It's the question of what's more important," said Ellis. "For you, you still view owning slaves as a display of power and wealth. Well, those off-planet are using them in the plantations to *make* their wealth. There is a happy medium though."

"What's that?" asked the first man, as he walked towards the Acquisitions cabinet.

"It's about collections. What makes a piece in a collection more valuable?" asked Ellis.

"Well, it's rarity and its condition, of course," said the first man, looking backwards at Ellis. He pulled out his key, then turned towards the cabinet. "The door's already open!"

"You know the keepers here, they're particular about dust mites. One of them likely forgot to close it," said Ellis. "You have a number of rare specimens in your collection, and they are all in excellent condition," he continued. Your collection's value isn't going to go down, just because people are acquiring common slaves. They're working them to the bone which devalues them even more."

The man pulled out the thick book, placed it on the lectern, and copied some notations into it. His foot was partly in the bottom of the lectern, were Cia was hiding. She was holding her breath trying not to breathe on his knees, hoping his foot wouldn't bump into her, giving her away.

He took a step backwards, turned around, and locked the book in the cabinet. "The lock's loose. They need to replace it," he said. "I don't know why they still operate with centuries old technology."

"It adds to the ambiance of the towers, don't you think?" The two men walked out of the room, and headed up the stairs, discussing architecture and antiques.

Cia crawled out of the bottom of the lectern, listened carefully, then made her way quietly to the hallway. She hoped no one decided to use the stairway while she was on it. She took a deep breath and dashed down the stairs to the room with the aperture. She scrambled on top of the cabinet, ready to crawl back through, when she saw one of the keepers, face powdered white, talking with Reagan. She backed down, looking for a place to hide, should someone come into the room. She saw none.

"Where is the fourth member of your party?" he was asking Reagan, strangely alert.

"Oh, we weren't sure if Z-Class Planets would be under Z or P," said Reagan in a relaxed manner. "So we split up to take a look."

"I didn't see anyone on that floor," the keeper stated to Reagan, before descending to check.

After the guard was completely gone, Cia climbed on the top of the cabinet again, and whispered to Reagan. He looked anxiety-ridden.

"Reagan!"

"Cia! Where have you been?" He reached up and carefully pulled her out of the hole.

"I got the info," she said quietly, "and a lot more. I'll show you when we get back."

The two of them started down the stairs and ran into the keeper a few flights down, as he was coming back up. He was surprised to see two of them.

"Sorry about that, I was checking out the different views from the balconies. The lights from the stained glass are so pretty," Cia explained.

Her explanation was acceptable to the keeper, and he smiled. "Yes, many come from all over to see the lights reflecting on the polished stone and mirrors."

They regrouped, thanked the keeper at the front entrance for the use of the library, and headed back to meet the rest of their party.

The challenge with rescuing slaves from Reimus 5 or any other planet, was that it meant the GIB would be announcing to the world they had not been destroyed. They needed the Shaula reinforcements to join them first, or they were vulnerable. They also wanted to keep the element of surprise for their confrontation with the alliance. So, instead of raiding the Tower of Records, they'd gone in undercover.

However, Reagan was not pleased with Cia's actions. He had entered her quarters, and she sat there, putting her shoes on. She was in a light pink dress, but it was unlaced at the back. They were having an emotional discussion about what had occurred on Reimus 5.

"No, Cia." Reagan was terribly upset. "The risk was too great. What if you'd been caught or worse? You know firsthand what those from Elanissia are worth on the black market."

"There was no other way we could have got in, Reagan. Besides, I know those towers like the back of my hand. Remember? I was stationed there as a greeter to be shown off to all those who visited," she stubbornly replied.

"Cia." Reagan was choked up. "Please listen to me."

"No, Reagan, you listen to me. I'm not some frail woman who can't stand up for herself. You forget that I *am* Elanisse, which gives me defensive capabilities if I'm cornered. Besides, I would give my life for Katryn." Cia wouldn't back down.

"Cia," Reagan said quietly. She turned towards him and saw the tears in his eyes.

"I couldn't bear it if anything was to happen to you," whispered Reagan. Cia suddenly felt a flood of emotion. She walked towards Reagan and held his hands.

"Reagan, what I got from that book far outweighs the risk I took. It was a small risk, if you really think about it. What would I have faced? Some older politicians and bookworms. That's not much of a threat. Besides, if that group took me they would never actually harm me. You know that." Cia spoke quietly.

"But they could have taken and hidden you before we even knew you were missing. That's their trade, remember?" Reagan was pleading with his eyes.

"Shhhhh, it's okay, Reagan." Cia put her finger over his lips. "If it was someone else doing it, you would have considered it a low-risk mission, right?"

Reagan had to be honest with himself. He slowly nodded.

"The risk was far less than what we gained today. Let me show you in the debriefing. Now, could you help lace my dress up?" she asked him, as she turned around.

Lady Cia stood before the council regally, as she explained the images on the screen.

"These photos were taken from a book in the Tower of Records, labelled 'Acquisitions'. This specific book contains a record of all transactions between slave traders over the course of this year. If you compare the books, the volume containing transactions from the last five years is a fraction of the size of this year's book. Which means the slave trade is suddenly flourishing.

"Slaves used to be paraded as status symbols, to display power and wealth. Now, without the threat of the GIB hanging over them, people are using them for forced labor." Cia flipped to a specific image. "For example, take a look at the Caviena Company. They acquired these slaves one month ago, to work their plantations."

Cia flipped to the next image. "Here's another cava bean plantation that is using slavery to 'cut costs' when it comes to their competitors. The problem is going to get out of hand, if something isn't done to stop it soon." Lady Cia nodded to Deputy Governor Shaw.

Tarek Shaw opened the subject for discussion among the council members. There were a lot of questions, most of them directed towards Lady Cia, since she was the most knowledgeable on the subject, and could predict certain outcomes since she had more variables.

"Well, we're faced with several options," said Lady Cia. "The first is to leave it alone until our reinforcements arrive, and deal with it either before or after we deal with the alliance. However, if we deal with it before the alliance, we lose our element of surprise with the alliance. After the alliance, then we've lost our element of surprise with the slave traders, and there will be a purging of records, and likely of the slaves themselves.

"Another option is to send in tactical units to take out the slave traders, and free the slaves. However, with the current volume of slaves, there would be no way to keep the operation small, or quiet. It would be like announcing that the GIB is right here in Sector 3. And, we are currently vulnerable until our reinforcements get here."

"Any other options?" asked General McKenna.

"We could pose as if we were from Ezio Prime again," suggested Officer Beckett.

Reagan faced Officer Beckett as he spoke. "The problem with that is it could start a war. No, posing as another race or planetary group is out of the question because of that possibility."

"An additional option would be to think 'outside the box' and come up with a non-military way to free the slaves," said Cia.

"What do you have in mind?" asked Officer Beckett.

"Well, we're dealing with money and trade. We need to disrupt those two things. The corporations are dependent on traders and public opinion in order to sell their product. If we hit them hard there so they lose their profits, it might be effective."

"Go on," said Deputy Governor Shaw.

"One idea is to run a media campaign," suggested Lady Cia.

The council was confused. "Media campaign? What do you mean, Lady Cia?" asked Officer Jennings.

"Well, the majority of forced labor is on the cava bean plantations. If someone not known to have ties with the GIB makes a documentary, showing the living and working conditions of the slaves, the public may stop purchasing cava beans from those companies."

She continued, "If they lose their profits due to public outrage, then they'll have no choice but to go back to hiring laborers. This ensures that the GIB stays hidden. The companies will attempt to sell their 'acquisitions' for whatever they can get for them. We then have 'wealthy citizens' purchase them at low cost and free them."

"That's a very interesting plan," said Officer Beckett, thoughtfully.

"It's just an idea," she commented.

"What about also targeting the traders with this information?" asked Officer Jennings. "Let those who are ethically driven choose which companies to deal with, after they have all the facts."

"Between this and the next meeting, let's think on options, especially non-military options, since we want to remain hidden," said Deputy Governor Shaw. The council nodded. They had been given a lot to think on.

"Meeting adjourned."

The council decided to run a media campaign and see what kind of effect it had. There was no risk to themselves and minimal cost. They authorized a team to travel to Reimus 5 to photograph and video worker conditions on the cava bean plantations. Their team was headed by a seasoned documentary filmmaker, Keira Pacrill.

There was no security on the plantations, and they were using slaves openly, so they had no trouble getting the footage they needed.

On the edge of the Caviena Plantation, the team was able to catch a worker and interview him about conditions. Somari agreed to this as long as there was no identifying information. He took them to their living area, where they took footage of rundown buildings where the slaves had been forced to live.

There was no safe water to drink. The rain wells had no covers, so dead rodents were constantly being removed from them. The slaves had attempted to rig covers from what little material they could find, but they were unsuccessful at preventing the small animals from getting in.

As a result, they boiled their water before they drank it or cooked with it, and before they washed themselves or cleaned their items with it. The amount of time it took to cover the basic necessities left them with no time for anything else, since they were picking or processing cava beans from dawn until dusk.

The original employee residences were occupied by contractors and enforcers. The slaves were packed into the old, dilapidated housing, eight people to a room on average.

The working areas for those processing the beans lacked equipment which would make their jobs less demanding physically. Everything had to be done by hand, with only the most basic equipment. This included separating the cava beans, stripping the pulp, and turning the damp beans to avoid mildew during the drying process.

The team was able to get in and out without being noticed by the enforcers, who were drunk, as usual. They had all the footage they needed of the true conditions at the prestigious Cavienna Corporation. Plus, they had proof of their "purchases" from the photos Lady Cia had taken from the Acquisitions book.

A couple of days later, the footage had been put together as a documentary, and previewed by the council. It was an eye-opener for them. They thought it was well done and would be effective. There were no identifying characteristics regarding who had done the documentary, and it was broadcast from a temporary radio setup on Reimus 5 itself. When investigators came looking for the source of the signal, they were long gone.

The documentary was sent out unencrypted to the planets in both the Paikahale and Antares systems, source unknown.

Bartholomew Sullivan had picked up an interesting broadcast about the Caviena Corporation as he approached Reimus 5 to trade. He usually dealt directly with Caviena and purchased their product to be resold across all four quadrants, but refused to deal with them after he saw the broadcast and verified the information was true.

He spent the next two days inspecting plantations until he was satisfied that the corporation he dealt with didn't use slaves, and had excellent quality cava beans. The Cava Java Corporation was about to become a very popular source of cava beans.

"We were able to buy and free several hundred slaves that were being kept on Reimus 5, working the plantations," reported Reagan. "Since images in the documentary connected the slaves with specific corporations, they weren't about to 'dispose' of them, in case they would be called up on murder charges in the future. Even though they believe the GIB is no longer in this quadrant, they know there are active authorities in other quadrants."

"Well done," said Deputy Governor Shaw.

"All those rescued have been given places to live on Calderra for now. They will be able to make the choice of where to settle permanently in the future. We still can't let the GIB's existence be known, and we weren't about to leave them on Reimus 5," said Reagan.

The Deputy Governor nodded.

"I'm glad to hear that the mission went well," commented General McKenna.

"Looks like we have a new spy in our midst." Officer Beckett teased Lady Cia. She blushed.

"Let's make sure those rescued have medical exams and proper care as needed." Reagan steered the conversation back on track. "Those with skills who would like to help with the pioneering of Calderra are welcome to do so, but let's not make them feel obligated. It's voluntary only, as they recover from their ordeal."

"Agreed," nodded Officer Jennings. The others nodded.

"Any more business on the table?" asked Shaw. There was no response.

"Meeting adjourned."

BUILDING

CHAPTER FIFTEEN

No one starts by thinking they want to eliminate an entire planet of people. First there was the manipulating of the contract terms to skim money, second stealing land as a platform to taking over a planet, and finally the attempted elimination of an entire planet's people. Monetary greed was the motivator for the first action, and lust for power the motivation for the second. The third action involved a combination of motivators that weren't clear then and may never come to light.

Lady Cadrius of the Aeaqualis

Director Finley was in an excellent mood. He sat back in his new glass office, surrounded by leather and mahogany, sipping a cup of cava. The previous occupant had good taste. At one hundred-and-forty-nine stories up, he had full view of the city and surrounding area.

He was the highest occupant in the tower, apart from those at the military post one floor above him. Having a pilot one floor up made things convenient for Director Finley. He could be flown wherever he wished in the heliplane on the roof's landing pad.

It was nice to finally get off his ship and set his feet on the ground. This time on his "own" planet. He smiled.

The sunlight shone through liquid crystal spectral filters, attached to the corners of the building. As a result, light refracted into colors, bounced off mirrored walls of surrounding buildings, and was projected over the entire city. Ten minutes later, the color pattern would be completely different. Yes, he'd made an excellent decision, choosing Belhandelar as the capital for the Corporate Alliance. In addition to being practical for their uses, the infrastructure was well-planned out, and it was aesthetically pleasing.

240,000 colonists had been displaced from the Inner Circle, but Director Finley knew they'd be back on their feet in no time. They just needed to find new office space and housing. Since he knew that productivity equals profits, he was not averse to having the military provide temporary housing for them outside the city, and transportation to their employment. Some would be able to find new housing and office space inside the city. However, because property values and rentals had skyrocketed overnight, it would only be the super-rich.

As a temporary solution many of the companies began sharing office space with other companies. Sometimes that meant a disadvantaged company only had access to space during the night. For now.

Not wanting to cause a complete disruption in trade and profits, he had decided to give the colonists in the second circle two weeks to prepare to move out. After that the military was to move into the second circle to permanently surround, and protect, the inner circle. Until then, the military was situated in the outer ring, where the displaced colonists were.

However, business was booming for those in architecture, and soon would be for those in the construction industry. Director Finley wished to see architectural options for an outer ring, and

approve them himself, as he wanted to keep the city developing in an aesthetic way. He had teams of architects working night and day to complete the design, and he personally ensured they were paid very well. After all, this was to be the alliance's permanent home. *His* permanent home.

Plans were approved for the new outer circle, which would be the new business and residential district. Within minutes of being put on the market, the building units were pre-sold at an astronomical price. More profits for the Corporate Alliance.

Now the blueprints had been completed, Director Finley wanted the new Outer Circle completed within two weeks. It would take tens of thousands of workers working around the clock to complete, but the military would also assist with their aircraft, heavy machinery, and manpower. For incentive, if the job was done within that time frame, the 50% profit grab would be bypassed, and everyone would be paid 100%. Director Finley just wanted it done. Quickly.

Everyone was in place to start. Architects set the hologrid around the outside of the city, which showed exactly where each labelled piece was to be placed. Now it was just a matter of building it. The clock was ticking.

Lord Bartholomew and his fleet had been travelling towards Quadrant 2 and the solar systems of Weixiuer and Xamidimura, to continue trading. He was glad to leave Quadrant 3. All the chaos there had troubled him. Two days into his journey, he was surprised to pick up a convoy of ships on his scanners. They were from the Shaula system.

He hailed them to see if they were interested in trading.

"Lord Bartholomew." Archduke Nizet of the Elanisse was an old friend. Bartholomew had been trading in Quadrant 1 for many years, and had met many citizens who lived there. Nizet had straight, long blonde hair, and the elven look that all Elanisse had.

"Nice to see you, Archduke Nizet," he smiled. "What brings you this way? Heard about trouble at Antares I suppose?"

"Exactly. We're meeting with the remaining forces of the GIB, then will decide what our next move is," said the Archduke.

"The GIB?" Bartholomew was confused. "You did hear they were destroyed?"

"That was just the outpost fragmenting. Many of the forces have regrouped and are ready to embark on a rescue mission to free prisoners on the Colonists' Planets."

"I haven't heard anything about their existence or whereabouts, and I trade for information," insisted Bartholomew.

"They've been keeping their heads low, since they aren't ready for a confrontation with the Corporate Alliance," said Archduke Nizet.

"Well, that's good news then," said Bartholomew. At that moment, he made a decision, a change in direction.

"I'm going to travel back with you," said Bartholomew. "In the least, I'll be able to trade with you along the way. At best, I might make myself and my fleet useful to you somehow. I don't like what I've seen from the Corporate Alliance, and it's only going to get worse as time goes on."

"You're welcome to join us, Friend," said Nizet. "Let's have dinner tonight and you can fill us in on your latest travels."

"Absolutely," said Bartholomew. "I do have a fair amount to report to you. I'm sure you know most of it, if you're in contact with the GIB, but you might glean something from my information."

"Excellent." Archduke Nizet was looking forward to exchanging information with Bartholomew. "Transmission end."

Bartholomew knew the five directors would be happy to know there was hope of rescuing their friends on the Colonists' Planets. He ordered his fleet to change course. It would take several hours to reach the Shaula convoy.

"Calderra? Neo Terrene? I was just there! Well, only one planet away. I had *no* clue the GIB was hiding out on the moon there. They've erased their presence entirely," laughed Bartholomew as he sipped chilled white wine.

"They've rebuilt their base there, or at least given it a good start," smiled Archduke Nizet.

"Amazing." Bartholomew was impressed by their stealth.

"By the way, I understand that Lady Cianna is on Calderra. Do you know anything about the whereabouts of Lady Islanda?" Archduke Nizet asked, looking at Bartholomew with his piercing light blue eyes.

"Last time I saw Lady Isla was nearly a month ago on Vitaari, living on K'vaal Ianov's estate along with Lady Cianna. She looked well taken care of," Bartholomew reported.

"Ah, I must thank this K'vaal then. He is one of the Vitaari I suppose?" the Archduke asked.

"Yes." Bartholomew paused.

"What is it?"

"Well, unless I'm mistaken, he seems very in love with Lady Isla," Bartholomew said cautiously.

"What about Lady Isla?" asked Nizet, quietly. "What are her feelings for him?"

"I think she believes she owes him a debt for returning Lady Cia to her," said Bartholomew. "I don't know the details, but I believe he had something to do with finding her after they were separated, and has treated her as a Lady of his household, under his care."

"Then I must thank him for what he has done for Lady Cia, as well," said Archduke Nizet. "I will give him a gift worthy of his deeds."

Bartholomew nodded.

It was time for the GIB fleet to pull back from Calderra and Neo Terrene, keeping out of sight of Ezio Prime and Reimus 5. They would travel towards the Shaula reinforcements and rendezvous with them in twenty-four hours.

Taylor gave Jesse a quick hug goodbye and turned to leave. "Wait a sec, you forgot something," Jesse said. Taylor turned around. That's when Jesse gave Taylor a real kiss. She felt all dreamy, like she was melting inside. Then Jesse whispered in her ear as he held her arms, "Come back safely." He let her go, she nodded, and was on her way.

"Really going to miss her, aren't you?" asked Kyler.

"Yup, sure am," said Jesse.

"Well, you have us guys to hang out with now," Kyler smirked. Then his voice went an octave higher as he tried to imitate Taylor's voice. "We'll keep you company." He dodged just in time, before Jesse could smack him with a lettuce leaf.

Reagan knew there was no use trying to talk Cia out of going with them. He was learning that there's no use fighting a losing battle with a girl like Cia. Sometimes you just had to go with the second best option. He would just have to keep her close.

Secretary Cohen, Jack, and Taylor planned on spending some time together on the trip out, before their jobs would require all their time and concentration. Of course, Jack was planning on asking Taylor a *lot* of questions regarding Jesse. Actually, "teasing her about Jesse" would be a more accurate way to put it.

It was time to start their journey.

Both groups reached the rendezvous point on time. Their plan was to swing wide of Reimus 5 so the sun was on their left, and travel through Sector 6, an empty sector without a solar system. In the meantime, they would scan for transmissions and gain intel before they chose their ground. The GIB hadn't been in the Antares sector for a few weeks now, and needed fresh intel. Anything could have happened while they were away.

After a few days of putting pieces together from broadcasts and transmissions, they gathered that the Corporate Alliance had taken over and were now based on Aleph, and their fleet was between the planet and the sun.

On Bethel, there had been some type of natural disaster or epidemic. Details were vague, but it was suggested that people stay away and treat it as a quarantine zone.

Gamuel had stopped an invasion by the alliance, and the governments were working together to prevent future attacks. It looked like this was the best place to start for intel, so they planned to send out a scouting team. Hopefully, they would learn more about the other planets' fates on the scouting mission.

Lord Bartholomew gave use of his ships for the scouting mission so they wouldn't be recognized. Although one of the corporation leaders wanted to go, he was told he would have to wait until it was "all clear". He would have to wait to check on the colony he was worried about.

Rather than just volunteer, Taylor *insisted* on going on the mission and that was that. The Secretary had anticipated that, and they already had Taylor on the list. They needed a pilot, and she was happy to fly a shuttle. Although Jack wanted to go as well, he had other duties he needed to carry out as Squadron Leader.

When they were prepared to leave, Taylor launched the shuttle, and they carefully made their way to Gamuel from Sector 6. As a known trading ship, they had no problems landing in Laetus, Corusco.

After they arrived, the team sought news at the large library in the busy town square. They scrolled through news stories on tablets to get the gist of what exactly had happened, and how the invasion had been countered. The City of Aeaqualis was where they would find the GIB survivors. Taylor didn't spend any time waiting around, and nearly dragged them all off to the shuttle. They headed to Aeaqualis.

Taylor landed on the opposite side of the city to the mountain range. *There has to be a list of survivors somewhere,* she thought. Although the chances were slim that her mother was on this planet, Taylor kept her fingers crossed. The anxiety of not knowing was difficult, so narrowing things down at least helped her to feel like she was doing something.

They approached the Hall of Records in the Town Square and went inside. Taylor asked if they had a copy of the list of GIB survivors, and was sadly disappointed. She suggested they keep trying government buildings until they found a list. The team split up. Half of them went to research in the library, while Taylor and the rest went next door to City Hall.

"Would you happen to have a list of the survivors from the GIB Outpost?" Taylor asked the prim and proper lady at the reception. She checked on her computer, unsuccessfully.

"The document has been protected and deemed confidential for the protection of the survivors. They are here under the care of Lady Cadrius and this city," she said.

"Then how do I reach this *Lady Cadrius?*" Taylor asked somewhat rudely.

"Lady Cadrius isn't available right now, but you could talk with one of her assistants who would have the information you are looking for."

"*Fine* then," Taylor said petulantly, arms crossed.

The lady pressed a button, and Taylor heard a chime in the distance. After a minute, she heard the sound of shoes walking down the hallway.

Janine, now on the Intel Team as well as working as one of Lady Cadrius' assistants, was incredibly busy sifting through information when she was called to the front. She lay down the file she was perusing, stood up and smoothed the red slacks under her black blazer, then headed out of her office. Her black heels made a tapping sound as she walked.

As she turned the corner by the front desk, she felt like her heart had done a double leap. She grabbed onto the receptionist's desk to steady herself. "Taylor?" she whispered. But Taylor was already flying towards her.

"Mom! It's you!" She buried her face in her mom's jacket, trying to stop the tears from coming. There had been so much anxiety built up that Taylor couldn't help it, and the tears started flowing.

Janine put her hand on Taylor's hair and smoothed it.

"How did you find me?" she asked.

"I was just looking for a list of survivors, and found out this was the city to come to," Taylor answered. "But never mind that. How are you doing? Are you hurt?"

"No I'm fine. Have you seen Dad or Jack?" Janine asked.

"Yes! I can fly you to them." She was tugging on her mother's sleeve. It brought back a memory to Janine of how Taylor used to tug on her leg because she wanted to go somewhere when she was little.

Janine laughed. "Hold on, you. I have to notify Lady Cadrius first. Give me five minutes." She walked into the back and was gone for a few minutes. When she came back she had her briefcase and coat.

They picked up the rest of the team next door, and headed back to the shuttle. It was time to have a family reunion.

Janine was before the council, discussing the details of what had occurred on Gamuel, starting with their experience working in the mines, and how one of the brave young men went to find the closest settlement with prisoners, and instead found a thriving city, willing to help them.

"Lady Cadrius was wise to deal with the alliance presence before they became a menace," commented Reagan with appreciation. "From what you've told us, and what we've seen about Aleph, things could have gone completely differently, had she not acted immediately."

Janine nodded. "She is very wise, and I have the privilege of being on the Intel Team with her, as well as acting as her assistant."

"Well you're now in the perfect position to act as Liaison between Gamuel and us," said Deputy Governor Shaw.

"Tell us what happened on Bethel. Do you know if it was a natural disaster or an epidemic? The reports are so vague that we haven't been able to pin down what exactly has happened there," asked Magistrate Kian Anderson.

"We're really not sure ourselves. We've just been told that it's best to treat the planet like it was under quarantine," Janine replied.

"So we need to do some investigating then," said Officer Beckett.

"Let's do some planetary scans for seismic activity, changes in the oceanic levels, or anything else indicative of natural disasters. We can do that from here, without having to move into visual range," said Officer Jennings.

"Good suggestion. Let's get the results in for next meeting, so we can plan our next step," said Shaw.

The meeting was adjourned.

The Cohens were having a family reunion. It had been difficult for the Secretary and his wife to be in the same room doing a formal debriefing, but now they were together and could say whatever they wanted to.

Janine took turns holding each one of them, and Taylor saw tears in both her dad's and Jack's eyes. They had all missed her so much, and the worry was finally being washed away by relief.

"Mom, you're amazing," said Taylor, quietly, after hearing her story. "Without you staying strong and giving others courage, the entire planet may have been jeopardized. You saved the planet, Mom."

"Well, I had a *lot* of help," laughed Janine. "So many courageous people. Think of the young man who spent nine days crossing over 450 sectars on foot to get help. Now *that's* a real hero," smiled Janine.

"You're my hero, Mom," said Jack, as he took her in his arms. This time he couldn't stop the tears. "You're my hero," he said in a softer voice. They held each other for a couple of minutes, then Jack was drying his face with his sleeve.

After a while, Taylor and Jack left, to give their parents some alone time to catch up with each other.

"Hmmm...no seismic activity right now or major changes in oceanic levels compared with the maps on file," said Sergeant Trevana, who was doing the scanning from the bridge.

"Let's find out where all the people are. Try heat," suggested Officer Jennings.

The sergeant switched to heat signatures. "That's strange," he said. "They're all gathered in these areas," he pointed at the screen. "Once sec." He overlaid it with a climate map.

"Look at that," he said, satisfied. "I thought I recognized a pattern. A good amount of people from the west have migrated to the coldest areas on the planet."

"It couldn't have anything to do with the sun, or it would have affected the other planets as well," said Reagan. "Maybe their climate regulator has had a serious malfunction. Can you get temperature readings of the areas they vacated?"

The sergeant got the temperature readings. They were all normal.

"Any more overlays?" asked Reagan.

"Sure, I can flip through them to look for matches," said Sergeant Trevana. He started flipping through elevation overlays, radiation overlays, weather overlays, and more.

"Wait a minute," said Reagan. "Flip back a few."

The Sergeant flipped back.

"Stop," Reagan said. "Let me take a look at that one."

"Oh, that's not an overlay," said the Sergeant.

"The people are missing where that yellowish-orange glow is in a streaked pattern," said Reagan.

"This one's a scan for organic matter," said Sergeant Trevana.

Reagan bent in closer. He gave the scan a long, hard look. Then he startled. "Oh no," he said in a quiet voice. "Can you get visuals? Of the western side of the hemisphere. The one that's completely covered with the organic matter."

"Sure. Hacking into a Bethel satellite..." After a few minutes of key-tapping, the sergeant zoomed in on the planet.

"Overlay the visual with the organic matter for a sec so we know where to look," Reagan said.

The sergeant lined up the overlay.

"Ohhh," said Officer Jennings. "Vines."

"Zoom in on that intersection," said Reagan, pointing at the scan.

Sergeant Trevana zoomed in on a huge mass of transparent green organic material. "What is *that*?" he asked. The vines were attached to the giant mass.

"The seed mass," Reagan said in almost a whisper. He could see liquid surrounding something solid inside the giant mass. It was pulsating very slightly. "The report from the lab said it had the equivalent of lower brain functions, which was why it could feel its surroundings and sense pain.

"Zoom in on that right there. The seed mass looks as if it broke out of some type of metal room. There's some writing on that piece." Reagan pointed to the one he was referring to.

Sergeant Trevana zoomed in on the metal. Although some of the letters were obscured, they could all see that it read "CORPORATE ALLIANCE".

Reagan had called an emergency meeting. He felt badly about disturbing the Secretary and his wife who had just been reunited, so he tried to keep things brief for their sake.

Reagan projected the images on screen.

"There's been no epidemic or natural disaster on Bethel," he stated. He showed the visuals with the overlays, then finally the actual video footage of what was down there.

Once he was at the part with the seed mass, the video zoomed in on the writing. Everyone gasped.

"Delaney Walker had an interaction with General Parker Channing a few weeks ago. He warned us recently that the general's plan was to weaponize the creatures from the Z-Class planet," said Janine quietly. They all turned their heads towards her. "Del seemed more concerned about the dromasaurs, since the general was already working on that project. But clearly the bigger threat was this creature, and General Channing's willingness to attempt genocide."

Heads were shaking. They couldn't fathom why someone would go so far as to eliminate an entire population, regardless of their grudge against them. There was a feeling of overwhelming sadness, due to all the lives that must have been lost. Lady Cia was terribly upset.

"Could you zoom in on the metal?" asked General McKenna. Reagan zoomed in. "That's a carrier ship. You can tell by the serial numbers. It split a *carrier* ship open."

When the meeting ended, everyone was in a sombre mood. No plan had been put into action yet. They had to consider that they needed to stay undercover until the strike on the Corporate Alliance.

Janine estimated that their numbers were fairly evenly matched, now reinforcements from Isidore and Elanissia were with them. That meant a drawn out battle, and potential colonist fatalities, depending on where the fight took place. They needed to choose a plan and a battleground that would limit collateral damage.

Lady Cia needed to be held. Reagan took her in his arms and held her, while gently rocking her.

She finally lifted her head, and Reagan helped to dry her tears with a tissue. She blew her nose.

He sat on a chair, and placed her on his knee, so he could still cradle her. He kissed the top of her head. She felt very warm, overheated from crying.

He understood how she felt. It was difficult to understand the "why's". Was it on a whim? Was it due to a grudge? Why would a person attempt to kill off an entire planet? There was no answer.

Reagan wished he had Cia's Elanisse ability, so he could calm her. Instead, he lay her down on her bed, and covered her pink and white eyelet dress with a blanket. He tucked her in, and rubbed her back until she fell asleep.

Taylor took Janine back to Gamuel, since it was vital to get information about Bethel to the Intel Team immediately. They called an emergency meeting of the planet's leaders, and showed the video footage that Reagan had presented to the GIB council, without revealing the source. The fewer people that knew there was a force sitting close by, the less chance of leaks.

At first there was shock and disbelief that even the Corporate Alliance would go so far. But then, as they retraced the steps the alliance had taken down their "slippery slope", it wasn't that surprising at all.

"If they've gone this far," said Lady Cadrius, "who knows what their next step will be."

The other leaders nodded in agreement.

"What are our options?" asked a representative from Corusco.

Janine had the floor. "We make sure no ships from the alliance get through, and do a visual confirmation check of the occupants of every ship trying to dock. Occupants would never survive if there is a creature on board. When occupants arrive, we scan them to ensure that there is no creature growing inside them. The governor alerted us to that possibility before the outpost fragmented."

Lord Ehzen wrote up the new protocols to be followed, to be distributed to all landing bays on the planet. Private landing bays were to be shut down and locked out until the impending crisis was averted.

By the end of the third week, Connor and Mia had been moved into a small apartment that consisted of a bedroom, bathroom, kitchen, and living area. They were happy to get their privacy back.

They'd had the opportunity to look loss straight in the eye. They had lost so much -- their home, their work, their personal possessions. But they were still alive and together, which far outweighed any material loss.

Some of those who had shared the large tent with them that first week had truly lost much. Several people had either seen their loved ones taken, or they were missing. Those were true losses. Connor was thankful that he and Mia had been together when the chaos started, or they would be in the same situation.

As Mia was fixing lunch with her back to Connor, he slipped his arms around her and kissed her on the nape of the neck. She relaxed in his arms, then turned around to face him. She planted a kiss on his lips.

Connor picked up the plates and placed them on the table. He pulled out Mia's chair for her, and she smiled as she sat down. They were both quiet while they ate.

After lunch, they went for a walk hand-in-hand, to where the military had been stationed. Things were looking good for the colonists, now they were settled. They now had a small school, and a large community building with a big screen where they showed movies each evening.

Mia had started teaching at the school, helping the younger children to settle. Some of them had been frightened and still acted out because of their experiences. Mia was very gentle and understanding, yet firm when dealing with disruptive behavior.

Connor assisted the military however he could. He was "another pair of hands" they could call on when they needed more workers for a job. He'd helped to construct the apartments the colonists were now living in.

"Hey Connor," one of the soldiers greeted him with a serious face. "The Colonel has been looking for you." Connor kissed Mia goodbye, and she walked back to the schoolhouse to teach afternoon classes.

Connor went looking for Colonel Kevin Strait. He found him in the communications tent.

"Connor! You worked communications, right?" Connor nodded. "Would you mind assisting us with this?" he asked.

"Sure, I'll do my best. What's up?" he asked.

"We've lost our coms, and could use some assistance getting them up again. Since you have experience, we were hoping you could give us a hand," Colonel Strait said.

Connor took a look at the decryption device. "Sure, I'll give it a go," he said as he got to work.

Mia came by to the military area after teaching was done for the afternoon. Connor had been hard at work on the decryption device, and was now tweaking the software for specific channels.

"Hi hun," Connor briefly glanced up. "Just finishing this up. I'll be a few minutes."

"Meet you at home?" Mia asked.

"Sure thing."

Connor showed the officers how to set each channel to encrypt and decrypt.

"What are our most recent codes?" Colonel Strait asked one of the other officers. "Could you enter those in for us?" he asked Connor.

"Sure. Just one sec." Connor took the codes and entered them in. The coms were restored for local and long-distance communication on the planet. There were smiles from the officers and pats on the back, as communications started coming through again.

The colonel took Connor aside. "You know we've been without a skilled Communications Officer? How would you like to give it a try? It would involve installing and maintaining our systems. Most of the tasks would be basic for you, but there would be the odd job like this one today that's more challenging. Up until now, fixes have been slow, and we've been just getting by."

"I'd be honored," said Connor. "Mind if I talk it over with Mia? She won't mind, but you know women..." Connor didn't have to complete his sentence.

Colonel Strait laughed. "I sure do. Get back to me as soon as you know."

Connor jogged the short way home.

"Publicizing the info may play right into their hands," said Lady Cadrius. "We have a plan to prevent a catastrophe, by following the protocols that Lord Ezhen transmitted. If we publicize what actually happened on Bethel, then there would be mass panic on our planet, and other planets may feel intimidated to giving them whatever they demand."

The debate between the leaders was going back and forth.

"However, if we do publicize it, we could gain more allies that we could use right now. We are on our own, Lady Cadrius. We may have a deal with Kitsuana, but what's that in comparison with what the Corporate Alliance can do to us? If they chose to take over this planet, they could. They'd sustain losses, but they don't seem to flinch at that," said Lord Tadriel of Corusco. "We *need* more allies, and this may be the only way to obtain them."

Lady Cadrius motioned to Lord Ehzen and whispered to him.

"Clear the room," intonated Lord Ehzen. The room was cleared of aids, security, and clerical staff. The only ones to stay, apart from the world leaders, were those on the Intel Team.

Lady Cadrius stood. "What we are about to tell you is classified at the highest level. This is not to leave or be discussed outside of this room," she emphasized.

Janine stood. "We are not without allies. There is a force that can match the Corporate Alliance in close range to our position."

There was sudden alarm among the representatives.

"What force? And how do we know they are allies?" asked Lord Tadriel.

Lord Ehzen had to stand to bring order back to the group. He motioned them to calm down, and let Janine finish speaking.

"There is a force made up of Quadrant 3's Galactic Investigations Bureau, and reinforcements from Isidore and Elanissia. They have come to assist us because of what has happened with the Corporate Alliance," said Janine.

"The GIB? But they were destroyed! And you say reinforcements have travelled all the way from Shaula to assist us?" Lord Tadriel looked incredulous. "Why hasn't the Corporate Alliance picked them up on their scanners? Why haven't we?"

"The GIB is made up of many resilient individuals. They regrouped and called for assistance, rather than rushing headlong into another battle," stated Janine. "Currently, although I cannot disclose their location, I can disclose that they are nearby. We have allies of the highest caliber, and with the highest ethics." Janine was proud of her association with the GIB and Shaula.

The room settled down.

"And we are only now being told this?" asked Lord Tadriel.

"Yes, although everyone here has our utmost trust, the less people who know, the better. Not just in case something 'slips', but if it was suspected that one of your aids had information, then they would be in more danger than if they did not know," Janine explained. "The reason why I've explained this now, is because I sensed that panic was to settle in here, with this group. Let's keep cool heads as we make decisions and see how we can assist in the big picture."

Lord Ehzen smiled. The rest of the council looked reassured and nodded. It looked like Janine had settled down the ruffled feathers. Now, instead of talking in circles, they could do some *real* planning.

LIBERATION

CHAPTER SIXTEEN

Common goals are what brings us together with others joining our paths with theirs for a time. When our goals change and are no longer the same, our paths change and become diverse.

Lady Isla of Elanissia

As the closest planet to the sun, Vitaaria had revolved around Antares from being closest to the planet Azram to now being closest to Kitsuana. Reagan suggested that he and Cia travel to Vitaaria to see Lady Isla and exchange intel.

Their shuttle docked at K'vaal's estate. Reagan and Cia descended from the shuttle platform. Lady Isla was waiting to greet them.

"I'm so glad you're safe, Cia." Lady Isla smiled as she wrapped her arms around Cia and held her close.

"It's wonderful to see you, Isla!" Cia kissed her sister impulsively on the cheek.

"Governor, it's good to see you alive and well. Especially after all the reports that were circulating."

"Thank you. Please, just call me Reagan," he said.

"We have so much to talk about, Isla," said Cia.

"Indeed we do," said Lady Isla. "Let's go into the study. K'vaal is waiting for us."

K'vaal greeted them. He hadn't realized it, but he was fond of Lady Cia. He was glad she was safe, not just for Lady Isla's sake.

Reagan and Cia discussed everything they were authorized to discuss with K'vaal and Isla. When they brought up the cause of the calamity on Bethel, K'vaal jumped in.

"Do you have a plan to defeat it? Do you know how?" he asked, sitting up straight.

"We only know that cold slows it down and makes it go dormant. Half the remaining population is now situated in the coldest areas of the planet.

"There is a way to kill it." K'vaal was excitedly pacing back and forth.

"How's that?" asked Reagan.

"I don't know my*sss*elf, but the Elders finally came up with a way after *ccc*enturies of re*sss*earch," said K'vaal, looking at Reagan.

"Centuries?" exclaimed Lady Cia.

"Ye*sss*, *ccc*enturies," K'vaal said absentmindedly. "If I can just arrange a meeting with them..." K'vaal trailed off.

Reagan nodded, "I'd be honored to attend."

Three hours later, K'vaal was introducing Reagan, Lady Isla, and Lady Cia to the Elders in a dark, mossy cavern farther out than Reagan and Cia had travelled for their outings.

"Welcome Governor, Daughters of the Elani*sss*se, K'vaal," said the Chief Elder in greeting.

"Thank you," the four of them replied. Reagan noticed the Chief and the Elders sat in stone chairs tailored to their size.

Reagan outlined the conditions on Bethel for the Elders. The Chief Elder arched an eye.

"Elder E'oghan, could you give the governor the details regarding killing the creature?" the Chief Elder asked.

He nodded and said, "It's*sss* not a 100% guarantee that it will die, *sss*ince we don't know the exact proportions. However, if enough liquid nitrogen is pumped into the protective liquid in its *sss*eed mass, then it will die. The 'if' part is determined by the word 'enough'," he said. "We don't know the exact quantity. We ju*sss*t know that it would be a large amount, ba*sss*ed on the *sss*ize you're de*sss*cribing."

"Thank you very much, Lord Elder," Reagan bowed in respect.

"Who is going to attempt to kill it?" asked Elder E'oghan.

"I will be putting a tactical team together. Since we know where the seed mass is, that's one issue already solved," Reagan said. The Elders nodded. Reagan said cautiously, "There are many excellent men and women among the GIB and their allies."

"The GIB and allies?" asked the Chief Elder with interest.

Reagan made the decision to tell the Elders about their current standing. "Yes, we've regrouped and called for reinforcements which have now arrived."

"You have reinfor*ccc*ements as well?" The Chief sat up straight in his large, stone chair.

"Yes, reinforcements from the Shaula system," he said. "Together we match the alliance in numbers."

"Impre*sss*ive," said the Chief Elder. "Let u*sss* conver*sss*e alone for a few minute*sss*," said the Chief Elder.

Reagan, and the two ladies left the stone room. A few minutes later, K'vaal came out to get them. They walked back inside together.

"It's unanimou*sss*," the Chief Elder smiled. "We and our followers are willing to a*sss*i*sss*t you as you go up again*sss*t the Corporate Alliance."

"Thank you," said Reagan, somewhat surprised.

"We have an interessst in Azram, the planet of our origin, which is currently being mined by the Corporate Allian*ccce*," explained the Chief Elder. "We are ready to take the planet back now that we have the remedy, but the Corporate Allian*ccce* is too much for us*ss* alone." The Chief Elder cleared his throat. Reagan nodded.

"Not all Vitaari follow the old ways," said the Chief. "*Ssso* do not trus*sst* any Vitaari who isn't present in this*ss* room right now. There is a faction who has been paid off by the Corporate Allian*ccce*, but we doubt they will go as far as partic*cci*pating in this*ss* war. However, information could get pass*ss*ed on."

"Understood," said Reagan. "We will be in touch with K'vaal about our plans."

The Chief Elder nodded, and the four of them took their leave.

Reagan brought the news back to the council.

"We have a remedy for Bethel, and we have new allies," Reagan reported.

He gave details of the meeting with the Vitaari Elders, and the decision they had made to ally with them against the Corporate Alliance. They had strong reason to, since they wanted their homeworld back.

Moving on to the discussion about the creature on Bethel, Reagan outlined what they would need. A tactical team experienced with air assault, high weapon accuracy, and good on the ground as well.

Secretary Cohen sighed, knowing that his daughter would insist on going. She had all the qualifications and more.

Reagan described what they would need for the projectiles to keep the nitrogen in its liquid form. A cooling system was

absolutely necessary, but would have to be small and of little weight. Since the projectiles would only carry a small amount of liquid, they would need many of them. Reagan also asked for jet injectors with the same coolant system, containing large amounts of liquid in them for backup, in case the projectiles weren't enough by themselves. Producing those would be a priority.

Reagan requested Jack Cohen as pilot, Taylor Cohen, Corporal Lucas Kim, and five others for the mission. They would approach in one of Lord Bartholomew's shuttles, and make the airdrop right over the seed mass.

"This is Gamuel. Can anyone hear me, Bethel? This is Gamuel. Please respond, Bethel."

Connor grabbed the handheld. "This is Bethel acknowledging Gamuel."

"Bethel, we're sending in a team to kill the creature, once and for all," said the voice.

"You are aware of what this creature is capable of?" asked Connor.

"Yes, the team has been briefed, and is on its way in. Hang tight."

"Copy," said Connor. He hoped the team knew what they were doing. Their forces on the ground had only been able to slow the creature down, airstrikes had enraged it, and it had still been able to take over half the planet over the last few weeks.

"It's now or never," Taylor yelled over her shoulder. She jumped. The team followed suit, knowing that soon it would be over. One way or another.

As his parachute floated downwards, Reagan prepared to take a direct shot. As long as he didn't touch the creature, it couldn't sense where he was. Or could it?

Reagan watched as it snatched a low-flying bird out of the sky and brought it to its jaws. It was then that he realized his team was in serious trouble.

"It just snatched a bird. It must be sensing the changes in the air currents," said Reagan to his team through his com. "Be careful, those central tentacles have a long reach, and they look to be guarding the seed mass." The tentacles were stretched out thirty feet from the seed mass, then curved upwards to the same height.

Taylor took the first shot, and the dart penetrated the thick transparent skin. There was a howl of pain, and suddenly all the curved tentacles snapped over the seed mass, protecting it.

Reagan groaned. There was no way to take a shot now, and Taylor's dart contained only a fraction of the amount of liquid nitrogen they needed to pump inside the creature.

"Steer to high positions, rocks, anywhere you can land that gives minimum vibration." The team followed Reagan's orders. They steered towards solid rock if they could, since they didn't know how many tentacles were underground that could sense them. The rock would slow the search from down below, if the tentacles couldn't crack through it.

One of the soldiers landed on a small rock surface and unhooked, but that was enough to alert the creature. It snapped out one of its tentacles from its seed mass and grabbed the soldier's leg, pulling it towards its jaws. At that moment, two darts were able to make it through the unprotected part of the seed mass. The creature dropped the soldier and snapped its tentacle back into a protective position.

Reagan could see a tentacle snaking back to the seed mass from further away. It was going to go after the soldier. The soldier saw it coming, and ran towards a tree and started climbing. The tentacle was stripping off branches as it made its way up the tree. Then suddenly there was a *crack!* and the tree started falling. The soldier jumped and rolled away, laying still on the soft ground.

The tentacle continued to feel up and down the trunk of the tree, and snapped it. Then it dragged it to its jaws, where it secreted the white liquid. It took a piece of the tree into its trap, and when it wouldn't dissolve, it shook itself, trying to get it out.

"Confuse it. Throw rocks, branches, metal, anything it won't eat onto the soft ground," said Reagan, as he landed on a rocky section. "If you have grenades, even better. Take out the traps if you can." More tentacles were slithering in from further away now. Those who had already landed were throwing objects in different directions.

The creature was like an infant, trying new items in its mouth. It was learning, too. After realizing that rock wasn't digestible, it felt rock with the cilia on its vines, and ignored it. The same with wood.

One of the tentacles picked up a grenade, and put it into its jaws, it exploded, sending a shower of organic matter all over the area. Some of the liquid hit Lucas' arm, and he quickly ripped off his shirt as the liquid ate through it. The creature was screaming now, in a frenzy. Tentacles were feeling all around on the ground, and it grabbed three of Reagan's team with the tentacles it had been covering the seed mass with.

The creature was pulling Taylor in, when Reagan made a bold move. He leaped onto the vines that were currently occupied, and ran up to the seed mass. He pulled out two large jet injectors, and used them on the seed mass. The creature wouldn't feel any pain, so the tentacles wouldn't snap back. He used all of his jet injectors and the gallons of liquid in his pack, and hoped they penetrated the thick, but porous skin in time to save his team.

Reagan tried shooting the seed mass with bullets, but they just bounced off the outer layer and enraged the creature even more.

Taylor was putting up a fight, slicing through a tentacle with her knife. Another vine grabbed her. The vines were coming in quickly now from further away. They weren't about to let their prey get away.

Reagan ran over to Taylor and started slicing through tentacles, trying not to get caught in the process. His other teammates were struggling as well, some helping each other, but if he could just get her free... The vines were pulling her closer, and she was fully wrapped up now and tightly. Taylor screamed, and Reagan was concerned she was being crushed.

He worked feverishly as he cut. His foot had been caught by a large vine, so he wasn't going anywhere.

"It's okay, Taylor! Hang in there!" he shouted as he cut. Until something white dripped on his knife. The next cut he made, the knife cracked.

Reagan didn't care. He tried to saw through the vine attached to the trap, with what was left of the knife, and it pulled back for a second before it approached him again. He was about to try destroying the trap, regardless of its liquid, when he noticed it was changing color.

He looked around him and saw that the traps were turning black. Although his team was still wrapped up securely, the vines were no longer reeling them in.

Reagan started working on the vines around Taylor's chest. He could see that she was barely breathing.

Suddenly, he heard something liquifying. He quickly looked towards the large jaws, but they were black, just drooping there. It was something else that was making the noise. As he was about to cut another vine from around Taylor, it became mush. The tentacles were turning into a mushy, gooey liquid.

Reagan checked Taylor's heart rate and breathing, then pulled Taylor out of the liquifying tentacles. She was okay, but still unconscious.

"Reagan!" Lucas called. "I'm okay! I'm going to check on the others!" Reagan heard a splooshing sound as Lucas stood up.

By that time, the last few members of the team had moved in. One of them examined Taylor and determined she had cracked ribs.

Taylor blinked her eyes, and saw Reagan and the team medic looking down at her. She tried to sit up but the pain in her chest was too great. The world started spinning.

"Whoa, sport, you don't need to be getting up so quickly," the medic smiled down at her.

Reagan stood up, and looked towards the seed mass. The outer skin had turned opaque and black, and looked brittle. Reagan heard it crackle, as gallons of light green liquid clouded with black poured out. Finally, some type of grey organic matter half as big as he was spilled out intact.

DISRUPTION

CHAPTER SEVENTEEN

Chief Elder N'kaam Dastoyl of the Vitaari

Steve Dixon was cleared to land his shuttle in Belhandalar, on Aleph. He wasn't sure if he was the right person for this mission and had said so when he was asked. But Secretary Cohen had personally recommended him for the job.

He docked, wearing a hardhat, and walked off with a toolbox. Underneath his tools, in a hidden compartment was what he really needed for the job, a miniature disruptor. He had personally developed the technology, being somewhat of a whiz, and it would scramble all signals within a fifty square mile radius.

He was surprised that he wasn't searched or scanned. The reason became clear as he made his way through the city by zoomcar.

Thousands of workmen were all over the city, and in the outer circle he could see several buildings near completion, with others well underway. No wonder he'd been told to walk in as a normal workman.

He had the zoomcar stop on the ground at a partly finished building in the outer circle, then walked outside the city to the

power plant. He walked through the front door, signed in, and was given a visitor pass on a lanyard to wear.

He made his way to the break room, and saw that he was the only one there. He took the disruptor out of his toolbox. He opened a lower cabinet door and the drawer above it, and stuck the device on the back of the drawer, pressing the activation button at the same time. It should give them twenty-four hours before it dissolved, and a two hour delay gave him time to finish his job and get off the planet.

He had closed the drawer when one of the staff walked in. Steve grabbed a paper towel roll out of the lower cabinet, and walked by him. "Washroom," he said, holding up the paper towel roll. He walked down the hallway, and put the roll in the men's washroom. Perspiration had built up and was dripping down the back of his neck. He wiped his neck with some paper.

He waited in a stall for five minutes, gathering his nerve. He had planted the device at the power plant in case it was somehow detected. It would be assumed that the power plant itself was causing the disruption.

He walked down the hall to the power control room. Once there, he glanced at his watch. It was time to create a bit of confusion, and spread some rumors. He flipped the switch and the power went out -- all over the city.

He heard feet running and saw the bobbing of flashlights. "What did you do?" one of the men asked.

"I think I flipped the wrong switch," said Steve, who then flipped it back on. "I need to turn it off for the section where the Redstar building is being built. It's one of the closest buildings to the plant," he said. "They're about to start wiring for the shield generator."

One of the men checked the map. "Section 7. Flip the third switch from the left," he said.

"Thanks man," said Steve, nodding at him. He flipped the switch, then headed back to reception to turn in his lanyard and sign out. He walked back into the city, and at the same building flagged down a zoomcar.

When he returned to the docking bay, he was stopped by security for a random check. The perspiration was rolling down his neck again. "What was your purpose for coming here today?" the dark-skinned guard asked, as if rehearsed. A second guard was searching his toolbox, then searched him.

"I had to drop off some plans for the shield generator in Section 7. Headed off now, because my wife is pregnant and having a rough day," he improvised. Steve felt like he was sweating profusely by now. He was sure they were going to search his ship. He wondered if he was about to have a panic attack.

The guards nodded to each other, and took him aside. Steve was sure he had been discovered.

"Just some advice, on days like this, call in sick and have someone else bring the darn plans in. Otherwise there will be hell to pay when you get home," one of the guards said. "Hurry up and get home to the missus."

Steve entered the shuttle, settled in, and took off. Now for the next part of his mission.

The military Communications Officer on the ground on Aleph was having a difficult afternoon. Hearing back from the runner he sent to the power plant, it sounded like the issue was due to a shield generator or some related issue. If that was the case, then there was nothing to do but to sit tight and wait until the problem was fixed.

In the meantime, he would have a runner sent to Director Finley in case he needed anything.

It had been over a week since the start of construction on Director Finley's project, building another ring around the city as a business and residential district. Progress was going well, and he was pleased.

However, he had lost contact with his fleet above, his military on the ground, with everyone in fact. He figured it had something to do with the power disruption earlier. It was a typical event over the last week while the construction proceeded. Oh well, he had plenty of reports to complete on his office computer. He would settle into a quiet afternoon, uninterrupted. It might not be that bad.

An unidentified shuttle was flying from Aleph to Azram, a common enough sight. However, before entering the atmosphere, the ship turned around and retraced its path.

When he was close enough to the shipyard, Steve sent out the magnetic bombs, as he passed over each ship docked in the building area. He had set them to blow in two hours from now.

He continued on his trajectory back into Sector 6.

Two hours later, Kalisanna was running down the hallway while the red alert alarm was going off. She had no idea why the ships in the shipyard had just exploded. There were no other ships in sight. She followed evacuation protocol, and packed into a shuttle, then launched into space with some of her colleagues.

Suddenly, there was firing, and she saw the whole shipyard explode. Looking through the cold glass, she could see there was a major firefight going on, further out. Closer to home, she watched as giant carriers passed over their evac shuttles.

Kalisanna held her breath until they passed. The carrier ships had ignored them.

The Corporate Alliance's fleet had moved closer to the shipyard, thinking they were under attack. That's when ships suddenly converged on them from behind and on the left flank. The fleet had been boxed in, thinking they were being attacked from three sides, with the fourth side being the sun.

They called for reinforcements, but were only able to reach the military on Azram, those overseeing the mining operation. General Channing told them to hold tight, and called in the spacejets that were waiting above Azram.

Why can't we reach the fleet on Aleph? General Eiden, the general under attack, was wondering.

Numerous carriers were attacking them from behind, and again while floating over them. They completely destroyed the shipyard. After that, they kept going towards Azram. But the ships on their left flank stayed on them, firing on them while pressuring them to move backwards towards the sun. They were fighting back as well as they could, but it wasn't enough.

Where did all these ships come from? he asked himself. "Identify ships!" he called out. One of his sergeants answered, "Carriers that just passed us are from Vitaari. Those on our left flank are from…" he hesitated. "From Isidore, Elanissia, and the Galactic Investigations Bureau."

Another set of ships was coming up behind them. "Ships behind us from Gamuel," he said.

They had been blindsided.

The Vitaari carriers were in Azram's atmosphere when they released their fleet. General Channing's spacejets still hadn't arrived. He had suspicions they had been intercepted and destroyed.

Fighter ships flew down from the Vitaari carriers, to intercept the heliplanes, and a large amount of very oddly shaped planes were gliding down gradually. They had a very strange flight pattern, General Channing observed.

General Channing and his fleet of heliplanes pulled up to meet the fighter ships head on, and their main ship planted on the rocky plateau below started taking out their fighter ships, one by one. The strange gliding ships were getting closer, and he laughed as he saw a group of dragons fly up to attack them.

But the dragons didn't attack the strange ships. Instead, they joined in with that strange flight pattern, gliding down towards General Channing's fleet. That's when General Channing realized what they were. They were *all* dragons, and headed his way.

He left those doing the flamethrowing at the dromasaurs, and started focusing on the dragons.

"Aim for the wings, less scales there," he ordered through his com. He tried to focus on their wings, but they were masters of evasion. His ammo went stray or bounced off their hard scales.

They were able to wound a few, but they moved to the back of their attack line. General Channing was amazed at how they just fell into formation, the dragons from the ship above and the ones from the planet below. He tried to stay facing them, tilted forward, to keep the rotors in their way. He didn't know if rotors could cut through the scales, but it was worth trying to use them as a defense.

Suddenly, from the right flank, he saw a dragon move from a majestic position, zooming straight at him. He had no time to maneuver his heliplane.

The horns went right through his heliplane, copilot, and partly through him. He could smell the hot, angry breath of the dragon as it yanked itself out of the side of the ship. It prepared to attack another heliplane. General Channing was losing blood, and his plane had been crushed in and torn open on one side.

"Going down!" yelled Channing. "Need medical support!" He landed on the plateau below, where the mining had occurred. He opened the door and stumbled out of the heliplane, holding onto his right side. A medical team rushed up to him right away and put pressure on the wound. One of the team checked his copilot in the heliplane, and was shaking his head to the other team members. They rushed the general into the main ship which had a decent med bay. The civilian workers had already fled to the ship when the attacks started.

More and more heliplanes were going down, as the dragons started flanking them in tandem, crushing the heliplanes from both sides. There were several explosions as heliplanes hit the ground on the rocky plateau. The med team inside the ship nearly lost their balance with all the shaking.

The only way off the planet now was in the main ship, unless the main fleet could evacuate them, and that didn't look like it was about to happen. General Channing wondered where the grounded fleet on Aleph was. He knew he was about to die. If not from his wounds, the dragons would take out the flamethrowers, and the dromasaurs would attack the ship.

The flamethrowers had dealt with almost all the dromasaurs, and once they were finished, they were planning on trying to keep the dragons back. But the dragons weren't willing to wait for that. They picked up the flamethrowers and dropped them, or pushed them forward so they stumbled. Anything to stop the burst of flames.

A couple of the dromasaurs that were left went for the fallen flamethrowers. The remaining three converged on the ship, trying to find a way in. They knew there was food inside. Lots of food. One was on the roof, and the others were slamming their bodies into the ship. The dragons knew the humans would stay occupied.

Hundreds of dragons converged on the other four mining sites and dealt with the military heliplanes. They then started searching the planet for the seed mass of the creature that had occupied their homeworld for the last five hundred years. Today they would put a stop to it and retake Azram.

Unfortunately, even though they had scanned for organic matter like the governor had suggested, they were still unable to locate the seed mass, because of the planitanium. That meant it was either on, inside, or under one of the rocky plateaus of planitanium. Looking for a pattern in the organic scans hadn't helped either, since the creature had been evolving, changing, and growing for hundreds of years. It no longer had a uniform pattern, and was different to the creature on Bethel. Besides, any pattern had been masked by the alloy.

They did a low flyby of each rocky plateau on the planet, but were unable to find the seed mass. That meant it was in a cave or underground. They may need the humans after all.

On the rocky plateau at "Site A", the dragons pried the top of the ship open like a tin can. The cowering and screaming made some of the dragons roll their eyes.

"Quiet!" growled the Chief Elder. A couple of people fainted. Jaws dropped. People were rubbing their eyes as if they were dreaming. A talking dragon?

"Lisssten up. We're looking for *sssomething* on the planet. Who deals with explosssives?" Twenty people partly raised their hands, unsure whether they should admit it. "Dissstribute the explosssives evenly." They shared the explosives between them. "If you help u*sss* with thi*sss*, we'll transport you all off thi*sss* planet to a *sss*afe place." They nodded. Without realizing it, they were about to have the experience of their lives.

Joshua was on the back of a dragon, flying to his fifth rock plateau. They landed, while thirty dragons circled the sky, watching for any sign of trouble.

Joshua found a crevice in which to put the explosive, lit the long fuse, then climbed on the back of the dragon. They soared up, out of the blast range.

The explosion created a tremor below the earth, and they saw four inch vines shoot out of holes, feel around, then recede. Then they were on to the next site.

Joshua was actually enjoying himself, soaring on a dragon, not having to be concerned about drilling or setting up equipment, just setting charges. At least he *had been* enjoying himself.

They landed on another plateau, and Joshua placed the charge as usual. They soared up, and there was an explosion. A second later, tentacles two to three feet in diameter shot up in the air, one grabbing onto his dragon's leg. Joshua was trying desperately to hang on.

The other dragons swooped down, attacking the tentacles. One of the dragons held the tentacle taut, while another rammed its horns through it. They could hear a loud scream mixed with a roaring sound. It let go and Joshua got his seating back. His dragon flew high, out of range.

Another tentacle had entangled a smaller dragon, and it slammed the dragon to the ground before it had a chance to pull away. Tentacles with jaws were being pulled onto the rocky surface, ready to go after the dragon. The other dragons swooped down, trying to untangle it, clawing at the tentacles, and biting off sections. The creature kept screaming and became more frenzied. By this time the smaller dragon was tight in its grip, and being squeezed tighter and tighter. It fell unconscious, blood coming out of its nose and mouth.

The other dragons were fighting for survival, so when a trap made its way to the smaller dragon, none of them were able to get to it. The trap secreted a white fluid, and started absorbing the dragon, taking longer than usual because of its thick skin. The foam turned pinkish red as the dragon disappeared.

The dragons finally got a handle on things, thanks to the largest dragons whose teeth, horns, and claws helped free them. They suspected this was the right place, that the seed mass was here.

One of the Elders was with this group, and spoke into his com to alert the other dragons where to come. Over the next thirty minutes, hundreds of dragons joined them in the sky overhead.

The tentacles finally relaxed and withdrew. Joshua noticed in awe that some of the tentacles had broken right through the planitanium. He knew then that the seed mass was underneath the rock.

"I have an idea," he said to his dragon.

"Mmm?" his dragon answered.

"If I can get close enough, I can drop an explosive down one of the holes where the tentacles broke through," he said.

The dragon chuckled, "You're a brave one, I'll give you that."

The dragons discussed the idea. If they put multiple explosives on the ground and down the holes, they may be able to cause a cave in.

Joshua duct taped a number of charges together that he should easily be able to drop into one of the three foot wide holes. Timing was important for this drop.

The dragon swooped down low, above the hole, and Joshua dropped the active charge into the hole, while they swooped back up. Suddenly, there was a huge boom, a scream, and the crumbling of rock. What they saw made Joshua's jaw drop.

A seething mass, two stories high, with transparent green skin, full of liquid, with something solid inside had been underground. This was the creature that had lived here for five centuries, keeping the Vitaari from returning to their homeland.

The explosives hadn't even damaged the creature. Its hide was that thick.

The next step was going to be rather difficult, since they hadn't anticipated it being as huge as it was. Injecting it with enough liquid nitrogen to kill it. They had prepared a large amount of jet injectors as the governor had suggested, otherwise the tentacles would snap around the seed mass to protect it if it felt pain. They decided to go with a non-stop barrage, even if one of them was caught. If they injected enough into the seed mass and quickly enough, then it would die before it was able to ingest any of them.

Forty dragons took position, ready to bombard the seed mass. The first dragon swooped low and was able to inject half a dose. The second dragon swooped down but was thrown aside by one of the tentacles. The next dragon was able to inject a full dose. They continued bombarding the creature in this way.

Finally, after two dragons had been ingested, and five more were caught, the seed mass liquid started to get cloudy with a black liquid. The outer skin became black and brittle, and the weight of the liquid became too much for the shell to handle. The liquid poured out, and then solid grey matter, larger than a human, spilled out. They had done it. They had freed Azram, and now they could return.

Back at "Site A", the humans had been guarded by five of the dragons, in case more dromasaurs came. They dealt with a few, but the dromas were no match for the dragons. As promised, they had the Vitaari carrier ships move in as low as possible, and the dragons carried the humans on their backs to the ships. The Vitaari joined them after picking up any stranded humans from other plateaus.

ENDINGS

CHAPTER EIGHTEEN

From slavery comes freedom. From death comes life. From war comes peace. We like to think that life is simple, but there are always forces for good and evil behind the scenes.

Lady Isla of Elanissia

The following day Aleph got their communications back. However, neither Director Finley nor the general on the ground were able to reach General Eiden of the fleet by the shipyard or General Channing on Azram. In fact, the ships weren't even on their sensors.

"Maybe they needed to move position?" suggested General Maveral, though he had no idea why they would need to do so. The director didn't know what to think.

It wasn't until Reagan hailed them that they knew what had transpired.

General Eiden had refused to even consider surrendering. In the end the military base and all ships above Aleph had been destroyed, with the exception of escape shuttles and pods, which were picked up by the GIB. As a result the corporations were left with only those military ships that were grounded on Aleph during the battle.

The Vitaari had taken the humans from Azram back to their planet, until communications opened up again with Aleph. K'vaal generously offered the use of his estate and the humans stayed as guests.

Under guard, General Channing received excellent care on Vitaaria, and although the dragon had ruptured his liver, he would live to face trial.

"For the workers on Aleph, they keep 100% of their profits. The corporations need to make their own profit and in an ethical way. The corporations will reimburse those forced out of the inner circle of the city, and there will be no more forced moves." Reagan was reading the terms of surrender to the directors and generals in a video conference.

"All prisoners from the GIB will be freed and transported to a place of their choosing. That includes those who were sent to Alniyat," said Reagan.

"The Corporate Alliance is now dissolved, and a new Guild of Mining Corporations is to take its place."

"All corporations belonging to the new Guild of Mining Corporations have equal voice and voting power."

"Payment schedules to reimburse the mining colonists will continue as I outlined in my original report."

"General Parker Channing will be turned over to the GIB and tried as a war criminal for his acts against humanity, specifically those on Planet Bethel. Any others we find to have been involved in that tragedy will also be tried."

"We will be sending you a list of others to be turned over to the GIB for trial and sentencing."

Reagan laid out all the terms for them, and they had no choice but to accept them. Although the directors of the smaller corporations weren't looking forward to paying the colonists what they were owed, they liked the changes to the balance of power in the new Guild of Mining Corporations.

"As these changes are implemented, you will be continually monitored and audited to make sure you are complying. We will be available to help if you need any assistance with the transition."

The five directors who had been in Lord Bartholomew Sullivan's care met with their colonist associates to see how they had fared. They offered their assistance to those who had been displaced on Aleph, but the colonists on Bethel hadn't survived. There was both relief for those who had made it through the difficult ordeal, and sorrow for those who hadn't.

Director Finley was in his office when they came for him. The door opened quietly. Director Finley glanced up from his desk impatiently.

"I told you to hold all my calls and visitors…" he started, but never finished. Those were the last words he ever uttered.

The weapon was wiped off and placed in his right hand.

The Elanisse Archduke, Nizet, met with Lady Isla at K'vaal Ianov's estate, after the employees had been returned to Aleph. General Channing had been handed over to the GIB to stand trial.

"Lord K'vaal, I understand we are in great debt to you for keeping Lady Islanda and Lady Cianna safe during their stay in Quadrant 3. As Lady Isla and myself are betrothed to be married, I have a gift of great value for you." The Archduke motioned, and three chests full of treasures were brought in as a gift for K'vaal.

Although the value of the treasure was worth more than five times what he paid for Lady Isla and Lady Cia, K'vaal looked terribly unhappy. He was losing his Lady Isla.

"I appreciate your offer, Archduke Nizet. I would prefer you use the funds to recover the third lady that was in their party.

Lady Isla and Lady Cia often talked about Lady Katryn, who we now know is being held on Vodyanyov. You may face great difficulty recovering her."

"K'vaal," Lady Isla spoke softly as she approached K'vaal and held his hands. "Thank you. You are one of the noblest creatures I have known." She reached up and kissed him gently on his face.

Archduke Nizet smiled. "You are truly noble. If there is anything you may need of the Elanisse in the future, please just ask. We owe you a debt." the Archduke bowed to K'vaal.

As Lady Isla and the Archduke parted hand-in-hand, K'vaal stood there, watching, longing. The time he had spent with Lady Isla had been of great value to him. He had changed because of knowing her.

Lady Isla and Archduke Nizet boarded the shuttle, and launched, setting a course to the Archduke's Elanisse ship.

"Why did you allow things to progress as they did?" Archduke Nizet asked Lady Isla, as they travelled.

"I had a string of foretellings," Lady Isla answered softly.

"What did you see in these foretellings?" the Archduke asked.

"Slavery, freedom, death, life, war, peace. The three of us were in the middle of something pivotal, and we needed to allow it to take its course," said Lady Isla.

"Where are you in the progression now?" asked Archduke Nizet.

"All three of us still have roles to play in this quadrant," replied Lady Isla. "There is still something sinister at work behind the scenes. Something that longs to enslave and dominate, not just here, but all across the galaxy."

"It is done, Lord," reported the man clothed in black, posed on one knee. "The director is dead, and I staged it to look like he took his own life."

"Good," said the deep voice that belonged to the darkness. Then the voice said disdainfully, "He failed at his simple task, to pave the way for our return."

"What would you have me do, Lord?" the man in black asked.

"We will proceed with a different plan," the voice said. The voice began laying out the new plan it had devised.

The Vodyanyov had pulled out of discussions with the Kitsuine, whom they despised. They'd spent the last two weeks reinforcing and strengthening their military, and going over strategic plans.

Eventually, they were going to war against the Kitsuine.

The Vodyanyov "palace" looked like a giant lump of clay. It was surrounded by marshland that could suck an attacker below its murky waters, as it had done many times in the past. The drawbridge could be opened remotely, but also had a system with chains and wheels, in case they needed to open or close the bridge manually.

On the main floor, the Vodyanyov royal family and guests were having a feast. Sauteed roachlets, warmed flutterbrie with hoppersauce, and grassaloni pie were all on the menu. The wine was flowing, and so was the conversation.

"I say we attack the Kitsuine sooner, rather than later," croaked a young, round, inexperienced prince, as he gobbled down a stack of panflied patties. He let out a huge belch.

"Don't eat so fast," chided his mother, a large, fat, frog-like creature with lips she had colored jade. "You are always too hasty."

The young prince pouted.

"We have had to change our plans since the GIB has dismantled the Corporate Alliance," croaked his father, a muscular creature, weathered by battles. It was his father, the king, who had finally united the clans under one banner a decade ago. Before that, civil war had been rife on the planet.

The young frog shrugged and served himself a large dish of lice cream.

"There is also talk that the Kitsuine have made allies in this system. If that is the case, attacking them would bring nothing but destruction to our military," his father croaked. "We need allies. Powerful allies. And I've just made a deal that will help bring powerful allies to this quadrant."

The young prince brightened.

"In the meantime, we will be building up our military, preparing our troops, and going over strategic options. We won't be attacking anytime soon," the Vodyanyov king declared.

The young prince sulked and went back to eating. He looked over at the Elanisse girl that his family had purchased on Reimus 5, and sneered at her. She didn't respond so he stuck his tongue out at her.

Lady Katryn had been taken by the Vodyanyov after she, Lady Isla, and Lady Cia were captured and sold on Reimus 5. She knew that Lady Isla had been bought by one of the Vitaari, and Lady Cia was bought locally, but that is all she knew of their fate.

Lady Isla had another foretelling the night before their capture. The three of them were about to part ways, and they must allow it to happen. They each had roles to play in the days to come, and those roles would play a huge part in the deliverance of this quadrant from the shadow.

Katryn had no idea what her role was or what she was to do. So she waited patiently, until she knew she was supposed to act.

Right now she was standing, ready to serve the Royal Family on Vodyanyov, should they call her. It looked like the youngest frog-like prince was making faces at her. She ignored him and looked away.

BEGINNINGS

CHAPTER NINETEEN

Dr. Jesse Bartell, Galactic Investigations Bureau

A week later Taylor was back on Calderra, still feeling bruised, but more upset that she hadn't been able to participate in the takedown of the Corporate Alliance. She and Jesse were walking through a grove where the sunlight danced, and the trees were full of beautiful, deep pink flowers.

"I'm just happy that you're safe. It must have been scary when the vines grabbed you," he said.

"Not really. I was trying to hack them to pieces with my knife," said Taylor. Jesse laughed. They both smiled shyly at each other.

"Well, it's time for the autopsy. Hopefully this won't take too long. I'm sure it will be fascinating, though," he said. "Dinner tonight?" Jesse asked, his bright blue eyes shining at her.

"Sounds like a date." Taylor reached up and gave him a gentle kiss on the lips.

Jesse cradled her face in his hands, gently brushing a stray strand of hair off her cheek, and brought his mouth down to hers for a longer, more intimate kiss. Taylor didn't know which way was up or down; she let the kiss completely envelope her. At the end, she was breathless, and clinging to Jesse.

Taylor had to peel herself off him.

"Okay, have to run now. How about we continue this later, after dinner?" Jesse winked at Taylor as he left to board a shuttle. Taylor nodded, still speechless. She walked inside the base so she could watch the broadcasting of the autopsy.

Both the GIB and the Vitaari Elders thought it was important to investigate the life forms further. The Vitaari took the large grey matter found inside the creature on Azram and the GIB took the smaller one found on Bethel.

It was suggested that the laboratories be in space and not on any inhabitable world. Although the creatures were dead now and these were autopsies, they weren't taking any chances.

The objects were preserved in formalin until the labs were set up and they were ready to do the autopsies. The Vitaari in particular needed to set up a larger lab for their specimen.

Both labs transmitted information and observations to each other before the first autopsy was started.

The GIB moved their lab to the space around Calderra. They were going to do their autopsy first, since they were first set up and ready.

Jesse was the one to do the autopsy, since he was both a physician and biologist. He put on his hazmat suit. Then he entered the autopsy room and started recording.

"So what we have here is the grey matter that fell out of the liquid in the seedmass pod. It is a bit more oblong than a sphere, and resembles a brain. We've never done an autopsy of one of these creatures, so it will be interesting to take a look. We'll be taking note of how it functions and is comparable to the human brain or brains of animals we are familiar with.

"We are assuming that the fluid around the brain was cerebral fluid much like ours, and that the thick skin provided protection like a skull and skin.

"First of all, I'm going to do some scans on the brain, before we do any dissecting.

Jesse scanned the brain, and it showed soft neural tissue wrapped around an oblong object.

"Well, the structure of this brain is very different than anything we've seen before," he said slowly. In fact, I'm starting to wonder..." Jesse switched to a scanner with more depth.

"Ummm," he said. "We've got it all wrong." He looked visibly shaken.

"What we're looking at...it isn't what we thought. What we're looking at is a protective outer covering with neurological connections surrounding...a soft bubble, in which is a partly drained sac.

"Inside the soft bubble...attached to the sac...there is a small living creature."

The scientists had to completely change their suppositions. What they thought was a brain did have neurological connections as they had supposed. Although it lacked direct connectors to the infant, ultimately it must have been connected to the mind of the infant. An infant that was always hungry.

The partly drained sac must be the remaining food source for the baby, now that it was completely detached from the large creature. The Vitaari scanned the grey mass they had in their lab, and the results were the same, except their creature was four times the size of the tiny creature in Calderra's lab.

Calderra and Vitaari pulled together their best scientists to discuss how it was best to proceed. Both infants were scanned, and it was found that they were both fully formed, just different in size. The one in the Vitaari lab had a much larger food sac than the one by Calderra. However, it was going to run out of food much faster, due to its rate of consumption.

The scientists were left with the questions: Should they wait? Should they operate to get the infants out? Or should they attempt to put them in stasis? Also, what type of safety precautions did they need to take? It seemed that choosing to have their labs in space was a good call for this "autopsy".

The scans were broadcast to the scientists' work areas at all times. One day Taylor called Jesse into the biology lab on Calderra. "Jesse look!" Taylor was very excited. "It's sucking its thumb!"

When the infants were scanned in more depth, it was discovered they had similar physiology to humans. They had beating hearts, lungs, and similar organs.

There was much debate over the fate of these two infants, both on Calderra and on Vitaari. Video scans showed them acting similar to humanoid infants. In the end, the scientists felt it would be safer to remove the smaller infant from its bubble first, and study it. That way if these organisms were a physical threat, then they would be dealing with a creature six inches long, instead of a creature two feet long. The small one was as fully developed as its counterpart, so there would be no issues that way.

Jesse was the lead on the procedure, and he was accompanied by a team of physicians and biologists in hazmat suits. Military personnel stood by.

Before they started, Jesse pressed on the neurological tissue covering the bubble, to see if the baby felt anything. In order to get the infant out, they would have to cut through the neurological tissue, and they had all agreed to stop the procedure if the infant showed any distress.

There was no response from the infant after pressing on the tissue. Jesse took a deep breath and picked up a scalpel, watching the scan of the infant closely while he started the procedure.

He inserted the scalpel in the tissue, and glanced up. No signs of distress from the infant. He began cutting through the tissue, careful not to puncture the bubble. Scientists from Vitaari and Calderra held their breath as they watched the procedure and scans simultaneously.

Jesse was able to peel back the thick neurological tissue, and they finally got a look at the tiny infant. The infant scrunched up its eyes, as if there was too much light, and the tissue slapped back over the bubble. Jesse was startled, and one of the other biologists jumped. Jesse started peeling the tissue back again until it was completely off. One of the physicians carefully placed the bubble on a soft towel, away from the neurological tissue, so they could take a look at it.

The baby had two arms, two legs, a tiny tail, and buds on its back. They could see that it had two very large eyes, a tiny nose and small mouth. It was a pinkish-white color.

The physicians had all agreed that the bubble looked similar to an amniotic sac in a womb. It wasn't connected to the little creature in any way, so shouldn't cause any pain if punctured. A basin was placed on the table, and the bubble was placed in it. It was up to Jesse to drain the fluid.

Jesse took the scalpel again and cut through part of the bubble that was furthest from the infant. Liquid started seeping out of the bubble into the basin. He made the incision longer, then placed the scalpel on the table, and started peeling back the bubble to grasp the infant.

He picked up the infant who had started to cry, and placed it in a warm, soft blanket. They sealed and clipped the cord to the feeding sac, and took the feeding sac to be analyzed right away. One of the other physicians used an aspirator to clear the infant's airways, and took it to be weighed. The baby was just over six ounces.

The initial examination took quite some time, as the physicians and biologists documented a lot of information. They kept the warm blanket handy as they measured the infant. They examined it completely and tested responses. They used an infant jet ejector to remove blood painlessly, but were very cautious of the amount, since the baby was so tiny. They did a full examination as they would with any human newborn, taking into account that "norms" would be different.

After a thorough examination, the baby was swaddled, and brought back to Jesse. He held the infant close in the warm blanket, wishing he wasn't wearing a hazmat suit. He was thinking that it was possible this was the only infant of its kind. After a while, Jesse placed it in an incubator.

When the analysis of the feeding sac came back, the report said they should be able to feed it with human formula and it would get the proper nutrition it needed. Batches of human formula were made up and readied. Jesse was there to feed the infant each time it woke up crying.

Jesse was so taken in by this miracle of life. He hadn't realized he'd been in the lab for over twenty-four hours. It was time for him to go back to Calderra. One of the other doctors took over. Jesse went through the decontamination chamber and took a shuttle to the surface. He found his way to the sleeping area, and crawled up onto his cot.

Taylor found him there a couple of hours later, but didn't wake him. She settled in her bunk for the night. She lay there, thinking of everything she'd seen on the video transmission. It was amazing, this tiny new life.

The next morning, Jesse had breakfast with Taylor, then obtained clearance for her to go up to the lab as his assistant. She was nervous, but excited to go.

They put on their hazmat suits, and entered the lab. There were still a few scientists observing and documenting, but not like on the previous day. The physician on duty saw Jesse and was introduced to Taylor.

"I'm guessing that you want to be introduced to the little guy," smiled Doctor Leila Yu. She carefully passed the swaddled infant to Taylor. It turned towards her and started snuggling.

"He likes you," smiled Jesse. Taylor giggled.

"So tiny. It's amazing," she commented.

"You guys came at the perfect time. I'll go get the formula. I'm off now, so enjoy your afternoon." The doctor brought the formula over, then headed to decontamination.

Taylor took the bottle and started to feed the infant.

"Wow, so much like a human baby. You can't tell the difference," said Taylor.

"Well, there are a couple of differences. The tail and the little buds on its back. Plus we're uh, not sure how it reproduces or if it can reproduce," said Jesse.

"Really?" asked Taylor.

"Really," said Jesse.

Taylor was watching how the baby sucked on the bottle. She pulled the bottle a couple millimeters back and the baby's suck became stronger. She laughed. "Hungry little guy. Gosh, Jesse. He's so adorable."

Once the baby was done with the bottle, she put him in a position to burp him, using just one finger on his back to tap with. The baby burped, then started cooing, and opened its eyes slightly, trying to focus, but looking a bit cross eyed. Taylor was fascinated.

They took turns through the day and night, chatting about the baby, watching it sleep, talking to it, stroking its head. When stroking its head towards the back, it looked like its eyes were rolling back at the same time. Both Jesse and Taylor laughed.

The baby was asleep, and the two of them had a few moments to themselves. Jesse held Taylor's gloved hand, and she had her head up against his shoulder. He put his arm around her.

"So I'm wondering about the other infant. Do you know what's going to happen with it?" asked Taylor.

"Not sure yet. Its food supply in the sac is depleting, but now we're aware that formula will meet its nutritional needs, it's likely set the team in Vitaari at ease. So far, taking care of this little one has been easy, apart from the three hour feedings around the clock, of course." Jesse smiled. He still looked ragged from spending twenty-four hours in the lab the day before.

"This little guy fits right in your hand. The other one is going to be big for a newborn," Taylor laughed. "Wow, life's amazing," she commented with a sigh.

They had both nodded off, and before they knew it, it was time to feed the baby again. It was also time for another daily exam, so the doctor did that before the feeding.

"The little guy is doing really well," the doctor commented. "He's up a quarter ounce from yesterday. That might change when he fills his diaper though," he smiled.

Taylor laughed. Then she became serious. "You know, I think for now, we should call it a girl."

"You have a good point," said the physician. "It's difficult to tell what it is, because there are no standard X or Y chromosomes we can identify to verify its gender, and the reproductive organs aren't there."

Taylor nodded.

"Right now it's not an issue, but as the baby grows, it will become an issue, not knowing what gender it is in a social context," commented the doctor. "I'm sure by then we'll have learned more about it and will have more light shone on that aspect."

Jesse squeezed Taylor's shoulder. "I'm sure we'll learn a lot as the little one grows."

"Well, for now I'm going to call her a 'she'," said Taylor. "She really doesn't like those exams does she?" The baby was protesting with her little cries.

"Most infants don't, because they are exposed to the air during the weighing and measuring. They like to be tightly swaddled," said the physician. He handed Taylor the infant when he was done. Taylor took the tiny baby into her arms to start the feeding.

"Hey, I thought it was my turn," Jesse joked.

"You can play with her, keep her awake until it's time for her to sleep again," Taylor stuck her tongue out at him.

"You guys okay to look after the little one for the next while?" asked the physician. "If so, I'll take a break after I tidy up this station."

The scientists on Vitaari had decided to follow Jesse's lead, and strip off the neurological tissue to get to the infant. The first incision was made. The bubble was eventually unwrapped.

They drained the bubble of fluid, just like in the earlier procedure, grasped the baby, sealed and clipped the cord, and examined the infant. So far things had gone smoothly. Apart from the difference in size, the two babies were very similar. They both had very large eyes and similar facial features.

The Vitaari had called over some of the physicians from Gamuel to do the procedure, when they saw the baby had similar physiology to humans. It felt more comfortable handling the second baby, since the first one had been so tiny. The second baby was twenty-four inches, which was the same size as a human infant, but larger than a newborn. Its development was the same, humanoid, with two buds on its back and a tiny tail. Its gender was also indeterminable.

One of the Vitaari physicians commented on the buds and tail. "They are very similar to what you see after one of our infants hatches. The buds on the baby may develop into some type of wings eventually, or they may disappear. The same is possible with the tail. We can track the size of the buds and tail as the infant grows."

One of the Isidorian physicians asked a question, and the same Vitaari physician answered. "Yes, the newer generation of Vitaari rarely develop wings from the buds. The older generation, those born on Azram centuries ago, have wings. Some of those in the newer generation no longer have tails, as the cartilage dissolves after birth, but so far that is rare."

The second baby was also doing well, and was cared for around the clock by physicians in the Antares system. Taylor and Jesse were also able to follow along with its progress, due to the broadcast sent to all medical research personnel.

CHANGES

CHAPTER TWENTY

Life is about embracing change. When the winds of change come we have a choice. We can adapt and bend. We can oppose and possibly break. Or we can ride the winds of change. We choose which winds to stand against -- the cause must be worth breaking for.

Governor Reagan Vasilios, Galactic Investigations Bureau

"So when can we stop wearing these hazmat suits?" Taylor was putting on her hazmat suit in the decontamination chamber.

"Not sure," said Jesse. "I think all the tests have been run for contaminants. The baby's chemical makeup is similar to ours, so there doesn't seem to be issues that way."

They entered the lab in their suits. Taylor asked the attending physician about getting out of the hazmat suit. "I just think the little guy could use some closeness, some human warmth."

"Yes, it's all clear and you are welcome to remove your suit. Most of us will still be wearing ours though as a precaution. After all, this is a new type of life form, one we've never seen before," cautioned the physician.

Jessie and Taylor went back to decontamination, stripped off their suits, and returned. The physician gave them both bracelets to monitor their vital signs, since they were the first to go without suits in the lab.

This time, when they picked up the crying infant, the crying stopped immediately. "She senses my skin," said Taylor excitedly. She held the baby close against the skin on her arm, and fed it a bottle of formula.

When the baby was done, Taylor burped her. She started cooing, and opened her eyes partway. Jesse put his pinky finger where she could easily grasp it. She grasped his finger, and had quite the tug for such a tiny thing.

"Wow, she's strong!" commented Jesse. They both stroked the baby's skin gently, and she responded well to the touch, trying to rub up against their skin as they stroked her. Jesse vaguely noticed that the infant's skin had darkened to a pinkish-beige color.

"Look at her beautiful blue eyes," said Taylor as she stroked the baby's cheek. The baby started to turn its head, rooting. Taylor allowed her to suck on her finger. "Does she have a name yet?" she asked.

"Just her catalogued name, 0-1," replied the doctor.

"I think we should name her, Jesse," said Taylor.

"I think that's a great idea," he responded. "What did you have in mind for a name?"

"Well, I haven't had time to think of one yet," she laughed. "I just came up with the idea."

"Hmm." Jesse was thinking. "Well, we could go with a traditional name, or come up with our own."

"What about Aria?" asked Taylor. "Like a piece of music."

"That's a beautiful name," said Jesse, looking at the little one. "It suits her. Aria it is."

"Hello, little Aria. Do you like your new name?" Taylor asked. The baby turned to the sound of her voice, looking up at Taylor with partly unveiled blue eyes. "She has your eyes, Jesse," Taylor laughed.

The two of them stayed on baby duty until they were exhausted again. It was a happy type of exhausted. They went through decontamination, then headed back to Calderra.

The older generation of Vitaari were moving back to Azram. It would take some time for their homeland to be restored, but they were hopeful. They brought plants, clippings, bulbs, and seeds from the outskirts of the Vitaari cities, the foliage they themselves had maintained.

The Vitaari scientists were mapping out the ecosystem, based on the original ecosystem. They had a lot to work on, to reestablish balanced life on Azram.

Reagan was pleased the Vitaari Elders had reclaimed Azram as their homeland. He met with the Elders after the battle, congratulated them, and offered future aid. Keeping Azram safe from intruders was in everyone's best interests, since the planitanium could pose a threat to them all.

"Thank you, Governor Vasilios. And if we can ever assist, please call on us," offered the Chief Elder.

Connor and Mia had finally been able to move back to their home city on Bethel. The military helped the civilians settle into temporary housing. Apartment buildings cleared by structural engineers were used as emergency civilian housing. Flashlights were handed out. Water was available on the main floor, and latrines and garbage disposal were set up outside.

Connor was helping to set up communication systems. He had a full team working for him on site. There were also several teams offsite who could check equipment around the city. The teams were able to assess damage, and sent in reports of what was needed. They were aiming to get the civilian emergency system up first.

The military and civilians were repairing issues with the water, solar power, and sanitation. Some homes, although in excellent shape, were uninhabitable since they lacked those three things.

Assistance from the untouched hemisphere and from offworld was abundant. They brought materials, equipment, and volunteers to help them rebuild. One group focused on making hospitals fully functional, and another focused on emergency buildings. Some of the Vitaari, Kitsuine, and colonists from Gamuel assisted with rebuilding.

It would take time, but the inhabitants of Bethel would get back on their feet.

Although the final numbers weren't in, it was estimated that less than a tenth of the population of the western hemisphere had survived.

Among the volunteers were medical personnel and trauma counselors. Everyone who had survived had lost people they had known. Family, friends, neighbors, and coworkers. The visiting Elanisse helped with the trauma, since they could calm anxiety and soothe emotional wounds.

Mia started seeing the Elanisse for anxiety, and the trauma that was so rapid it hadn't registered until now. Returning home brought remembrance of neighbors and acquaintances she had lost. She felt guilty that she had survived when so many others had died.

Being able to grieve was important, but the Elanisse made it easier to cope with day-to-day tasks while Mia was grieving. Instead of being overwhelmed by it, she was able to process the losses piece by piece.

A good portion of GIB ships stayed in the Antares system to help the colonists rebuild. Reagan and Cia decided to stay with the GIB and Elianisse fleet instead of returning to Calderra immediately. They knew that the need was highest on Bethel, so assisted there.

Since they were both on the council, they knew there was a Vitaari lab close by in space, and why it was there. Reagan still shook his head whenever he thought of the infant. He was still in disbelief.

"I think we should go and see it," insisted Cia. "It would help you to reconcile things."

"Maybe," shrugged Reagan. "I don't think we could get clearance though." In all honesty, Reagan was feeling reluctant, after his encounters with the creatures in their other forms.

The following day, Cia met with Reagan in the morning. She was all smiles.

"You look radiant today, Cia." Reagan held her hands, and kissed her on the cheek.

"Guess what I did?" she asked. Without waiting for him to guess, she blurted out, "I was able to get clearance for us. We can go see it. Here's your tag." Reagan was too surprised to say anything.

They boarded a shuttle and flew to the lab. After decontaminating and putting on their hazmat suits, they walked into the lab to see the infant. It was sleeping in an incubator.

"For some reason I thought it would look scarier, and that it would want to attack me as soon as I walked in," commented Reagan wryly.

"He's really cute. He looks just like a human baby," Cia observed. The baby woke up and started crying. "He sounds like a human baby, too."

"You guys are just in time for feeding," the attending doctor smiled. "Would you like to feed him?" he asked.

"Oh, I don't think…" started Reagan.

"Absolutely," said Cia.

"I don't think it's safe, Cia," Reagan said quietly. There, he had finally told her his thoughts.

"Reagan, it's just a baby. It's not going to *eat* you."

"Well last time I saw it, it would have," muttered Reagan under his breath.

Cia accepted the baby in her arms, and it settled down as soon as she sat down and started to feed it the bottle.

Reagan was attentive the entire time. He didn't want to take any chances. He felt really uncomfortable letting Cia feed it. What if it attacked her?

"Here, let me feed it, Cia," said Reagan.

"Sure," she said slowly. She gave Reagan a strange look, and handed him the baby.

Reagan started feeding the baby. His adrenaline was flowing. Once in a while the baby peeked up at him with its light blue eyes, and then its eyelids slowly closed.

After the feeding, the baby started squirming. "Here, you have to burp it, Reagan." Cia held her hands out to accept the baby.

"It's okay, I'll do it," said Reagan. He still didn't trust it.

He sat the baby in his lap, and gently patted its back. After thirty seconds, the baby spit out a strange, white liquid all over Reagan's arm. Reagan panicked.

"I knew it! It's going to burn!" He couldn't remember what happened next, just that he was by the sink, ripping off his glove.

The physician rushed over to Reagan. "What happened?" he asked. Reagan held up his glove so the physician could see the urgency. Reagan had drenched his arm in the sink, hoping to stop the chemical from liquefying his flesh.

The physician visually examined both Reagan's arm and the glove.

"You stripped your glove off because the baby spit up on you? That's normal during burping, you know." The physician was trying not to laugh.

Reagan looked at the glove. There was no hole burnt through it, just some white formula the baby had spit up. His arm was absolutely fine. He started turning red.

"Well, you've already been exposed, so it doesn't matter now. People are caring for the other infant without hazmat suits on anyway. It seems safe enough," said the doctor.

Reagan glanced over at Cia. Her eyes were wide, and she had that same strange look on her face. She held the baby on her lap. He couldn't remember her taking it. Reagan walked back over to Cia.

"Uh, sorry about that," said Reagan, sheepishly.

"It's okay." Cia was trying not to laugh.

"I'll take him." Reagan held out his hands for the baby again. Cia placed the infant in his arms. The baby started cooing at Reagan.

Suddenly Cia exclaimed, "Reagan! Look at his hair!" The tiny swirl of hair on the baby's head was going from blonde to brown. Reagan didn't know what to think.

Cia took off her glove and touched the infant's skin.

"What are you doing, Cia?"

"Just wait." They waited for a minute. "Reagan, look at his eyes."

Reagan could see they had changed to a deep purple, the same color as Cia's.

Delaney Walker finally had the opportunity to meet with Reagan. Janine Cohen and her husband were hosting a dinner party on Gamuel and had invited both of them.

"Wow, I'm honored to finally meet you, Governor." Delaney and Reagan shook hands. "After seeing your courage, the way you stood up for the colonists, and the way you carried yourself on Planet Z, I just had to meet you."

"Well actually, on Azram all I was doing was running for my life." The group laughed.

When dinner was ready, the group sat down at the table. They shared stories of their experiences that month. Reagan shared the story of the takedown of the creature on Bethel, and Delaney talked about the mining operation and Aurora Corporation's mixed up priorities. Cia told how she copied the records of slavery on Reimus 5, and Jack recalled the battle at the outpost.

Janine was talking about the prisoner escape. "It was Lucas who got us out of that situation. He travelled 450 sectars *on foot* to get to the next settlement."

Lucas felt a bit awkward. "Well, if it wasn't for Nolan and his maps, I wouldn't have been able to get out of the camp or find the city."

"And if it wasn't for Janine encouraging us to make a plan and fight back...let's just say it was a group effort." Nolan winked.

"I think everyone here played an important part to ensure our freedom," declared Janine.

Nolan stood up and raised his glass. "To freedom." He toasted.

"To freedom." Everyone raised their glasses.

A spheric ship, the size of four carriers, had approached from the outerworld and was now situated between the Iklil and Antares systems. It hadn't crossed into GIB territory, and instead lingered outside Quadrant 3, Sector 9. No need to trigger alarms that pointed to their location. Deception was part of their strategy.

From the starlight, it could be seen that the outer hull was composed of reddish-brown organic matter, scaly and nearly indestructible, and that a tail followed behind it. The ship made an odd grunting sound.

Four more tadpole-shaped ships were closing in, propelling themselves slowly by swishing their tails back and forth. The "tadpoles" each had a mouth covered with a membrane, behind which were many rows of razor sharp teeth. This membrane controlled what passed through, and vibrated when the creature vocalized sounds. Instead of eyes, each creature had one large, tight circular membrane on the front of its head.

Inside the skull, on the "bridge" was a burgundy winged creature, humanoid, but with thick, twisted horns and claws. Its wings and thin, pointed tail were scaly, and it had eye sockets but no eyes.

It pulled its arms out of two organic holes that allowed it to sync with the large tadpole creature, slopping gooey organic matter all over. The organic goo was absorbed, sucked into the floor.

The creature inside the "tadpole" and the tadpole creature itself had a symbiotic relationship. They coexisted and benefited from each other's existence. Although neither had eyes, when the two were linked, they could "see" what was ahead, being instinctively drawn in the direction of what they desired. Malevolence.

When they had a unified neural connection, the immense neural network of the larger creature could amplify and project sensory data. Right now their goal was to deliver a message to the inhabitants of Alniyat.

The inside of the circular membrane started to glow. Six long ivory-colored tendrils snaked down from the ceiling, and suddenly jabbed themselves in vertical rows into the sides of the humanoid creature's neck. The humanoid creature cringed in pain.

The circular membrane shone brightly. The winged humanoid creature spoke, and a low-pitched voice reverberated through the skull of the large creature. Its image and voice was being projected halfway across Quadrant 3, and would be seen and heard in the system of Alniyat.

After the message was delivered, the humanoid creature's face contorted into a wicked grin. It could hear the large creature's low rumbling, as if it was chuckling to itself.

A vision had appeared in the sky to all those living in the Alniyat solar system.

Alarms were going off, and the planets' militaries were on the move. Some inhabitants were headed to underground shelters or strongholds.

Many others were headed to sacred ground, led by spiritual and religious leaders. They believed their faith would save them. They prayed to their ancestors for protection, or chanted mantras to invoke the gods to come down from heaven.

Some believed that military might would not protect them, but the angels from above could. They couldn't understand how so many others put their faith in weapons and things created by their own hands. How could they ignore the spiritual significance of the situation?

After all, the one who spoke in the vision was a demon.

The council was reporting on how the rebuilding was going on the planets in the Antares system. The meeting was about to be adjourned when there was a knock on the door.

"Come!" called Deputy Governor Tarek Shaw. It was one of the com officers. "What is it?"

"A distress call has come in from Sector 7," said com Officer Muier.

"What's happened?" asked Shaw

"The system of Alniyat is about to be invaded," the officer said. The council members were all suddenly on their feet.

"By whom?" asked Reagan, holding his breath.

Officer Muier answered, "They call themselves...the Hashain."

GLOSSARY

ABIGAIL HAWKING: Fighter pilot. Blue Squadron Leader.

AEAQUALIS (AY-KWAH-LIS): City on colonist planet Gamuel, in the Antares system. Council run. The current council leader is Lady Cadrius.

ALEPH (A-LEF): One of the colonists' planets in the Antares system.

ALNIYAT (AL-NIE-AT): Star in Quadrant 3, next to Antares, named after the mythological "Twin Goddesses", Alena (AL-EEN-A) and Naya (NIE-A).

ANTARES (AN-TAHR-EES): Large red supergiant with seven planets in orbit. Star in Quadrant 3 of the Scorpius constellation.

ARCHDUKE NIZET (NI-ZET): One of the Elanisse.

ARIA (AH-REE-A): A mysterious being.

ASHER CORPORATION: One of three large mining corporations that started the Corporate Alliance.

AURORA CORPORATION: One of three large mining corporations that started the Corporate Alliance. Led by Director Rowan Finley.

AZRAM (AZ-RAM): Z-Class planet, uninhabitable by life, in the Antares system. Also known as Planet Z.

BARYCENTRIC CELESTIAL REFERENCE SYSTEM: Navigation system used in space, based on the center of the Milky Way galaxy.

BELHANDELAR (BEL-HAN-DE-LAR): Beautiful city on the planet Aleph in the Antares system, known for its "rainbow projections".

BETHEL (BETH-EL): One of the colonists' planets in the Antares system.

BOTS: Robots used to help with assigned tasks.

BRADY NASH: Tech at the GIB. However, is in the pay of the Aurora Corporation as a spy.

CALDERRA (CAL-DER-RA): Moon that orbits Neo Terrene, in the Paikahale star system in Quadrant 3.

CAMERON: Alpha Team member during the alloy recovery by the Corporation Alliance.

CAVA (CA-VA): A popular drink, usually enjoyed hot, and by some with milk and sugar.

CAVA BEANS: Aromatic beans that can be ground to flavor water.

CAVA JAVA CORPORATION: A lesser known corporation that sells cava beans to traders.

CAVIENA (CA-VEE-EN-A) CORPORATION: Popular corporation that sells cava beans to traders.

CHIEF ELDER N'KAAM DASTOYL (NI-KAHM DA-STOYL): The highest Elder of the Vitaari. Known to be over nine hundred years old, possibly older.

CLAY: In a specialized military tactical unit for the corporations.

COLONEL ALAN CAMPBELL: Captain of a large carrier that hosts the Red and Green Squadrons.

COLONEL KEVIN STRAIT: Working in the Bethel military relief project.

COLONISTS' PLANETS: Aleph, Bethel, and Gamuel in the Antares star system. There are others in the Alniyat system.

CONNOR: Bethel resident and communications expert. Married to Mia.

CORPORAL JANERRA (JAN-ER-RA): Bridge officer for the Corporate Alliance.

CORPORAL LENNOX (LEN-IX): Bridge officer for the GIB.

CORPORAL LUCAS KIM: GIB prisoner with elite survival skills.

CORPORAL SAYAN (SIE-AN): Military officer of Aeaqualis.

CORPORAL VINAY (VI-NAY): Military officer of Aeaqualis.

CORPORATE ALLIANCE: Dictatorship comprised of fourteen of the corporations with mining operations, backed by the three militaries of the Aurora, Leo, and Asher Corporations.

CORUSCO (COR-OOS-CO): Province on the colonist planet, Gamuel in the Antares system.

CROCODYLIA (CROC-O-DILL-EE-A): Reptile predator that spends its time in and out of the water.

DAVIS COOPER: Leader of Epsilon Team during the alloy retrieval by the Corporate Alliance.

DECOPIDIA (DE-CO-PEA-DEE-A): Exquisite dish served on Vitaaria, also known as lobster.

DELANEY WALKER: Leader of Alpha Team during the alloy retrieval by the Corporate Alliance.

DEPUTY GOVERNOR TAREK (TA-REEK) SHAW: Temporary governor of the Galactic Investigations Bureau in Quadrant 3, during the one month absence between transfers. Served with Reagan Vasilios' father.

DIRECTOR ROWAN (ROW-EN) FINLEY: Director of the Aurora Corporation.

DR. ELENA HARLOWE (E-LEE-NA HAR-LOE): Botanist and BioTech department head on Aurora's military base.

DR. JESSE (JE-SEE) BARTELL: Physician and biologist for the Galactic Investigations Bureau.

DR. LEILA YU (LAI-LA YOO): Physician in a space lab.

DRAGON: Flying reptile thought to be a mythological creature.

DROMASAUR (DRO-MA-SORE): Carnivorous dinosaur that grabs its prey with its front claws, keeping it at arm's reach, balances on a back leg, then slashes with its other hind leg's middle sickle claw.

DRU (DREW): In a specialized military tactical unit for the corporations.

DSCHUBBA (DE-SHUB-BA): Star system in Quadrant 4 of the Scorpius constellation.

ELANISSE (EL-A-NEESE): Race of beautiful and powerful beings that have elven characteristics. Their full capabilities are yet to be revealed.

ELANISSIA (EL-A-NEESE-EE-A): Planet in the Shaula star system in Quadrant 1.

ELDER E'OGHAN (O-WEN): Elder of the Vitaari. Known to be over six hundred years old.

ELDERS: Older generation of Vitaari who watch from the shadows.

ELIZANA (EL-I-ZA-NA) CORPORATION: Corporation on Aleph that treats its colonists fairly.

ELLIS: Wealthy slave acquirer on Reimus 5.

ESTEVAN (E-STEE-VAN) DIXON: Commonly known as Steve. Works in the Tech Department for the Galactic Investigations Bureau. Makes an interesting discovery.

EZIO (E-ZEE-O) PRIME: Planet of the Paikahale solar system.

FORETELLING: Mysterious gifting of the Elanisse. Lady Isla is the most proficient "Reader" of the threads of the future and an "Interrupter of Fate".

GALACTIC INVESTIGATIONS BUREAU: Also known as the GIB, a government agency extending from Shaula that helps regulate fair practices in the four Scorpius Quadrants.

GAMUEL (GAM-YOO-EL): One of the colonists' planets in the Antares system.

GENERAL EIDEN (AY-DEN): General of the Asher Corporation's military.

GENERAL MAVERAL (MAV-ER-EL): General of the Leo Corporation's military.

GENERAL MCKENNA: General of the Galactic Investigations Bureau military. Served with Reagan Vasilios' father.

GENERAL MILEN (MILL-EN): General of Aeaqualis' military.

GENERAL PARKER CHANNING: Military General of the Fleet, works closely with Director Rowan Finley in the Corporate Alliance, with the Aurora Corporation's interests in mind.

GIB: *See* Galactic Investigations Bureau.

GOVERNOR REAGAN VASILIOS (RAY-GUN VA-SILL-EE-OSE): Sent from Isidore to keep the peace in Quadrant 3. Future Protector of the Throne of Isidore.

HASHAIN (HA-SHAYN): A mysterious race that is somehow connected to the Vitaari's history.

INTERNAL AFFAIRS: Also known as IA, investigates members of the GIB when there is wrongdoing.

ISIDORE (IS-I-DORE): Planet with powerful connections in the Shaula solar system in Quadrant 1, led by the House of Vasilios.

JACK COHEN: Son of Secretary Jaylen and Janine Cohen. Yellow Squadron leader.

JANINE COHEN: Wife of the Secretary of Bureau Investigations, Jaylen Cohen (GIB). A woman with strength of will and resilience.

JORATI (JOR-A-TEE) CORPORATION: Corporation on Aleph that treats its colonists fairly.

JOSHUA: Explosives expert originally working for the corporations to extract ore.

K'VAAL IANOV (KA-VAWL IE-AN-AWV): One of the Vitaari, a lizard-like creature. Has fallen in love with one of the Elanisse.

KALISANNA (KAL-I-ZAN-A): Shipbuilder for the Corporate Alliance. Metallurgical expert.

KEEPER: Guide and guard responsible for ensuring the safety, order, and organization of the tower of records on Reimus 5.

KEIRA PACRILL (KEE-RA PA-KRILL): Famous creator of documentaries.

KITSUANA (KIT-SOO-AN-A): Planet where the Kitsuine live.

KITSUINE (KIT-SOO-EEN): Formal race of fox-like creatures, who oil their golden-red fur with pleasantly scented oils.

KRISTINA: GIB mediator working with the Kitsuine and Vodyanyov.

KYLER (KIE-LER): Friend of Dr. Jesse Bartell.

LADY CADRIUS (CAD-REE-US): Leader of the council of Aeaqualis on Gamuel.

LADY CIANNA (SEE-AN-A): Sister of Lady Isla, and one of the Elanisse. Also known as Lady Cia (SEE-A).

LADY ISLANDA (IE-LAND-A): Sister of Lady Cia, and one of the Elanisse. Also known as Lady Isla (IE-LA). Gifted with the rare talent of Foretelling, she is also known as the "Interrupter of Fate".

LADY KATRYN (KAE-TRIN): Close relative of Lady Isla and Lady Cia. Her whereabouts are unknown.

LADY KIARA (KEE-ARR-A): Lady from Corusco on Gamuel.

LADY LISKA (LIS-KA): Leader of the Kitsuine, and head of the Kitsuine Dynasty.

LADY MADDY (MA-DEE): Lady from Terelina on Gamuel.

LAETUS (LAY-A-TUS): Capital city in the province of Corusco, on Gamuel.

LEO CORPORATION: One of three large mining corporations that started the Corporate Alliance.

LIAM (LEE-AM): Alpha Team member during the alloy recovery by the Corporate Alliance.

LINCOLN: Linking android on Reagan Vasilios' ship.

LORD BARTHOLOMEW SULLIVAN: Owner of the Nicos Trading Company that trades between the four Scorpius Quadrants. A man of unknown age.

LORD BRENDAN: Lord from Obsanitale on Gamuel.

LORD EHZEN (AY-ZEN): Chair of the Council of World Leaders on Gamuel.

LORD MYKEL VASILIOS (MIH-KEL VA-SIL-EE-OSE): Current Protector of the Isidorian Throne, and Reagan's father. Previous governor of Quadrant 4.

MAGISTRATE KIAN (KEE-AN) ANDERSON: Magistrate of the Galactic Investigations Bureau military. Served with Reagan Vasilios' father.

MARIAN (MARE-EE-AN): Friend of Janine Cohen's.

MARTY: Alpha Team member during the alloy recovery by the Corporate Alliance.

MASON GIBBS: Slave acquirer who has welcomed mass trade of slaves.

MEGACERATOPS (ME-GA-SER-A-TOPS): Nine feet tall hoofed creatures, used by the Aeaqualis as cavalry.

MERIT CORPORATION: Corporation with good intentions. Contracts with Aeaqualis.

MESARCHYDS (ME-ZAR-KIDS): Six feet tall canine creatures, used by the Aeaqualis as cavalry.

MIA (MEE-A): Bethel resident and primary school teacher. Married to Connor.

MINERS' GUILD: Made up of colonists who have contracts with the mining corporations.

NEO TERRENE (NEE-O TER-REEN): Planet in the Paikahale solar system with three moons, one being Calderra.

NICOS (NEE-KOSE) TRADING COMPANY: A stable company that has been doing trade between the Scorpius Quadrants for two centuries, owned by Lord Bartholomew Sullivan.

NOLAN: GIB prisoner with excellent tactical and analytical skills.

OBSANITALE (OB-SAN-I-TALL-E): Province on the colonist planet, Gamuel.

OFFICER MARSHALL JENNINGS: Civilian officer. Served with Reagan Vasilios' father.

OFFICER MUIER (MY-ER): Communications officer for the GIB.

OFFICER SLATE BECKETT: Civilian officer. Served with Reagan Vasilios' father.

PAEGA (PAY-A): Tigras, giant catlike creature found on the moon Calderra, to the east of the mountain range.

PAIKAHALE (PAY-KA-HALL-AY): Star in Quadrant 3, next to Antares.

PHALASAT (FA-LI-SAT): Aeaqualis scout.

PLANET Z: Z-Class planet (uninhabitable by life) commonly referred to as Planet Z. Also known as Azram.

PLANITANIUM (PLAN-I-TANE-EE-UM): Alloy with strange properties.

POLARIS CARDINAL DIRECTIONS: Navigation system used on planets, based on the Polaris star as "north".

QUADRANTS: Divisions of space in the Scorpius constellation that contain more than one solar system.

REIMUS 5 (RAY-MUS): Planet with rumor of slavery surrounding it.

RHYS (REESE) COPELAN: Alpha Team member during the alloy recovery by the Corporate Alliance.

SCORPIUS: Constellation that resembles a scorpion.

SECRETARY JAYLEN COHEN: Secretary of Bureau Investigations. Served with Reagan Vasilios' father.

SECTAR: One kilometer.

SECTOR: Unit of division of a quadrant.

SERGEANT MONROE: Eager sergeant on the Aurora military base.

SERGEANT OF INTERNAL AFFAIRS: Investigates members of the GIB when there is wrongdoing.

SERGEANT TREVANA (TRE-VAN-A): Bridge officer for the GIB.

SHAULA (SHAW-LA): Star system in Quadrant 1 that includes the planets Isidore and Elanissia.

SOMARI (SO-MAR-EE): Slave on the Cavienna Plantation on Reimus 5.

STEVE DIXON: Full name is Estevan Dixon. Proclaimed a hero after discovering something in the Secretary's office.

TASERBEAM: Weapon used by the Aeaqualis to stun their opponents.

TASERLANCE: Weapon used by the Aeaqualis to stun their opponents.

TAYLOR COHEN: Daughter of Secretary Jaylen and Janine Cohen. Yellow Squadron pilot.

TERELINA (TER-A-LEEN-A): Province on the colonist planet, Gamuel.

THRACE: Dr. Jesse Bartell's lab assistant.

TIGRAS (TEE-GRUS): Giant catlike creature.

TOWER OF RECORDS: Reknowned group of three adjacent white, stone towers on Reimus 5, where significant historical records are kept.

VAMPIRICA (VAM-PEER-I-CA): Vampiric blue star in Quadrant 3, amassing energy from Antares.

VITAARI (VI-TAR-EE): Lizard-like people who live on planet Vitaaria. The modern Vitaari are generally known to be greedy and calculating.

VITAARI (VI-TAR-EE) COUNCIL: Council of young Vitaari politicians seeking power and wealth.

VITAARIA (VI-TAR-EE-A): Planet where the Vitaari live, located in the Antares system in Quadrant 3.

VODYANYOV (VOE-DEE-AN-EE-OV): Round, frog-like creatures, who have rude manners and give off a muddy scent.

VULPES (VUL-PEZ): Second-in-Command of the Kitsuine.

WEIXIUER (WY-EX-EE-ER): Star in Quadrant 2 of the Scorpius constellation.

WILSON KARTER: Works in the Tech Department for the Galactic Investigations Bureau. Was cleared of suspicion of espionage due to his injury.

XAMIDIMURA (ZAM-I-DIM-UR-A): Sstar in Quadrant 2 of the Scorpius constellation.

Z-CLASS PLANET: A planet that is uninhabitable by life.

ZOOMCAR: Vehicle with the ability to move both horizontally and vertically in traffic.

ABOUT THE AUTHOR

Anjula Evans is a writer living in the Toronto area. She started writing and illustrating children's books in 2014, and this is her first full length novel for Young Adults.

She enjoys time with family, writing books, and composing music.